THE
GREY GIRL

She never sleeps...

[signature]

THE
GREY GIRL

ELEANOR HAWKEN

HOT
KEY
BOOKS

First published in Great Britain in 2014 by Hot Key Books
Northburgh House, 10 Northburgh Street, London EC1V 0AT

A CIP catalogue record for this book is available from the British Library.

ISBN: 978-1-4714-0195-4

1

This book is typeset in 10.5 Berling LT Std using Atomik ePublisher

Printed and bound by Clays Ltd, St Ives Plc

Hot Key Books supports the Forest Stewardship Council (FSC),
the leading international forest certification organisation, and is
committed to printing only on Greenpeace-approved FSC-certified paper.

www.hotkeybooks.com

Hot Key Books is part of the Bonnier Publishing Group
www.bonnierpublishing.com

For Victoria, thank you

Sunday 7th September 1952

I saw a ghost today. A grey girl. She was standing at the window of the top-floor dormitory, looking down upon the world below.

I'd never seen the girl before and today was the start of my fourth year at Dudley Hall. My long summer on Uncle Jack's farm already feels like a million years ago. As the car pulled up to the school this afternoon it felt as though I'd never even been away. The stone gargoyles, the twisted ivy and rattling old windows have been my only real home since Mother and Father died.

Mistress Johnson was waiting at the main entrance, ticking off our names as we arrived and telling us which dormitories we're in. Once again I'm sharing with Lavinia, Margot and Sybil. That's not altogether a bad thing, I suppose. Better the devil you know.

We're in a room on the second floor that looks out onto the school grounds. I had to do two trips to get my trunk, tuck box, hockey stick and heavy winter cloak upstairs and because I was the last to arrive I'm stuck with the bed by the draughty old window. Sybil has the bed by the door, and Margot and Lavinia have beds up against the far wall, either side of the fireplace. Lavinia said that because Sybil's nearest the door she has to be the lookout girl. It's her job to peek out onto the landing at night to check that Matron isn't coming whilst the three of us prepare things for the Rituals.

I hadn't even thought about the Rituals all summer. I don't think Lavinia has thought of anything else.

After we unpacked, Mistress Johnson said we could have some free time outside to enjoy the last of the summer air (as if we need reminding that winter is on the way; the windowsill by my bed is already mouldy with damp!). So the four of us sat underneath the weeping willow tree by the river, took off our long socks and dangled our naked feet into the brook. Margot told us all about her summer with her aunt and uncle in Devon, and Sybil told us how her guardian had forced her to volunteer in a London soup kitchen at weekends. Ghastly.

'Am I the only one who did any reading at all over the holidays?' Lavinia complained with her nose in the air. 'I took any book I could find on Rituals from the Oxford library. Good job one of us is serious about this stuff.'

'When do you want to do the first Ritual this year?' Margot asked.

'Tonight, of course,' Lavinia replied, as she splashed her feet about in the cool river water.

We sat and spoke about the Rituals until the air grew colder and we were called in to clean up for supper. As we walked back through the school grounds something compelled me to look up towards the attic dorm rooms that sit above the row of gargoyles. The rooms that the prefects in final year sleep in.

That was the moment I saw her. A horrid shiver ran along my spine as the small grey face stared down at me from the last room on the right. She looked as though she had been carved from frosted glass. As though someone had spat on a hankie and scrubbed out all her colour. It truly felt as though I was staring at a ghost, into the very face of death. I froze as the others walked ahead, and the ghostly girl looked down at me and waved. I quickly found my feet and ran to catch the others up as fast as I could. I didn't look up again. I didn't want to see her. She unnerved me, whoever she is. I don't like her – the grey girl.

Supper time now, and then the Rituals later tonight.

Until I write again,

Annabel

I

Ghosts are all in your head. That's what I keep telling myself, over and over. She's dead and buried. She didn't come back.

I was only in Warren House for five weeks before I was discharged. That's nothing compared to how long most people are in there for.

'You're going to spend some time with Aunt Meredith,' Mum announced down the phone shortly before I left Warren House. 'Your father's being deployed to Afghanistan for the next few months, and my nerves are playing up again, Suzy. You need to be somewhere you can be looked after properly. After everything that happened to you at school you need some stability.' Aunt Meredith and cousin Toby are my only relatives in the UK. Dad has a brother but he's in the army too, and my grandparents all died years ago.

That's the story of my life. Mum passing responsibility for me on to someone else. When I was a kid we had an au pair. The au pair did everything with me; played with me, brushed my teeth, helped me with homework and put me to bed. My childhood is filled with memories of Olga the au pair whilst Mum was lying in bed 'suffering with her nerves'. As soon as I was old enough to brush my own teeth I was packed off to St Mark's College, a boarding school. Mum was probably thankful that I was carted off to a loony bin after I had to leave school – that way she didn't have to look after me.

'You look tired, Suzy,' was the first thing Aunt Meredith said when she picked me up from Warren House. She loaded my single bag into her car boot and slammed it shut. 'I think you've lost some weight too – I hope you've been eating properly.'

Trust me, an eating disorder is a problem I don't need at the moment. The truth is the food at Warren House was so disgusting even a hogzillar pig would drop a few pounds.

'Dudley Hall is a few hours away,' Aunt Meredith said as we began the long drive through the English countryside. Dudley Hall – Aunt Meredith's new house – was going to be the closest I'd come to a home in the UK for years. 'Toby's finished school for the term so at least you'll have some company during the day,' she rattled on. One of the only things that Aunt Meredith had in common with my mother was the need to fill silence with inane prattle. 'The doctor told me you've been keeping a diary? Well, I think that's excellent. I had a diary when I was younger. I used to keep an elastic band around it, thinking it would keep your mother out. Foolish of me, I found out a few years ago that she used to steal my diary every night and read what I'd written each day.' Typical Mum – not caring one iota about someone else's private thoughts and feelings. 'The village is quite small,' Aunt Meredith went on, 'but there are a couple of shops. There aren't many people your age, but one of the women who works for us has a nephew who's a bit older than you. I thought perhaps –'

'I don't need help making friends,' I cut in. 'And actually I'm not keeping a diary any more.' Aunt Meredith's eyes quickly flicked from the road to me. 'I'm writing a screenplay.'

Her eyebrows rose and she said, flatly, 'Really?'

'Yes, about my time in Warren House. One day it's going to be made into a film. I'll probably play the lead part. I might direct it too. If they won't let me direct it then I'll have someone like Robert De Niro or Ben Affleck do it instead.'

Aunt Meredith smiled to herself and then continued to drone on about everything and nothing whilst she drove. I noticed that the one subject she didn't touch upon was Warren House. I suppose she was afraid to ask me what they did to me there. I suppose it didn't matter, so long as I was cured. So long as I'd stopped believing in ghosts.

I stared out of the car window and tuned her out as the world outside whizzed by. After weeks of being locked up I had felt sure I was ready for freedom. But sitting in Aunt Meredith's car I suddenly wasn't so sure that I was ready. When I'd arrived at Warren House I'd been a shell of who I once had been. Everything that had happened to me at school had nearly destroyed me. When the doctors sent me to Warren House I thought it would be the final nail in my coffin. But instead it had turned my life around. However horrible it had been, it had been safe. But the outside world was full of limitless possibilities, and the thought of all that unknown waiting for me tightened my belly and filled me with dread. I'd counted down the days until the doctors released me, and now that I was free it felt as though it had all happened way too quickly. It felt surreal, as though it was happening to someone else.

I could have been an actress in a movie, playing a part that someone else had written for me.

'Nearly there now,' Aunt Meredith chirped, after we'd been driving for hours. We were passing through the small village of Dudley-on-Water. Cobblestone houses, manicured gardens, a small river with an ancient stone bridge and a market square. I wondered if Dudley Hall had been named after the village or if it was the other way around. I looked over at my aunt and considered asking her, but she looked deep in thought, chewing the inside of her cheek and frowning. I had weeks to force conversation, I'd save the question for when I was really desperate.

'Can we make a stop here?' I asked, pointing at a small chemist by the piddly excuse for a village green. 'There's something I need to buy.'

Aunt Meredith pulled up outside the village chemist and I jumped out of the car. The chemist door chimed as it opened and an old lady frowned at me from behind the counter. I made my way down the central aisle to the shelf at the back of the shop. What I needed was on the top shelf. I lifted myself onto my tiptoes and reached for the box. The box was covered in dust – that told me volumes about the people who lived in Dudley-on-Water and the kind of things they shopped for. 'Just this please,' I said to the old lady as I put the box down on the counter and pulled out my purse.

A few minutes later I was back in the car and being driven towards my new home. Aunt Meredith didn't ask what I'd bought. Good – if she could manage to keep out of my shopping bags, my diary and my head whilst I stayed with her then maybe the next few weeks would be bearable.

We turned onto a gravel driveway, passing through rusted iron gates that had been pinned back against the hedgerows. The gravel path twisted around a corner before opening up onto a long straight drive that ended at a large, imposing country house.

'Dudley Hall belonged to the Dudley family for generations. The village and house are named after the family who once owned the land,' Aunt Meredith explained as the long gravel driveway scrunched beneath the weight of the car. Great, I thought, that's one conversation starter I'd just been robbed of. 'After the family sold the house it became a school for a while. But when that closed down the house was left derelict for years.'

My head snapped around to look at my aunt as my heart suddenly pounded hard. It felt as though my blood was thickening and my face growing hotter. Dudley Hall had once been a school. I was going to be living in an old school. After everything that had happened to me, everything I'd been through – how could anyone think this was a good idea?

Aunt Meredith ignored the look I gave her and continued, 'Richard managed to pick it up for an excellent price. A steal really.'

I didn't like the idea of a house being stolen from anyone.

Dudley Hall was both daunting and magnificent. Not like Windsor Castle or anything ridiculous like that. But it was bigger than any normal house. It was exactly the sort of gothic retreat a screenwriter should live in. It was the kind of ancient house that told a hundred stories as you looked at it. There were three storeys of large, wrought-iron windows capped by a row of gargoyles. Above the gargoyles was another storey of smaller windows peeping out of a sloped roof. Ivy crept up the crumbling walls and the windows towards the top of the house were cracked and frosted with age.

'We're working our way up with the renovations,' Aunt Meredith told me. 'One floor at a time. The guests only see the ground floor and the first floor. Our rooms are all on the second floor.'

'And the top floor?' I asked.

'Hasn't been renovated yet,' she replied.

The 'guests' Aunt Meredith was talking about were her murder mystery participants. Aunt Meredith has always liked a project. She'd run dozens of short-lived businesses in her time – a cupcake company, a dress shop, a villa in the south of France, and then she imported French foods when she got bored of living out there. She even took up charity work when husband number two got sick. And when Aunt Meredith decided to host murder mystery weekends, she wanted a traditional country mansion to do it in. So Richard bought her Dudley Hall. 'We have a party arriving tomorrow afternoon,' she said, as the car pulled up in front of the house. 'So you'll have plenty of time to settle in before then. I thought maybe you'd like a small part to play in the murder mystery. I actually wrote this one myself; it's called *Murder at the Mansion*.' Aunt Meredith flashed me a satisfied smile as she swung open the car door.

'Actually, I'd rather not be involved,' I said, getting out of the car. 'I know it would be good acting experience for me, but I'm not sure I want to be an actress any more. I think I want to be a writer now instead.'

'Maybe you could be both?' Aunt Meredith smiled proudly, as if the thought hadn't already occurred to me.

Staring up at Dudley Hall, my new home, I once again allowed myself to fall into the fantasy that my life is just one big film script. If I really was living in a movie, a butler or housekeeper would have been there to greet me as soon as the car pulled up outside Dudley Hall. They would have opened the car boot, 'Allow me, ma'am,' and carried my bags inside. But no, there was no one there to greet us and I had to lug my bag out of the car boot myself. I followed Aunt Meredith towards the large, oak-panelled door, heavy rucksack in one hand and my purchase from the chemist in the other.

'Richard's away at the moment,' Aunt Meredith said, as she reached out and twisted the large, rusted knocker and the ancient door opened with a groan. Obviously there was no need to keep your door locked when you lived in Dudley-on-Water. 'On business in Boston. He'll be back in a week or so. He's looking forward to seeing you.' That was a lie. I'd only met her new husband twice, and each time he'd barely said a word to me.

The hallway of Dudley Hall felt like something out of the Middle Ages. I'm not sure what parts of the decor were genuine and what was there for the murder mystery guests' benefit. There was a wide oak staircase at the back of the hall that wound around to the left. A life-size suit of armour stood at the bottom of the stairs clutching a sword as though it guarded the staircase. Light streamed in from a huge domed skylight that sat above the staircase, illuminating the tiny particles of dust that swilled about in the air. The place stank of polish and musk. Scattered around the hallway were large, wrought-iron candlesticks and the stuffed heads of various animals – deer, boars and pheasants. My nose scrunched up at the sight of them. There were four doors leading off from the great hall.

'The dining room, drawing room, library and billiards room.' Aunt Meredith pointed to the doors. 'The corridor to the left leads to further sitting rooms and studies, and to the right is the kitchen and store rooms.'

A large mirror sat between the two closed doors on my right. I caught sight of my reflection. My bright red dress that I'd made last summer hung off me like a sack. Aunt Meredith was right, I did look too thin. My hair was the colour of rust and my eyes looked sunken and hollow. Haunted.

'I'll take you straight to your room to freshen up. Then you can come downstairs and get something to eat,' Aunt Meredith said, tearing my attention away from my startling reflection.

The floorboards creaked beneath my feet as I followed her past the suit of armour and up the grand flight of stairs. The first-floor landing wound around the staircase, framed by a gold-trimmed balcony with marble arches that reached up to the floor above. The staircase then wound up towards the second floor, the floor that I'd be sleeping on. Four corridors led off from the second floor landing, two to the front and two to the rear of the house. Dudley Hall seemed far too big for one family to ever live in, and I could see why it had once been used as a school. There must have been thirty rooms on the first and second floor alone.

I tried to push the thought that the building had once been a school to the back of my mind and lock it away. I'd had enough of boarding schools for a dozen lifetimes. Just the thought of school shoes running up and down those grand stairs made my chest tighten. I imagined the chatter and giggles of schoolgirls, the sound of gossip in the halls and whispering in dormitories after lights out. Memories of my own school began to swirl into my head and conjure up thoughts of the ghosts I was trying so hard to lay to rest.

But Dudley Hall was silent; you could have heard a pin drop.

Aunt Meredith led me towards the corridor on the right at the back of the house. She stopped at the second door and swung it open.

'I've put you in here.' Aunt Meredith ushered me into the empty room.

It was large and painted stark white. An empty fireplace sat on one side of the room with a bare mantelpiece above it, a double bed with crisp white sheets sat on the other. The room was so white and sterile it burnt my eyes, and reminded me far more of an asylum than Warren House ever had. There was a door at the far corner of the room. 'You have your own bathroom.' Aunt Meredith pointed to the door. 'And I'll take you into the village tomorrow so you can buy some bits and pieces to put on the walls. Your mum's sending some of your things from school, your posters and photos –'

'I don't want them,' I said loudly. 'I don't want anything from school.'

Aunt Meredith looked mildly embarrassed and nodded quickly. 'I'll leave you to freshen up.'

She turned and disappeared from the room, closing the creaking door behind her. I put my rucksack and bag from the chemist on the bed and walked towards the large window at the back of the room. I could see the garden – a beautiful lawn, smart hedges. But best of all I could see a winding stream that ran through the grounds, and further along the stream I could see what looked like a boathouse. If nothing else Dudley Hall was going to provide me with perfect scenery in which to sit and write my screenplay.

I closed my eyes and tried to steady my nerves. I reminded myself that I'd waited five long weeks to finally have my freedom back. My life was mine once again, and this was where I needed to be. I needed time and space to breathe, to write and to recover from everything that had happened to me at school. And that's what I would get at Dudley Hall.

Opening my eyes, I stared blankly into the bare, white room. Alone, in between the white walls and the echoing silence, I felt so small and fragile. As if I might lose myself, like I'd done before. Memories of everything that had happened came flooding back … The Blue Lady who had haunted my school, the smell of her rotting flesh burning my nose when she crept into my room at night. The soft padding of her muddy footprints and the feel of her ice-cold hands as she gripped me like a vice. And for as long as I live I'll never forget her face, her dark eyes pleading for release. Her fear and her restlessness at being trapped in a world she should have left long ago. The doctors at Warren House had tried to convince me that I was crazy. That what I'd seen had all been in my head. For a while I had almost believed them. But stepping foot in Dudley Hall, I suddenly felt stupid for ever doubting myself. My mind wasn't playing tricks on me. I know what I saw. I saw her come back.

In that moment I knew that everything I had spent weeks trying to bury deep down inside of me was on the brink of resurfacing. The ghosts, the visions, the terror, it all began to creep up inside me and I wanted nothing more than to run away from that old house and never look back. There was something about Dudley Hall that wasn't right. I knew what it felt like to stand in a room that had a sinister story to tell. And standing in that room I knew, as instinctively as a dog knows to hide from a storm, that something in Dudley Hall wasn't at rest.

Closing my eyes and once again shutting out the world around me, I tried to push my dark thoughts to the back of my mind. It isn't the house, I tried to reassure myself, it's me. *It's all in my head*, I repeated like a mantra. All in my head. She's dead and buried. She won't come back.

2

I woke up the next morning to bright light flooding painfully into my room. I could have sworn I'd drawn the curtains the night before, but they were pulled right back. Someone must have come into my room whilst I'd slept and opened them.

I looked at the small travel clock I'd put on my bedside table. It was gone nine o'clock. I smiled lazily; I'd never been allowed to sleep that late in Warren House. The bottle of blue pills the doctor had given me sat next to the travel clock. I reached over, pulled out the bedside-table drawer, and placed the pills inside it. Out of sight, out of mind. I didn't care what the doctors said; I didn't need to take them. They fuzzed up my head and made it difficult to think, and I needed my mind to be as sharp as a razor if I wanted to spend my days writing.

As I pulled back the duvet and swung my feet out of the bed my stomach grumbled loudly. I'd hardly eaten anything the night before. I'd spent dinnertime quietly pushing a few potatoes around my plate whilst Aunt Meredith jabbered on about the Victorian-themed murder mystery party she was hosting that weekend. My cousin Toby was excited because he got to wear his Sherlock Holmes costume. He'd grown loads since I last saw him; he was eight years old now. Toby hadn't stopped talking the whole evening, which was good because it meant I didn't have to. I had too much going on inside my head to hold a conversation with someone. I was busy convincing myself that there was nothing strange about Dudley Hall, that my feeling of unease was all in my head.

Despite the fact that I was famished, I had something important to do before I went downstairs for breakfast. I should have done it the night before but I'd been too tired. The bag from the chemist in the village lay in the middle of my bedroom floor. I picked it up, along with a fresh towel, and headed for the bathroom. Forty-five minutes later I was ready to face the world again, looking like the old me.

'Why is your hair that colour?' Toby asked as I sauntered into the ginormous old kitchen with my head held high. 'It wasn't like that last night.'

I headed for the kettle, filled it up and flicked it on. 'I dyed it this morning. I actually prefer my hair this colour.'

Toby sniggered. 'You look like one of those Goth people.'

I threw up my hands in horror. '*Angels, and minsters of grace, defend us!*'

'What does that mean?' Toby laughed at me.

'It's a line from *Hamlet*, by William Shakespeare.' I smiled down at him. 'Don't tell me you haven't heard of Shakespeare?'

'Good lord, Dudley Hall has its own resident firecracker,' came a deep voice from the doorway before Toby could reply. I turned around to see a middle-aged woman with a bright orange scarf tied around her head. She was wearing a long purple skirt and a loose fitting red top that clashed with everything else she had on. I knew who the woman was without her introducing herself. Aunt Meredith had told me about her over dinner last night. She was once an actress but now lived in the village and helped out at Dudley Hall with the cooking and cleaning. She also worked at the murder mystery parties and pretended to be a psychic.

'You must be Old Nell,' I said, looking her up and down. She had a necklace of gold coins jingling around her neck, and large gold earrings dangling from several holes in each ear. She was shorter than me, and quite squat. Old Nell was obviously someone who dressed to get attention; either that or she inhabited the character of Dudley Hall's psychic in residence even when the guests weren't around to see her. Either way, my first impression of Old Nell was that she was someone who wasn't afraid to stand apart from the crowd. I instantly respected her for that, and it made me want to like her.

'Less of the old, please,' Nell said, walking into the room. 'That's only what the guests call me. And I'll have a cup of tea, seeing as you've got the kettle on. Unless you're running the water so you can put out the fire raging on top of your head.' She nodded at my head of freshly dyed red hair.

A scowl clouded my face. Maybe I'd been wrong about Nell. She wasn't someone who appreciated individuality, she ridiculed it.

'My hair is an expression of who I am,' I mumbled, as the kettle boiled and I reached for some mugs.

'Nell's taking me into the village to the joke shop today,' Toby announced. 'We're going to find a pipe to go with my Sherlock Holmes costume. Sherlock Holmes is always sucking on a pipe. But I don't want a real one – smoking stinks. Are you going to come with us?'

'No.' I shook my head as I handed Nell a cup of tea. I would have loved to have a brother or sister. I thought it was cruel that my parents cursed me with being an only child, so I've always liked Toby. But still, there was no way I wanted to spend the day with him trawling around Dudley-on-Water's lame excuse for shops. I had better things to do. 'I need to do some work on my screenplay today.'

Toby looked mildly disappointed and Nell gave me a patronising smile. I turned my back on her with a loud exhale of air and made my way towards the impressive-looking coffee machine on the kitchen counter. I'd never used a coffee machine like that before. In fact, I'd never really made a habit of drinking coffee, but as every writer seemed to drink coffee, it was time for me to start drinking it too. I flicked the coffee machine on at the wall and started to fiddle with the buttons and switches, trying in vain to make the contraption work.

Nell made a snorting sound. 'Need some help with that?'

'No,' I replied, making a mental note to practise making coffee once Nell had left the house so I didn't have the same debacle the next morning. 'I actually prefer instant coffee anyway.'

'Cupboard on the right,' she said. I stopped wrestling with the machine and reached inside the cupboard for the instant coffee.

'Aunt Meredith says you used to be an actress,' I said steadily to Nell, as I poured hot water over the coffee granules in the cup. 'But now you just stay here and help out with the murder mystery parties.'

24

'Nell is a psychic too,' Toby informed me before Nell could speak. 'And sometimes she helps out with the cooking and cleaning. But she only cleans downstairs, she won't go upstairs.'

'That's me,' she nodded, her gold earrings jangling. 'Jack of all trades and a mistress of many.'

'Was it you who came into my room this morning and opened the curtains whilst I was still sleeping?' I asked pointedly. 'Because I prefer to sleep late in the holidays. And the doctor did say I need my rest.'

Nell raised her painted eyebrows and they disappeared into her orange turban. 'I've not been anywhere near your room, my dear. Toby is many things but he's not a liar. I don't go upstairs in this house.' A stony expression fell across her face. 'I dare say no one has been near your room this morning. Your aunt left early, had to drive into the city to pick up some costume bits for this evening. That reminds me, the guests will be arriving from four so can you please be in your costume by then?'

Who did this washed-up old fortune-teller wannabe think she was? 'I'm going to sit this party out,' I told her indignantly. 'I actually have other things I need to do this weekend.'

'Suzy's writing a screenplay,' Toby reminded Nell.

Nell's eyes narrowed and she smiled like a cat. 'So she says.' I hated her already. 'Well, we'll get out of your red hair and leave you to it. Come on, Mister Toby, let's get you to the joke shop.'

Nell slurped up her tea like some kind of common washerwoman and yanked my small cousin's arm, pulling him out of the kitchen. 'Bye, Suzy, see you later!' Toby called.

I turned around and leant my elbows on the kitchen counter so I could gaze out of the window. The kitchen's large sash windows at the back of the house looked onto Dudley Hall's sprawling grounds. It was a similar view from my bedroom window, which sat directly above. I brought my cooling coffee to my lips and grimaced at the taste of it. I forced myself to swallow the bitter black liquid as my eyes glazed over and I started to daydream. The grounds really were beautiful, the perfect place to sit and write. I imagined myself in a film, where a montage of shots would capture me outside in the hazy sunshine, writing my screenplay. I pictured the camera panning in on me as I sat beneath the old weeping willow on the riverbank, bare feet kicking at the cool water as I wrote with a notepad on my lap, my pen working furiously against the paper.

The sound of a vehicle pulling up on the gravel driveway outside violently dragged me from my daydream. Through the glass panels of the kitchen's back door I could see a man pulling a motorbike to a halt. My stomach did a nervous flip as I tried to work out what to do. Aunt Meredith hadn't told me to expect a visitor this morning, and it was too early for any of the guests to arrive. My eyes anxiously flashed towards the telephone on the wall as I briefly considered calling the police. The man could have been anyone – a burglar, a murderer, a crazed kidnapper who'd been watching me and waiting to strike for years. A million and one scenarios flashed through my head, and I stood frozen to the spot as I watched the man swing his legs off the bike and onto the gravel, pulling off his helmet as he landed.

As soon as I had a clear view of his face I realised he was younger than I'd initially thought – not that much older than me. He was wearing worn jeans and a black biker jacket over a white T-shirt. His blond hair was cut short, but before I could take any more in I nearly dropped my cold, disgusting coffee all over the floor as I realised the boy was heading for the kitchen door.

My eyes flicked again to the telephone on the wall. I didn't have enough time to call the police. If the boy had come here to kill or kidnap me no one would ever get here in time to rescue me.

Horrified, I watched in slow motion as he walked right up to the back door, swung it open and waltzed straight into the kitchen. He nonchalantly placed his motorbike helmet on the kitchen table, along with what looked like a small, padded coolbag, without so much as a word or a look in my direction. 'You must be Suzy,' he said, brushing past me and reaching for the kitchen cupboard.

'What on earth are you doing?' I asked, my voice sounding more angry than scared.

'Getting a glass of water,' he answered without looking at me.

'You can't just walk into my house and pour yourself a glass of water.'

Still without looking at me the boy sauntered over to the sink, standing only inches away from me. His arm brushed against mine as he reached over to fill his glass with water from the tap. 'This isn't your house,' he said.

'It's my aunt's house,' I replied quickly.

He brought the glass of water up to his lips and took a long, slow drink. His light hazel eyes met mine. 'I thought it was your aunt's husband's house.'

'I have no idea who you are,' I shot back.

'I'm Nate,' he responded, taking another sip of water.

'Okay, Nate. Who are you and what are you doing here?' I looked him up and down. 'Are you the gardener?'

Nate shook his head. 'Digging about in mud's not really my thing. My aunt works here. I'm just here to drop off her crystal ball for the party tonight.' He nodded at the bag he'd put on the table before draining the last of his water and putting the empty glass in the sink. He didn't even bother to wash it up. 'Meredith said you've been in hospital. You don't look sick to me.'

Brilliant, now complete strangers knew my mental health history. I reached up and touched my newly dyed hair, feeling suddenly self-conscious. 'It's actually none of your business but I'm fine.'

'Glad to hear it.' He smiled. 'When I heard Meredith's niece was expelled from school, did a stretch in a head hospital and was now coming to town I couldn't help but be –'

'Excuse me? A "head hospital"?' I crossed my arms over my chest and glared at him. 'Just who do you think you are?'

'Well, that's a complex question.' He grinned. 'One I'm sure I'll have the chance to discuss with you at great length over the next few weeks, seeing as we'll be seeing quite a lot of each other.'

I let out a small splutter of outrage. 'What makes you think that?'

The boy crossed his arms over his chest, mirroring my body language. He gave me a slow, cheeky grin and my eyes momentarily rested on the dimples in his cheeks. 'Look around

28

the place, Suzy. Nothing ever happens in Dudley-on-Water. Trust me, you'll be bored senseless soon enough and wanting someone to distract you. I thought –'

'I don't care what you think,' I said quickly. 'I'm not interested. I'm not here to entertain you, or make friends, or do anything else you might have in mind. I just want to keep my head down. Besides, I'm only here for a few weeks, I'll be gone before you know it. And by the way, I wasn't expelled from school. It just wasn't the right place for me.'

The grin slipped from Nate's face as he studied me for a long, awkward moment. I held his gaze, determined not to be the first to look away. 'Suit yourself,' he said eventually, shrugging. He turned to go and I smiled to myself in triumph. 'Let me know if you change your mind. Tell Nell I said hello, and make sure she gets that.' He pointed at the bag he'd left on the kitchen table. 'Nice to meet you, Suzy.' And then he scooped up his helmet and just walked off. Out of the kitchen, onto the gravel driveway and away from me. My mouth hung open like a fly trap as I watched Nate climb back onto his bike, rev the engine and drive away without looking back.

3

The whole encounter with Nate had only lasted a couple of minutes, but it had been enough to completely throw me off-kilter. There was no way I was going to befriend the first motorbike-riding, leather-jacket-wearing, cocky cliché with a nice smile that strolled into the kitchen. And I made a mental note to complain to Aunt Meredith about the lack of security at Dudley Hall. If anyone was free to walk up to the house and let themselves in through the back door then it was a miracle no one'd been murdered in their sleep yet.

It took me ages to make myself breakfast, I was so flustered. I couldn't find a pan to boil eggs in. And then I burnt my toast and had to start again. Meeting Old Nell and her biker teenage nephew in the space of half an hour had not been the start to the day I had expected. No surprise that they were related – if the rest of the village were half as rude then it was going to be a long few weeks at Dudley Hall. And I couldn't help but feel betrayed by Aunt Meredith. Nate knew I'd been in hospital. She'd clearly blabbed about me being in Warren House to anyone who'd listen. By the time I had finally cooked my breakfast and eaten it, I'd already resolved to ignore Nell,

Nate and any other boorish villager I might be unfortunate enough to meet whilst I stayed at Dudley Hall. I couldn't afford to feel so distracted. I had to focus on getting better and writing my screenplay.

It was late morning by the time I finally made it outside into the sunshine with my notepad and a stack of pens. I needed to find a few good writing spots. I needed shade and I needed somewhere I wouldn't be easily disturbed, somewhere far enough away from the house. I briefly considered sitting underneath the old weeping willow by the stream, but it was still in view of the house. I wanted to be somewhere I knew no one would find me straight away. I followed the small brook as it wound its way through my new garden. Sure enough, after following the stream for a few minutes I saw the old wooden boathouse perched on the riverbank that I'd spotted from my bedroom window the night before. My face widened with a grin – a boathouse would be a perfect place to write.

The door bolt was rusted but unlocked, and after a few frustrating minutes of struggling I managed to pull it open and swing back the boathouse door. Inside was cool and damp and smelt of stale river water. One ancient-looking boat lay on the wooden decking of the boathouse. The boat was rotten and filled with holes, its paintwork long chipped away. I walked around the small vessel slowly. On its helm was the name *The Lady of Shalott*.

'Named after the poem,' I whispered to myself. '*"The curse is come upon me," cried the Lady of Shalott.*' I sat down on the boathouse floor, the wooden boards creaking as I leant against the rickety old wall and made myself comfortable. The gentle sound of water splashing against the boathouse gave me the perfect soundtrack to sit and write. I opened my notepad, clicked a biro into action and began to put pen to paper.

I sat and wrote for hours. There, on the floor of the rotting old boathouse, I began to stitch together the threads of my story. I decided not to set it at Warren House. I heard once that you should write about the things that you know best. And other than 'head hospitals' the one thing I knew best was boarding schools. I'd lived in a boarding school for most of my life – instead of parents I'd had housemistresses and matrons, and instead of home-cooked meals I'd had cold, stodgy school food to nourish me. So I started to write a story set in a boarding school – a school that had once been a grand country home. I created a set of characters based on girls I'd met during my time at school – orphans, spoilt rich kids and those other girls who'd just been put into school and then forgotten about until the holidays rolled around. I didn't get around to writing any proper scenes, I just jotted down my ideas about the characters that would appear in my screenplay.

By the time I re-emerged from the boathouse and headed back to the main house the murder mystery guests were beginning to arrive. The driveway was steadily filling up with cars, and the sound of feet scrunching down on gravel and car boots slamming filled the air as I came into the back of the house through the kitchen door. I'd been in Dudley Hall for less than a day, and I'd taken an instant dislike to the draughty halls and dramatic history of the place, but I suddenly felt uneasy at the thought of sharing the old house with strangers.

I suppressed the uneasy feeling in my chest as I walked further into the kitchen. Nell was sweating over a boiling pot at the stove. She'd ditched the colourful clothes she'd been wearing earlier and was now in what looked like a Victorian peddler-woman's outfit.

'Mmm, what's for dinner?' I asked her.

'Suzy!' Aunt Meredith stepped in front of me. She was dressed like a Victorian aristocrat. Her hair was pinned up elegantly on the top of her head and she wore a stiff cream dress with pearls sewn down the front of it. Her skirt pooled out like a lampshade and hovered just above the floor. She did not look pleased to see me at all. She spoke quickly, without a pause for me to interrupt. 'How are you? I've been looking for you everywhere. What have you done to your hair? Well, no time to worry about that now. You need to go upstairs and change please. And make sure you cover up that red hair. We can't have the guests seeing you like that, it's important that we all stay in character the whole time guests are here. Helps create a bit more atmosphere.'

I grimaced. This did not sound like fun. 'I told you, I don't want to take part in the party.'

'Well, I'm afraid there's no one else to play the part,' Aunt Meredith said bluntly, ignoring the daggers I was shooting at her with my eyes. 'As long as you're staying here then you need to pull your weight. Be thankful I don't have you scrubbing the toilets.' As if I'd let anyone make me scrub a toilet! 'Besides,' she sighed. 'The distraction might be good for you.'

Aunt Meredith was the second person that day to suggest I needed distracting. First Nate and now her. However, the thought of having something to take my mind off an evening alone in my stark white room with nothing but my haunted thoughts for company did seem appealing.

'I don't have anything to wear,' I pointed out.

'I've put a scullery maid outfit on your bed,' she said. 'Quickly go upstairs and change and meet us all in the library in half an hour so we can introduce all the characters to the guests.'

'A scullery maid?' I said with obvious disgust. 'Can't I at least have a nice dress like yours?' I complained.

'The scullery maid is the murder victim,' Aunt Meredith said with a smile. 'I know you said you didn't want a part to play, that you had too much to do. But all you'll need to do is come down for the meet and greet in half an hour and then do your best blood-curdling scream towards the end of dinner. Then I'll need you to act dead for twenty minutes or so whilst the guests inspect your body. Then you'll be free for the rest of the weekend. Although I'd prefer it if you could stay in costume for as long as the guests are here – just in case one of them sees you.'

There was no way I'd be spending the weekend in a scullery maid's costume. I'd sooner spend every waking minute locked away in the boathouse so no one saw me. But the opportunity to scream the house down and play a murder victim sounded too good to be true. However, I wasn't about to admit that to Aunt Meredith.

I rolled my eyes and stomped out of the kitchen. 'Fine! But just for this weekend. I won't do it again.' I slammed the kitchen door behind me for added effect and then allowed myself a small smile once I was out of sight. Spending an evening as a murder victim in Dudley Hall was going to be fun.

4

The costume was slightly too big for me, but it would have to do. At least there was a white maid's cap for me to hide my bright red hair under so I looked a bit more authentic. I quickly dabbed some concealer under my tired eyes and half an hour later I was standing in the grand library amongst a room full of excited weekend guests.

There must have been twenty strangers in total, all of them dressed up as Victorian aristocrats and wearing grins of anticipation. But the spectacle of the murder mystery party guests was not what drew my attention. It was the first time I'd been in the Dudley Hall library, and it was incredible. Dusty old books lined the walls from floor to ceiling, and a rickety old ladder was propped against the far wall so you could reach whatever volume you wanted to read. Aunt Meredith had told me the night before that some books belonged to the house – throwbacks from the days the house belonged to the Dudley family, and the time that it was a school. But some of the books Richard had had someone buy from second-hand shops so they all looked old and well read. I found it slightly hollow that Richard didn't have books of his own to fill the empty shelves with. I was determined to collect a library's worth of books by the time I got to his age. I wanted a room that looked just like the Dudley Hall library, full of books I'd actually read. I'd already been warned that Dudley Hall's library would be out of bounds at weekends – it was one of the rooms that the guests used. But I made a promise to myself to spend at least a day in there writing the next week, once all the guests had gone.

Aunt Meredith tugged on my arm and pulled me beside her so that I lined up with the other 'staff'. My eyes quickly cast over the gaggle of excited guests as they chatted away to one another, casting frequent glances in our direction for a sign that the drama was about to begin. Disappointingly, they were all roughly the same age as Aunt Meredith.

Aunt Meredith turned around and struck a huge gong that I hadn't previously noticed standing behind me. Silence descended upon the room and Aunt Meredith began to speak. 'My Lords, Ladies and gentlemen,' she said dramatically. 'Welcome to Dudley Hall. The year is 1885. Queen Victoria is on the throne. The first public train has just chugged along British train tracks, the Statue of Liberty has just arrived in New York, professional football has just been legalised and the Spanish King has just died. The British Empire is at its height and you are all fabulously wealthy. You have come to spend the weekend with the debauched aristocrat, Viscount Thomas Cavendish.'

'That's me!' waved a fat man from the crowd, pushing his way to the front.

'Would you like to stand here, sir?' Aunt Meredith ushered him to her side.

'Viscount Cavendish and his wife, Lady Charlotte…' a woman shuffled away from the crowd and stood by the man's side, 'will host a spectacular weekend of feasting, dancing and relaxing. But keep your eyes and ears open, as Dudley Hall has a fair few secrets that it is struggling to keep hidden.'

The crowd of party goers made a few 'Ooh, ahh' sounds. I tried desperately not to roll my eyes at how embarrassing the whole affair was.

'I am Mrs Jones, your housekeeper,' Aunt Meredith said, straightening her back and getting into character. She pointed at me next. 'This is Suzanne, our scullery maid.' I instinctively fell into character and sank into a deep curtsey. 'This is Old Nell, our cook and resident physic.' Nell took a step forward and gave the crowd a solemn nod. Her heavy jewellery was jingling away like some kind of Romany Gypsy, and under one arm she held the crystal ball that Nate had brought to the house for her earlier. Aunt Meredith then pointed to a thin woman who must have been in her thirties. I hadn't noticed her before. She was dressed like me – like a servant. 'This here is Katie, she'll be the maid who will serve you dinner and empty your bedchamber pots.' Poor Katie, I thought, she must be the part-time cleaner Aunt Meredith had told me about. 'And this here,' Aunt Meredith gestured at Toby, 'is the local county sheriff. On hand should any of you need any help at all.'

Toby stepped forward and sucked proudly on his new plastic pipe. The crowd gave him a patronising clap.

Thank God Katie was there to serve everyone dinner. I am many things but I am not a servant, even in the name of my art. Whilst the guests gorged themselves on the feast that Nell had prepared for them, I hid away in the kitchen and made myself a ham sandwich for supper. 'Suzy,' Aunt Meredith tutted as she came into the kitchen. A strand of greying hair had fallen out of her smart up-do and she pushed it back from her face with a sigh. 'If you'd waited half an hour you could have eaten what was left of the guests' food – there's always enough left to feed a small army .'

'I was hungry.' I shrugged.

'Well, they're halfway through their dessert course now. I should think you're good to go.'

'Good to go?' I raised a confused eyebrow.

'Scream. Die.' She smiled at me. 'At the bottom of the stairs please.' I rose to my feet. 'Oh, and make sure you're loud enough. We want them to be able to hear you through the dining room door.'

I obediently stood and walked into the grand hallway, made my way to the bottom of the staircase and cleared my throat. At the top of my lungs I gave my best, most blood-curdling scream. I then sank dramatically to the floor and quickly arranged myself in a graceful dead-person pose by the foot of the stairs, right next to the suit of armour.

There was a clatter of excited footsteps rushing out of the dining room and into the grand hall. 'The scullery maid has been murdered!' I heard one woman gasp with joy. They quickly gathered around me and began to speculate on how I might have died. I tried not to flutter my eyelids or sneeze in anyone's face as the guests stood over my 'dead' body exchanging their theories. 'Perhaps she was strangled?' one man said. 'Or bludgeoned to death?' said another. 'But there's no blood, and no murder weapon,' someone replied. I could feel their hot breath on my cheek as they bent down to study me, and could smell their perfume as they wafted about around me. The group must have been standing over me for half an hour, but it felt like days. 'I say she fell down the stairs and broke her neck,' said one man. 'I say she was pushed,' said a woman. This seemed to be met with a chorus of agreement, and gradually I felt the guests moving away from me and heading back towards the dining room. I lay there for a while longer, in case anyone was still watching. My arm was twisted beneath me in an awkward position, and I longed to roll over and free it.

Gradually, I heard the guests' voices grow softer as the dining room door was pulled shut behind them. Aunt Meredith hadn't told me when I'd be able to get up – I'd just assumed I'd play dead at the foot of the stairs until she told me otherwise. But my arm was killing me, and I was beginning to need the loo. Just as I was about to sit up I felt a swish of movement down by my feet.

Someone was still in the hall, watching over me. Someone had stayed behind from the rest of the group and was silently observing me, looking for clues as to how I died. I forced myself to stay put, to ignore the throbbing pain in my arm for just a few more minutes.

Whoever was standing there began to move around me as I lay still on the floor. I couldn't hear their footsteps but I could feel them moving close to me. I felt a presence by the top of my head – they must have been standing right above me, looking down onto my face. I willed my eyes to stay closed as whoever was there bent down and came closer to me. Suddenly the air around me seemed to thin out, and I became more aware of the sound of my own breathing. There were no draughts there in the hall, but it suddenly felt like an ice-cold wind was sweeping all around me. As I felt the stranger move closer to me, a chill crept along my spine and I couldn't help but shudder. With the other guests I had felt their warm breath on my skin, but this was different. It felt like icy tentacles were creeping around me and squeezing the breath out of me. I forced myself to lie still a moment longer, but the sensation grew more intense. I felt the hairs on my body stand up and my heart began to thump furiously inside me. The silence was broken by the creaking of the old staircase and the wind rattling against the domed glass skylight overhead. On impulse my eyes shot open and I sat bolt upright. I spun around, searching the hallways for whoever had stood over me, but there was no one there. No one in the hallway, no one walking up the stairs. I was completely alone.

Another shudder ran through me. I'd imagined the whole thing. The sensation of someone standing over me, breathing their icy breath over my face. Eventually I stood up, brushed down my scullery-maid skirt and headed towards the kitchen. I rooted around in the fridge for some of the guests' dinner leftovers and washed it down with a glass of cold water. I was alone in the kitchen; I had no idea where my aunt or cousin, Nell or Katie were. I tried to shake off the feeling of unease that crept through my veins. I tried to convince myself that whatever had just happened to me whilst I lay in the hallway had been in my head.

I put my dirty plate and glass in the sink and headed out of the kitchen and up the stairs towards my room so that I could change into my own clothes. I put on a short blue cotton dress that I'd made the summer before. I'd spent hours sewing sequins onto the straps – a few of them had fallen off in the past year but it was comfortable and cool.

Desperate to distract myself from whatever had just happened, I picked up my notebook and pen and climbed onto my bed. The light outside was soft as I sat on my bed and read through what I'd written that day – notes about the girls who lived in the boarding school in my head. I began to make notes on the side of the page about things I should probably change when I began to write it properly – who was friends with who, who was the bitchy girl and who was the doormat. I invented lives for the girls on my page, personal histories and wishes for their future. Thinking about them was so much easier than thinking about myself and the disturbing sensation I'd had whilst playing dead in the hallway earlier.

After a while I had to turn my bedside light on to write as it was getting too dark outside. I think it must have been gone ten o'clock when I finally put my pen down.

I walked over to the window to pull my curtains shut. The curtains that someone else had opened for me that morning.

As I stared out into the darkness, movement on the ground below caught my eye. In the moonlight I could see a small, cloaked figure running away from the house towards the river. It was a girl, probably about twelve years old. Her long cloak billowed out around her as she ran. I assumed she must have been one of the murder mystery dinner guests, although I couldn't remember seeing her earlier. As I watched her move through the garden a cold shudder ran through me, and my mind took me back to the sensation of lying on the hallway floor and feeling someone watch over me.

I tried to shake it off as I watched the girl run up to the riverbank and untie a boat. I thought it strange as I couldn't remember seeing a post to tie a boat to as I'd walked along the river that day. And as I watched the girl hurriedly untie the boat, I realised I hadn't seen another boat on the river either. I briefly wondered if she'd rowed the boat from upstream somewhere, docking it by the house for some reason.

Curiously, I watched as the girl waded into the river and began to push the boat away from the bank in a hurry. Her heavy cloak spread out around her in the water, dragging her back towards the bank. She turned and looked back at the house, as if she was looking at it for the last time. The hood of her cloak shadowed her face and I couldn't see her features properly. Instead, the space where her face should have been just looked like a grey void. The girl quickly turned away again and began to clamber into the boat, struggling with her heavy cloak as she did so. Once she was in the boat she took hold of an oar. As the girl began to row herself down the river, away from the house, the moonlight bounced off the name written on the helm of the boat.

The Lady of Shalott.

Friday 12th September 1952

The new girl's name is Tilly. Tilly the grey girl at the attic window. Apparently she's our age but she looks like she should be bunking in with the first years. No one knows why she's allowed to sleep upstairs with the prefects and why she's allowed to skip Games. Yesterday she was allowed to sit in the library and read for the whole afternoon whilst the rest of us had to run around in the rain battling it out with hockey sticks. It's not fair. Lavinia complained to Mrs Taylor, 'Why should we have to risk our health in this weather when she gets to sit in the warm? Why's she so special?' But Mrs Taylor just told Lavinia to stop being bitter and to stop complaining or she'll be sent out to weed the grounds next time it rains like it did yesterday.

Lavinia hates it when people tell her off. She blamed it all on Tilly. Last night, at wash time, Lavinia grabbed my hand. 'Come with me. We're going to find the new girl.' Even though Tilly sleeps upstairs with the prefects, she still has to wash on our floor. Lavinia cornered her in the washroom and told everyone else to leave. 'But you lot can stay here,' she said to me, Sybil and Margot. Everyone else left and Lavinia made sure the door was closed shut before she started to quiz Tilly. 'Who are you anyway? What makes you so special? Why do you never speak? And you're so small, I bet you're not even in a brassiere yet ...' Then she snatched Tilly's towel away from her so she stood there stark naked in front of us. Lavinia started sniggering but me, Sybil and Margot just looked

43

away. Then Tilly started crying, she snatched her towel back and ran for the door. I just let her through without stopping her, although Lavinia scolded me afterwards for letting her go.

We've been doing the Rituals every night this week. Last night the sky was too clouded to really see the moon, so we had to guess at its position in the sky. We chalked the pentagram on the floor and stood at four of the corners. Shrouded in our winter cloaks, we lit candles and chanted. Lavinia's convinced that summoning the Goddess will help us. She says it will help our hair grow long and luscious, our skin to bloom and shine and our breasts to swell like real women's. I've been checking every morning and my breasts are still the same. Although not as small as Tilly's. Lavinia says it takes a while for the Goddess to answer our Rituals, that's why we need to do them every night. Sometimes I wonder if it's ever going to work at all. But then I remember that I couldn't stop the Rituals, even if I wanted to. Every time I look down at my forearm I see the scar that binds me to Lavinia and the others, and the Goddess herself.

It was my job to throw the ashes out of the window after tonight's Rituals. I opened the window and something in the moonlight caught my eye. It was Tilly; she was wandering along the riverbank in her heavy winter cloak. She held her hands out in front of her as she walked and seemed to study them in the moonlight. How strange that she doesn't go outside during the day and yet is walking around at this time of night. I wonder if the teachers know. I didn't tell the others what I saw. I don't know why.

Until I write again,

Annabel

5

'Suzy! Phone for you!'

I jolted from my dreams to hear Aunt Meredith banging on my bedroom door. 'Suzy! Frankie's on the phone.'

Bright light streamed through the window. I knew I'd closed the curtains last night. Once again someone must have come into my room and opened them before I woke up. If I wanted to be woken up by offensive daylight blinding me then I'd be sleeping with the curtains open. But I don't. So I had them closed. I'd have to have a word with Aunt Meredith about respecting my private space.

'Suzy!' she shouted again.

'I'm asleep!' I croaked back. 'Tell Frankie I'll call her later.'

I could hear Aunt Meredith murmur down the phone at my friend, then she knocked on my door again and said loudly, 'She says you don't have her number.'

'Well, then ask her for it please.'

Frankie was my best friend but I didn't want to speak to her. Everything I'd been through at school – being haunted by the Blue Lady – Frankie had been through too. I knew that the sound of her voice would just take me back there again, and

I didn't need that. Even hearing her name made me think of the dark times we'd shared together. I pulled the duvet over my head and tried in vain to fall back asleep. But the thought of Frankie and the life we had back at school had woken me up like a cold shower.

An hour later I was washed and sitting at the breakfast table with Toby. Once again I was trying to force down a cup of instant coffee. I swear it tasted even worse than it did the day before.

'So how are you this morning, Toby?' I asked, trying to sound cheery.

'I feel discombobulated,' Toby said with certainty, not looking up from his book.

'That's a good word,' I congratulated him. 'Where did you learn it?'

'Dr Who,' he replied. 'It means that I feel confused.'

My lips curled into a smile. 'And what do you have to feel confused about?'

'I'm trying to work out who the murderer is this weekend. Mum won't tell me, she says I have to work it out for myself.'

'So how was the rest of the party last night?' I asked him.

'It was fun,' he said, half chewing a piece of toast and half flicking through his book. Once again he was wearing his Sherlock Holmes costume, but his cape was thrown over the back of his chair and the plastic pipe that he'd had glued to his lips all evening rested on the table. 'Mum made me go to bed before they got their first proper clue, though.'

'And how did they get that then?' I asked. 'My Oscar-worthy

performance not enough to convince them that someone was murdered?'

'Nell sat down with her crystal ball and told them all that the murderer was in their midst.'

'Ah, I see.' The very same crystal ball that Nate had brought round on his motorbike, I bet. 'And when do they get their second clue?' I asked, leaning in and widening my eyes playfully.

'They had it over breakfast this morning. A letter arrived saying that Dr Fletcher is a bigamist. Mum said that means he's married more than one lady.'

I nodded. 'So where are they all now? I haven't seen any of them since I woke up.'

'You can't go into the library, the billiards room, the music room or the dining room, or the apple grove – that's where they'll all be, trying to work out who did it.'

'And when will they find out who has "done it"?' I asked.

'We'll all find out at dinner tonight,' he said, still looking at his book.

'But I'm dead, Toby. I won't be at dinner tonight. If you find out who the murderer is before then you have to tell me. It's only fair – I was the one who died after all.'

Toby just nodded at me without looking up.

'What're you reading?' I asked. 'Is it *Hamlet?* Did you go and pinch a copy from the library?'

Toby shook his head and held up the cover of his book so I could see. *007 – Fact or Fiction?* 'I thought I could pick up some spy tips and spy on the guests. Then I can work out who's acting suspiciously and who might be the murderer.'

'Good idea, but I'm surprised you're in here reading and

47

not outside playing with that young girl who's here for the weekend.' He looked at me blankly. 'One of the guests.'

'Children aren't allowed at the parties,' Toby said, looking even more discombobulated than he did before. 'Apart from me,' he added, sitting up a little straighter.

'I saw her last night,' I said with certainty. 'From my bedroom window. Maybe she's here with the guests but just didn't come down to dinner.'

'Children aren't allowed at the parties,' Toby repeated, getting bored by the conversation and looking back down at his book.

I shrugged. 'Well, I guess one just slipped through the net. So, 007 ... you like secret agents, huh?'

'I'm going to be a spy when I grow up,' he said. 'Either that or a detective. Or a pilot. I haven't decided yet.'

'Why don't you be a spy who solves mysteries and flies planes?' I grinned.

Toby lifted his chin and looked at me, considering what I'd said. Then he nodded and looked back down at his book. 'That's what I'll probably be.'

Two voices came towards the kitchen, and I turned around to see Aunt Meredith and Nell deep in conversation about something as they walked in, both still wearing their costumes from the night before. 'The kettle's just boiled,' I told them.

'Ah, if it isn't the flame-haired teen.' Nell grinned at me. I really hate it when adults try to be funny. 'How's the writing going?'

'Fine,' I replied curtly.

Aunt Meredith walked over to the complicated coffee

48

machine and switched it on. 'Can you make me a cup please?' I asked, wide-eyed.

'I thought you preferred instant?' Nell winked at me.

I gave her my best glare and shot her my best comeback: '*Consistency is the last refuge of the unimaginative.*'

'And *I am so clever that sometimes I do not understand a single word of what I am saying.*' She smirked at me. 'I can quote Oscar Wilde too, you know.'

I turned my back on Nell in contempt as Aunt Meredith passed me a cup of steaming coffee fresh from the machine. To my annoyance it smelt just as revolting as the instant stuff. Still, I brought it to my lips and began to sip.

'Were you all right last night?' Aunt Meredith asked loudly so both Toby and Nell looked up from what they were doing and stared at me.

'I'm fine,' I said quickly.

'You just seemed to disappear after playing dead – which you did brilliantly by the way – I just, you know, wanted to check you're okay.'

'I'm fine,' I repeated, feeling my cheeks begin to burn slightly.

Aunt Meredith bent down and spoke quietly, so that only I could hear. 'You know if you need to talk to anyone about anything, I'm here. I don't want you to feel like you're alone, Suzy.'

'How could I be alone?' I tried to smile at her. 'The house is full of people.' I swallowed another rank mouthful of coffee and said, 'Aunt Meredith, what made you bend the rules about having children here for the party?'

Aunt Meredith reached for the sugar and stirred some into

her own cup of coffee. 'We only allow Toby to come along because he lives here. And he's not allowed to stay up past his bedtime.'

'But what about the girl who's here this weekend?' I asked.

Aunt Meredith frowned as she put the sugar spoon in the sink. 'There're no children here this weekend. It's a fortieth birthday party.'

I tried to ignore the unease that tightened my throat. This was exactly how it had all begun before, at school. I saw things that other people didn't. It couldn't happen again. I refused to let it happen to me again. I wasn't going mad. She had been real, not a trick of the moonlight or my overactive imagination. I know what I saw. And then I remembered the boat she was running towards, *The Lady of Shalott*. 'How many boats do you have here?' I asked.

'None at all,' Nell replied.

I shot her a dagger look. I wasn't speaking to her. 'That's not true; I saw a boat in the boathouse yesterday.'

'*The Lady of Shalott*? That old thing?' Nell laughed. 'That's been there for decades – since the building was used as a school, I imagine. It's certainly not river-worthy. No, there are no boats at Dudley Hall.'

'But I saw ...' I stopped myself quickly. I'd spent weeks and weeks convincing people I wasn't crazy. And somehow, at last, I'd succeeded. I'd left Warren House, I was finally free to live my life once again. The last thing I needed was to ruin all my hard work by admitting I'd seen some kind of ghostly child running towards a boat that's been in ruins for decades.

'You all right, Suzy?' Nell looked at me. 'You look like

someone's just walked over your grave.'

'I don't like that expression,' I said without thinking, pushing away the images it conjured up in my head. Those words reminded me of everything I'd lived through at school – walking over the shallow grave in the woods, again and again. I tried to ignore the familiar knot in my stomach and the sensation of ice cracking through my veins as I stood up from my seat at the kitchen table, all eyes on me. 'Please don't say things like that around me.' I put my coffee cup down on the counter with a loud clang, suddenly aware that I needed to get out of the room as soon as possible. I remembered what the doctors at Warren House had told me about removing myself from trigger situations, and about learning to think before I speak. When I say the first thing that comes into my head other people think I'm rude, or hostile or just plain crazy. Right then I couldn't have given a monkey's hind legs what Nell or anyone else in the room thought of me. I just couldn't bear talk of graves and walking over them, not after what had happened at school. 'It's this stupid costume,' I said feebly, pulling at the tight collar around my neck. A pathetic excuse, but it was all I had. 'It's too hot and heavy. I need to change.'

Aunt Meredith's eyes filled with concern. 'If you need to, of course. But if you're going to wear your own clothes then I need to ask you to stay out of the way of the guests please.' I nodded at her and ran out of the kitchen. I heard Aunt Meredith mutter something to Toby along the lines of, 'Suzy's not well.' Hearing that just annoyed me further. Aunt Meredith might pretend to care about me, but she seemed to care more about what clothes I'm wearing in front of the guests than anything else.

I slammed my bedroom door behind me, closed my eyes and took a long, deep breath. I pulled at the buttons on my stupid Victorian costume until it quickly pooled around me on the wooden floorboards. I threw on my blue, sequinned sundress I'd been wearing the night before and picked up my notepad and pen. I must have sat on my bed trying to write for hours. I tried in vain to return to the characters I'd been trying to create on a page – the girls living in a draughty old boarding school. But no matter how hard I tried to concentrate, the words I was searching for just wouldn't come. It was as though the story I was reaching for was crafted from smoke, and it disappeared every time I tried to touch it.

I stared at my bedside cabinet drawer and thought of the blue pills the doctor had given me, the pills I hadn't taken since leaving Warren House. Deep down I knew I wasn't crazy. I didn't need pills or shrinks. But I did need an explanation for what I'd seen from my bedroom window the night before, and if I wasn't going to get one then I needed to distract myself from the memory.

Putting down my paper and pen, I reached for my make-up bag and started to paint my face like a canvas. I wasn't a natural artist, not like my best friend Frankie who could draw anything she put her mind to. But I was creative. Using my black eyeliner I drew a small key in the corner of my eye, coming down onto my cheek. I painted my eyelids a bright orange colour and coated my lips in a deep purple. Using a silver eyeliner I drew a row of dots above my arched eyebrows. I found a large, colourful butterfly clip and slid it into my bright red hair. I sat back and looked in the mirror to admire my creativity and smiled. It felt good to dress up like me again after so long in Warren House trying desperately to conform. But a look that enigmatic needed to be showcased. I decided a trip into the village would be another good distraction from Dudley Hall.

I crept through the house, careful not to be seen by any of the murder mystery guests. I could hear their animated voices from behind the library door as I walked past it. I could hear them laughing and chatting away without a care in the world. At least someone in this house was happy, I thought to myself. Soon I was out the front door and onto the gravel driveway. I plugged my earphones in and blasted rock music into my ears, singing along loudly and not caring who might hear. As my feet scrunched down on the gravel, leading me away from Dudley Hall, and the spring breeze moved through my bright red hair I began to feel lighter than I had done in days.

The walk into the village only lasted about twenty minutes; all I had to do was follow the narrow country road away from the house, retracing the route Aunt Meredith had driven me along a few days before. With every step further away from the house I was beginning to feel better. By the time the cobbled houses and small market square came into view I was feeling like the old Suzy. Confident, charismatic and carefree.

The first shop I came to in Dudley-on-Water was a small newsagent. With music still blaring into my ears, I opened the door and marched in. I made my way to the shelves of chocolate and took my time picking out something I could sit and munch my way through whilst I walked around the village. I put the chocolate bar down on the counter and pulled my headphones out of my ears before reaching for my purse.

As I put my money down on the counter and reached for my earphones again I felt someone tap me on the shoulder. 'Hello,' came a voice that nearly made me jump out of my skin. 'What are you doing out here then?'

I swung around and saw Nate, Nell's nephew, standing behind me and smiling. He was wearing jeans and a white T-shirt, just like he'd been the first time I'd seen him. I briefly wondered if he even owned any other clothes. The way you dress and present yourself to the world says a lot about you. Clearly no one had told Nate that. 'What do you want?' I grunted at him.

'A pint of milk,' he grinned, turning to a nearby fridge and pulling a pint of milk from it. He looked me up and down with a lazy smile. I'm not sure why Nate or his aunt Nell found me so amusing, but it annoyed the hell out of me and all I wanted to do was walk away. 'Unless you have something more interesting on offer,' he smirked. 'I'm all ears.'

I rolled my eyes and went to walk past him. Nate moved in front of me, blocking my exit. I sighed at his persistence and rudely looked him up and down. Despite his lack of creativity in the dress department, Nate was undoubtedly good-looking. His skin was tanned and smooth and the golden flecks in his hazel eyes made him look like some kind of giant cat. I briefly wondered if that was why he chose to dress so boringly, so you were forced to look at his beautiful eyes instead of his clothes.

'Don't run off just yet,' he said apologetically. 'I just thought I'd come and say hello.'

'Great, so you're stalking me now,' I murmured.

He shrugged and moved towards the counter. He pulled out the correct money for the milk, placed it down on the counter

54

with a smile and then turned to leave. For some reason I found myself following him as he walked out of the shop. Nate held open the door for me and turned around to face me once we were both outside. 'I was going to take my bike for a spin this afternoon – fancy coming along for the ride?'

'Do I look like a girl with a death wish?' I replied. 'Actually,' I added, smiling to myself, 'don't answer that.'

'Come on.' He nodded at his motorbike, which was parked up on the side of the road. He began to walk towards it and once again I found myself following him. Nate walked towards his bike like he'd walked into Dudley Hall when I'd first met him – as if he was lord of the manor. He held his head high, pulled his square shoulders back and took long, lazy steps, once again reminding me of a huge and dangerous cat. 'Let's go cause some trouble.' He looked back at me with a dimpled grin.

'What makes you think I want to cause trouble?' I shouted after him, beginning to enjoy the attention he was giving me.

'You were expelled from school,' he reminded me.

I rolled my eyes again. 'It wasn't like that.'

'So what was it like then?' he asked, turning to face me and walking backwards as he spoke. 'Tell me all about it.'

I stopped walking and cast my eyes towards his motorbike, propped against the pavement. I'd never been on a motorbike before, and the thought of getting on the back of Nate's bike filled me with a mixture of terror and exhilaration. The idea of riding away from everything, the world falling away behind us as the bike's tyres headed for the horizon, was tempting. But I didn't want to tell Nate anything about myself – about school or why I'd come to live at Dudley Hall. 'I don't want to talk about myself,' I said before I could stop myself.

'Neither do I,' he said quickly. I noticed the smile had dropped from his face and his eyes had clouded over. 'I won't ask you any questions, you won't ask me any in return,' he said. 'Deal?'

I paused for a moment, suddenly curious as to what Nate could possibly have to hide about himself. But if he was willing to spend time with me and not try to dig beneath the surface, then the least I could do was return the favour. 'Deal.' I smiled back.

His face lit up, his dimples deep in his cheeks. 'So, let's go have some fun.' He nodded towards his bike.

I gave Nate my most flirtatious grin. 'So, what do you do for fun around here?'

Nate laughed deep in his throat and said, 'Oh, you know, the usual.' I raised my eyebrows playfully. 'Breaking and entering. Petty theft. A spot of light flirtation with arson. Digging up the dead on a full moon.'

The smile slipped from my face.

'And there's always this thing.' He pointed to his motorbike. 'Comes in handy any time you need to make a quick escape,' he said.

'Escape,' I echoed quietly, suddenly wanting to run away.

Nate noticed my change of attitude and began to shake his head at me and laugh.

'Why are you laughing at me?'

'I'm not laughing.' He held out his hands in mock surrender. 'I just can't work you out, that's all. Cold one minute, hot the next. So, um, why are you staying here at the moment?

Where's home normally?'

'None of your business, that's where,' I said sharply, feeling my heart begin to pound inside my chest. Nate was right, my moods were as changeable as the English weather. One mention of digging up the dead and I was freaking out big-time. I needed to get away. 'And you promised – no questions.'

'I know,' he sighed. 'Sorry for asking. I just wondered about you, that's all.'

'What's that supposed to mean, "wondered about me"?'

'I just wondered where you're from, you know. What you like to do? What music you're into. That kind of stuff. No big deal. You don't want to talk, I get it.'

'No, I don't want to talk. Not to you. Not to anyone. Okay?'

He shook his head and laughed again. 'You're a right mental-case, aren't you?'

Nate's words stung violently. He might as well have slapped me hard in the face. He must have seen the look in my eyes as regret flashed across his face as soon as he'd spoken. It took all the strength I had not to lunge at him and knock him in the teeth. 'What did you say?' I whispered. It hurt more than I thought it would, being called 'mental'. I suddenly felt so stupid. I wanted the ground to swallow me up. I wanted to run back to Dudley Hall, jump into the river and swim away until it reached the ocean.

'Look, I didn't mean to upset you.' He raised his palms at me in all seriousness this time. 'I was just joking around.'

'You don't joke with me. I'm not a joke!' I choked back the tears.

'I never said you –' I charged past him, knocking into him before he could finish speaking. I plugged my headphones into my ears so I couldn't hear him calling my name as I began to march back towards Dudley Hall.

I stopped suddenly, pulled my headphones out and turned to find Nate still staring at me, mouth agape. 'Look, Nate, just stay away from me, okay? If you knew what's good for you then you'd just leave me alone.'

He didn't say a word as I turned around and ran away without once looking back.

6

The rest of that first weekend passed by in a blur. I stayed out of everyone's way as they fussed over the guests and the murderer was finally revealed. Turns out it was Lady Charlotte Cavendish who murdered me – she discovered I'd been having an affair with her husband. But even finding out who dunnit couldn't bring me out of myself. On the Sunday morning I watched from the second-floor landing balcony as the guests wheeled their suitcases down the stairs, hugged each other and said goodbye. I thought I'd be glad that the guests had gone, glad that I could finally explore the library and roam around without having to wear a silly costume. But once the house was empty of guests I just felt numb. I spent the rest of the weekend sleeping and walking around in a daze. Nothing Aunt Meredith could say to me made me feel any less alone.

The days began to slip by and soon a whole week had passed. Frankie called me every day for that first week. Every day I made an excuse not to speak to her. I had no idea how she'd managed to get hold of my phone number. I hadn't given it to her – Mum must have. Traitor. It's not that I didn't love Frankie. She's the best friend I'd ever had. But Frankie reminded me of school and of the ghosts that I so desperately needed to lay to rest. Every morning I pulled the duvet cover over my head, burying myself away, pretending I was asleep so I didn't have to face Frankie when she called. And every day after breakfast I took myself off deep into Dudley Hall's grounds. I either sat beneath the weeping willow by the brook or in the boathouse where I knew Aunt Meredith wouldn't look for me when the phone rang. I didn't check my email or Facebook accounts. I hadn't turned my mobile on in months. Frankie had no way of reaching me. Sooner or later she'd stop trying.

Every morning I woke up in my stark white room to find my bedroom curtains wide open, even though I knew I closed them the night before. I stopped asking the others if they had come into my room and opened the curtains. They always said no. I didn't want to press the matter and give them a reason to think me insane and send me back to Warren House. So day by day I spoke less and less to Aunt Meredith, Toby and Nell. I threw myself into writing my screenplay.

I picked up where I had left off with the characters I'd been trying to create in my mind. Only now those characters had a story, and the story had a title: *The Ghost of Dudley Hall*. The story was set at the time that Dudley Hall was a school, and it followed a group of girls who'd seen a ghost haunt the school corridors at night. Only no one knew who this ghost had once been, and why it refused to leave their boarding school. Each day as my pen hit the paper, I hoped I could escape my own reality and live between the pages of the story I was creating. I hoped that if I created a ghost story on the page then I'd somehow escape a similar story in my real life.

Breakfast time was always the same and I was gradually getting used to the taste of coffee in the morning. I sipped my straight black coffee and listened quietly as Toby told me facts about spies, and Nell would make jokes about my red hair as she cooked up batches of food, freezing it ahead of the weekend guests. Aunt Meredith was the only one who seemed to really notice my quiet mood. I'd often catch her staring at me thoughtfully, and then she'd smile and ask me if I were okay. Every time I answered her I kept my words to a minimum and tried to convince her that I was fine, I didn't need fussing over.

During the day Toby would follow me around and pretend to spy on me. I nearly died of fright when I saw a small brown box peep through the boathouse door one day. I leapt up and swung the door open to find my cousin crouched down and peering into the end of the box. 'What are you doing?' I asked.

'It's my periscope,' he explained, handing it to me to inspect. 'I made it myself.'

The boathouse was my favourite place to write. I hadn't left the grounds once since my run-in with Nate. There had been the briefest of moments whilst I was speaking to him where I almost thought that we could be friends. Ask no questions, get no answers – that's what we both seemed to want from each other. But I couldn't help but wonder again what Nate might possibly have to hide; obviously he felt the same way about me as it hadn't stopped him from asking. There was no way we could be friends – I didn't need that kind of complication in my life. I convinced myself I'd be happy to never see him again. He probably thought I was insane and I hated the fact that I cared. It was easier to pretend he didn't exist than entertain

61

the thought of explaining myself and apologising to him.

Friday came around soon enough, and a new batch of murder mystery guests was due to arrive in the afternoon. The sun shone down on Dudley Hall all morning, and I sat outside beneath the old weeping willow tree on the side of the stream as I wrote *The Ghost of Dudley Hall*. I found it hard to concentrate on my story that morning; I was easily distracted by the sunlight bouncing off the water, the smell of the flowing brook and the reflections in the stream. I stared for what felt like hours at the weeping willow's leaves as they swayed in the water, collecting the weeds and rotten petals that carried on the stream. I daydreamed about Ophelia from *Hamlet*, who'd drowned herself in a river, and the Lady of Shalott who had died as she floated downstream. Whether I was staring at the stream and daydreaming, or writing down the words of a ghost story on a page, my mind kept bringing me back to thoughts of death.

The sun began to sink in the sky, it was getting colder and I knew that the guests would soon be arriving. I pressed my palm against the willow's tree trunk to steady myself as I stood up, and felt deep grooves in the wood beneath my fingertips. I moved my hand and looked at the tree bark. There was a scar on the side of the tree; it had been covered by moss but was still partially visible. I picked off the moss to reveal deep etchings into the tree trunk. It was a five-pointed star – a pentagram – with five letters around it, one at each of the points: A, M, S, L and T. I stroked the carving thoughtfully, wondering what it meant and who had put it there.

The wind blew and a shiver gripped hold of me. It was time to go inside, get warm and prepare for the evening ahead.

I heard the first of the guests' cars pull up into the gravel driveway as I came in through the kitchen door. I quickly rushed upstairs to my room to shower and change before anyone could catch me in my regular clothes. That weekend's theme was the swinging sixties. Aunt Meredith had let me read through the premise of the party the night before. A sixties rock star, Graham McGroove, had invited a bunch of artists, models and musicians to spend the weekend at his country pad. But an aspiring model – once again to be played by me – is murdered on the first night of their stay. I had a black and white miniskirt and a black polo-neck vest to wear. I smiled as I looked at myself in the mirror – it was certainly an improvement on the scullery-maid costume.

I left my bedroom and made my way to the grand, winding staircase. Something stopped me suddenly, a noise coming from the floor above. It sounded like muffled crying. I was sure Aunt Meredith had told me that the attic floor hadn't yet been renovated, and that guests weren't allowed up there. But I could definitely hear someone – it sounded like a child. 'Toby?' I called out. There was no answer. I moved to the foot of the attic staircase and looked up towards the gloomy landing above me. My foot hovered over the bottom step. Part of me was desperate to investigate, to see where the crying was coming from. But I was running late for the beginning of the party, and I didn't have time. Turning away from the sound, I ran down the stairs towards the library.

My eyes fell on Toby as soon as I pushed the library door open. Despite the weekend's theme he was wearing his Sherlock Holmes cape and holding his plastic pipe. He smiled broadly at me as I walked into the room, and I smiled back, although feeling uneasy as I realised the crying couldn't have been him. Just as I'd done the Friday before, I lined up with Aunt Meredith, Nell, Toby and Katie – the part-timer who only ever showed up at weekends – in the library as Aunt Meredith welcomed the guests and introduced the staff and characters. Once again there was no one under the ancient age of thirty-five in the party. And once again during dinner I screamed a blood-curdling scream in the hallway and collapsed to my death. The guests came hurrying out and pawed over my 'dead' body, wondering aloud who could have killed such a pretty and promising young thing.

I made sure to get up as quickly as I could as soon as the guests had left me. I didn't want to be alone playing dead on the cold stone floor. I hurried back to the kitchen and helped Katie clean away the dinner plates and pack away the leftover food. 'Katie,' I said carefully, as she passed me the last of the plates to be put away. 'There are no guests staying on the top floor, are there?'

'No,' she replied, pushing her fair hair away from her face. 'It hasn't been renovated yet. It's not safe up there so I wouldn't go exploring if I were you.'

'I thought I heard –'

'It was the wind,' she said quickly, before I could finish. Her face had paled and her eyes darted away from me, as if she was hiding something. 'The wind will play tricks on you up there in the attic. Don't go up there.'

'I won't,' I replied, although I didn't believe what I was saying.

I spent the next day avoiding the guests and keeping as far away from the house as I could. I sat in the boathouse writing for hours. The afternoon was muggy, the air desperate for a thunder storm. I wrote scene after scene, tearing each page that I'd completed from my notepad and setting it aside into its own little pile. Needing a break, I took myself back to the house and into the kitchen, my completed pages in one hand and the notepad in the other. Nell was sitting at the table; Toby was sat next to her reading his 007 book. I put my notepad on a shelf by the sink so I could use my free hand to run the tap. I gulped down a glass of cold water greedily.

'I don't suppose you want to help me?' Nell said, chopping a lettuce into shreds. That annoyed me. She'd already made up her mind that I'd say no before she asked, so why bother asking at all?

'I don't suppose I do,' I muttered back.

'You know, Suzy,' Nell said thoughtfully. 'Sometimes you can sound very rude. You really should think before you speak.'

I nearly exploded all over the kitchen. I could have lashed out at her and torn her throat out at that moment. How dare she say such a thing to me? 'Just because you can hear what comes out of my mouth doesn't mean you know me,' I said sharply. Toby looked up from his book, his little body rigid at the sound of my outburst. 'You don't know the thoughts in my head. You don't know what I think and feel,' I accused Nell.

'All the world has to go on is what you give them, Suzy,' Nell replied so calmly it only made me angrier. 'You're a girl with shocking red hair and an arsenal of Shakespeare quotes at the ready and a whole lot of attitude. It doesn't take a genius to know that something is troubling you. I'd much rather you spoke to me about it than snap.'

'What makes you think I'd speak to you about anything? You're not my friend. You're not my mother,' I shouted. 'You have no idea who I am or what I've been through in my life. I don't care what you think of me. You or your stupid, stalker nephew. Don't speak to me ever again!'

I stormed out of the kitchen, trying desperately not to cry. Why couldn't Nell just keep her big mouth shut? Was I that transparent? Was it that obvious that I was walking around with a grey storm cloud over my head? I raced up the staircase to my bedroom on the second floor and slammed the door behind me. I collapsed onto the bed and sobbed into my pillow. I didn't want to feel like this. And I didn't want other people to notice how I was feeling. For the first time in my life I wished I was invisible, I wished I could just disappear and no one would care where I was or what had happened.

I cried and rocked myself to sleep, falling asleep on my bed without changing or showering.

When I woke it was pitch dark outside and the air was crackling with thunder. It must have been the middle of the night. No one had come in to wake me for dinner, no one had come to check that I was okay. Suddenly I regretted my wish to feel invisible; all I wanted was for someone to care.

My bedroom window swung on its hinges and specks of rain spattered through the open window. I pulled myself up and walked over, reached out for the window latch and before I knew it I was looking down towards the river. I felt my heart thud as the memory of the girl running to the river bank surged up within me. But this time there was nothing to see. No boat, no girl. Just the sloshing rain hitting the swollen river. I closed the window and drew the curtains. I pulled the hair band from my red hair, scrunched the edges of the curtains together and tied them into a knot with the hair band so they couldn't be pulled open easily.

The travel clock on my bedside table said one a.m. The rest of the house would be sleeping, but I felt horribly awake. I'd heard a lot about writers who do their best work in the middle of the night, and I wondered if it would be the same for me. I walked over to the small desk in my room and sat down. I began to look about for my notepad when I realised I must have left it on the shelf by the kitchen sink when I was last downstairs. After arguing with Nell, picking up my notepad had slipped my mind.

Still in my clothes from the day before, I left my bedroom and went out onto the dark landing. The only light came from the waning moon glittering through the central skylight above. Rain pattered down on the glass, the droplets looking like diamonds in the moonlight. As I slowly descended the grand staircase lightning flashed through the skylight overhead, illuminating the suit of armour standing guard at the foot of the stairs. As I reached the great hall I saw that there was a light on in the library, and I could hear the drunken and muted chatter of a few of the party guests – who'd obviously stayed up drinking into the night – coming from behind the closed library door. The dim glow escaping the library was enough to light the way for me as I went through the grand entrance hall and towards the kitchen at the back of the house.

The back corridor was cloaked in blackness. I made my

way into the kitchen in the darkness and quickly reached for the light as soon as I was in there. The place was pristine; Nell, Katie and Aunt Meredith had done an impeccable job of clearing up before they'd retired for the night. I walked over to the sink and looked up at the shelf where I was certain I'd left my notepad. I still couldn't see it. I quickly checked the other shelves, the spotless surfaces, the kitchen table – it was nowhere to be seen. I did a second sweep of the room, of the shelves and surfaces, and it wasn't there. There were no piles of clothes, papers or magazines that it could have been tidied away into. I swore under my breath and promised to really make a point of complaining to Nell and Aunt Meredith for touching my stuff. Annoyed, I turned out the light and made my way back down the dark corridor and into the dimly lit entrance hall. As I walked towards the stairs a square of white on the bottom step, next to the suit of armour, caught my eye.

My notepad.

The breath was knocked out of me as though someone had punched me in the gut.

The notepad had certainly not been there when I'd walked down the stairs only minutes before. And Aunt Meredith wouldn't have put it there for the guests to see as they walked up and down the stairs.

Horror tickled my insides, like small insects scuttling through my veins. Someone must have known I was looking for it. They had put it there after I'd walked down the stairs. I picked up my notepad with shaking hands and clutched it to my chest. I turned around, expecting to see someone watching me in the shadows. But there was no one.

I turned sharply at the sound of murmured voices coming from the library. Without thinking, I charged towards the library door with my notepad in my hands. I pushed the heavy door back and stepped into the dimly lit room. A man and woman sat together on the old chesterfield couch. They pulled apart from one another as soon as I came into the room, as if I'd caught them doing something they shouldn't have been. 'Did you move my notepad?' I blurted out.

The couple, both as old as my parents, looked at me as though I had just clawed my way out of an asylum. I repeated myself, louder this time, 'Did you move my notepad?'

'We didn't touch your notepad,' said the man, bemused.

'Did you see anyone out in the hall a minute ago?' I asked, suddenly realising just how crazy I sounded. 'Did you hear anything?'

The woman shook her head and looked up at the man as he said very firmly, 'No.'

I stood there, staring at them in silence for a few long moments before I turned and left them to whatever they had been doing before I interrupted.

I quickly ran up the stairs, moonlight still pouring through the skylight above. As I stepped out onto the second-floor landing, ready to head into my room, another square of white caught my eye. This time it was above me, on the third floor – the un-renovated attic floor where no one stayed. It looked like a swish of white material, but it was gone as quickly as I'd seen it. Determined to prove to myself that I was imagining things, I forced my legs up the next flight of rickety stairs. Soon I was standing on the third-floor landing.

It was dark, and the corridors were narrower up there, not as open and grand as they were on the floors below. It struck me that in over a week at Dudley Hall I'd never been up to the third floor. I had no idea what was up there. At the top of the stairs a corridor led off to my left, and to my right was a closed door. I assumed that behind the door was another corridor, similar or identical to the one on my left. Slowly, with my back to the closed door, I began to walk down the dark corridor to the left of the stairs. Where there should have been a door like the one behind me were rusted hinges and a splintered doorframe. The right-hand side of the corridor was lined with small glass windows, which strobed with the lightning from outside. There were three doors along the left-hand side of the corridor – all closed. I found myself walking towards the door at the far end, and it was as I was walking that I began to hear the sound of crying. Not loud, grief-fuelled wails. It was a small sound, a muffled sob. The same sound I'd heard the night before, the sound that Katie had told me was the wind. But it didn't sound like the wind. It sounded like a child, a girl.

The noise was coming from behind me. From the landing at the top of the stairs.

I looked back and to my horror saw that the closed door on the other side of the building was no longer closed. It stood open, inviting me to walk through. The sound of the crying grew louder, and I realised that it wasn't coming from the landing, where nothing could be seen. It was coming from the far corridor, the corridor that had sat behind a closed door only moments before.

Before I could stop myself my feet were moving towards

the sound of crying. I walked past the three doors, past the rusted hinges where the corridor door should have been, and out onto the landing. The sound of thunder and rain lashed against the domed skylight, flashes of lightning illuminating the dark attic corridor.

Without thinking, I walked towards the open door. The corridor was a mirror image of the one I had just walked down. This time the three closed doors were to my right and the small windows to my left. The floorboards creaked beneath my feet and my heart beat a furious rhythm in my chest as I followed the sound of crying to the last room on the right.

As I came face to face with the door, my chest rising and falling as if I'd just run a marathon, I clutched my notepad to my chest so tightly my fingers numbed. The unmistakable sound of crying seeped through the closed door. I pressed my ear to the wood and listened. I could hear someone crying as clear as thunder. I reached for the doorknob, ready to open the door and confront an empty room, confront my madness. Part of me wanted to see an empty room. I needed to know that what was happening wasn't real. Closing my eyes, breathing deeply to steady myself, I turned the doorknob.

It wouldn't turn. Wouldn't open. It was locked. I rattled the handle, wanting desperately to open the door and see whatever was behind it. But it wouldn't budge.

A loud clap of thunder shook me and my hand flew from the door handle. The next thing I knew I was running back down the corridor, down the stairs, and along the second-floor landing. I burst into my room and shut the door behind me loudly. I pressed my back against the door and slid down it, onto the floor. I closed my eyes and focused on steadying my breathing. In, out. In, out. Breathe, breathe, breathe. It's not real, not real. It's all in my head, in my head. Ghosts aren't real. She's dead and buried. She didn't come back.

I opened my eyes and stared at the window.

The curtains were wide open, drawn apart like they were every morning.

Shaking, I rose to my feet and walked towards the window. It was the middle of the night and someone had come into my room, taken my hair band from the curtains and drawn them apart in the darkness.

I stood at the end of my bed and gaped in horror at the open curtains. Something on my pillow caught my eye and I turned to look.

There, placed very purposefully on my pillow, where I'd slept every night since arriving at Dudley Hall, was my hair band.

Wednesday 17th September 1952

The moon was strong in the sky last night so Lavinia, Sybil, Margot and I stayed up late doing the Rituals. Margot burnt her finger trying to drip wax onto our prayers to the Goddess, and Sybil had to sneak her down the hall to the washrooms so she could bathe her hand in water. 'Honestly, they're such schoolgirls,' Lavinia complained. 'If we're ever going to summon the Goddess and make her answer our prayers it's going to have to be you and me that do it, Annabel.' Whilst Margot and Sybil were down the hall and Lavinia was clearing up the room I looked out of the window. That's when I saw her again – Tilly. She was walking through the grounds with her cloak pulled over her head. The moonlight bounced off her pale skin as though she was made of diamonds. Just what is she doing out there? 'Shut the window, Annabel,' Lavinia moaned. 'I'll catch my death!'

We had Games in the rain again today. Lavinia and I were making our way outside with our hockey sticks when we saw Tilly heading towards the library. 'Let's follow her quickly,' Lavinia said. We slipped into the library where Tilly was getting a heavy book out of her satchel. A few of the other girls looked up but no one said anything as Lavinia marched towards Tilly and snatched the book clean out of her hands. 'What do we have here then?' Lavinia said spitefully, opening up the pages of Tilly's book. 'The Complete Works of Tennyson. What a bore you are, Tilly. Who reads poetry for fun? Just as well you can't come outside – we'd beat you to death with our hockey sticks if we could.' Then Lavinia threw the book at Tilly's face and it hit her on the nose before falling onto the table. Lavinia swished her hair as she stormed off.

Tilly scrambled about for her book and wiped the tears in her eyes. 'Don't cry,' I whispered to her. 'It's what she wants; it'll only make it worse.' Then I had to leave with Lavinia so we didn't miss Games.

We have another late night meeting for the Rituals tonight. Sybil swears that her skin is clearing up. 'Of course it is, the Goddess is finally listening to us,' Lavinia snorted. But I can still see Sybil's pimples when she stands in the sunlight. I don't think the Goddess is listening at all. But I daren't tell that to Lavinia. I wouldn't want her to start throwing books at my face. Mind you, at least I wouldn't cry, I know how to handle myself with Lavinia. And at least I have other friends. Tilly doesn't have any one.

Until I write again,

Annabel

7

I didn't sleep that night. I sat by the foot of my bed until it was light outside. My eyes drifted between my notepad, the open curtains and the hair band on my pillow until I was nearly blind from the tears streaming down my numb cheeks. I could make no sense of anything. Exhausted, I eventually lay down and pulled the bed cover over myself. I lay at the tail end of the bed. I couldn't bring myself to rest my head on the pillow. The pillow was where they had placed my hair band. Whoever 'they' were.

As the night slowly gave way to the morning, I listened to the sound of the party guests downstairs. I could hear their suitcases thudding down the stairs, and their cars pulling away outside as they left. I waited until gone noon before I finally went downstairs. That way I could be sure that all the guests had left and it would just be my aunt, Toby and Nell left in the house. Still wearing the clothes I'd worn the day before, I walked down the winding stairs. I could hear the sound of a vacuum cleaner whirring away in one of the guest bedrooms, and in the cold light of day the staircase looked like it belonged in a different world from the night before. The spot where I'd found my notepad didn't look sinister, and when I looked up towards the bright sunshine streaming through the glass-domed ceiling, and drew my gaze to the third-floor landing, nothing seemed strange or in any way frightening.

Nell was in the kitchen. 'Coffee?' she asked, fiddling with the machine. 'You look like you could use some.'

'No,' I said. The last thing I wanted was the rank taste and heady rush of caffeine running through me. I still felt bruised from the night before, I needed something comforting. 'Got any hot chocolate?' I suddenly remembered that the last time I'd seen Nell I'd told her never to speak to me again. I looked down at the floor, feeling stupid; my teenage outburst felt so trivial compared to what had happened to me in the hours afterwards.

'One hot chocolate coming right up.' Nell smiled. I sat down at the table and rubbed at my tired eyes as Nell pottered about. Every noise she made was like an assault to my senses – the boiling kettle, the tinkering of a teaspoon – I just wanted to thump my fists on the kitchen table and beg for silence.

Nell put the mug of hot chocolate down in front of me wordlessly, much to my relief. She sat down opposite me and began to shuffle a deck of cards she had pulled from her pocket. I watched as she spread the cards out in front of her, touching them with great care, a look of absolute concentration on her face.

They were tarot cards. Even I could see that. I'd never seen a deck of tarot cards before but I knew what they looked like. The death card, the lovers, the magicians, the two of swords and cups. 'You can read tarot cards?' I asked her.

She nodded. 'The guests love it.'

I waited for her to offer to read my cards, but she didn't even look up at me. Whatever she was seeing in the cards must have been far more interesting. I watched on silently as she patiently lay out the cards in a formation on the kitchen table. She carefully lay them on top of each other, touching each one almost lovingly and taking a moment to study it before she moved on to the next. I wondered if there was any truth to them, and what they might be telling her. I absently started picking at the skin around my nails, my eyes glazing over as the cards blurred into a puzzle of shapes and colours.

'Trouble sleeping?' Nell said without looking at me. 'I find it difficult to sleep during storms too. My mother used to say I was a sailor in a past life, died at sea in a storm. Even as a baby I couldn't bear the sound of thunder, that's obviously why.'

'Obviously,' I said dryly.

She smiled warmly at me and looked back down at her cards. It dawned on me that someone like Nell must be used to people thinking she's crazy. It clearly didn't bother her. I wished I could be like that. Our school chaplain used to preach to us in his sermons, saying that everyone we meet in life has been put there by God to teach us something. If that's true then maybe Nell's lesson for me is not to care what people think.

'What's on your mind?' she asked, once again without looking up.

'You mean you can't see that in the cards?' I snorted. Nell said nothing, and I immediately felt like a bitch for being such a predictable teenager. 'Sorry,' I mumbled apologetically. 'I'm just tired.' Nell looked up and smiled. 'Will you read the cards for me?' I asked before I could stop myself.

Nell hurriedly scooped up the cards from the table and began to shuffle them in her hands once again. 'Do you know what you're asking me, Suzy? Tarot cards are powerful things, they're not a game.'

'You don't need to treat me like a party guest,' I said, annoyed. 'I'm big enough to know what I'm asking. But if you're too scared of my aunt…'

'Your aunt?' Nell snorted. 'No, Suzy, Meredith doesn't worry me. Unlocking flood gates do, though.' As the mental image of gushing floodgates swept through my mind I realised that I didn't care. I've always been attracted to fire, I've always wanted to walk on the wild side. Ouija boards, seances, tarot cards – they might be a gateway to darkness, but they're also part of who I am. There was nothing Nell could say to deter me once I had my mind fixed on something. And my mind was fixed on having my tarot cards read.

'I'd like you to read for me,' I said with certainty. 'Please.'

'Very well.' She sighed and sat back thoughtfully. 'What do you want to ask them?' As if the cards were a sentient entity unto themselves.

The answer to Nell's question came as simply and as suddenly as a dream. 'I want to ask if I'll ever be happy.'

Nell frowned and then nodded in understanding and passed me the cards. 'Shuffle them and then fan them out on the table, face down.' I did as she instructed.

The back of the cards had a symmetrical pattern of the moon at its various stages against a midnight-blue background. 'I want you to repeat the question over and over in your mind and then pull out three cards.'

'Any cards?' I asked.

She nodded. 'The three cards that are pulling you towards them.'

Will I ever be happy? Will I ever be happy? I repeated in my mind, over and over. As I repeated the question and stared at the cards, I let my focus drift so the deck blurred into one. Slowly, I reached out and tugged on the corner of three cards, one from either end and one from the middle.

Nell pulled out the three cards I had touched and flipped them over. She pointed to a card with the Roman numeral VII and a picture of a golden chariot ridden by a woman with flames in her hair. 'This card represents the road you have walked.' Next she pointed to a card of an older man with a flowing grey beard; in one hand he held a golden chalice, in the other a silver spear. 'This card is the path you stand on now. And this card is the road that lies ahead.' The final card had an image of a plain, ashen-faced girl standing alone in a field, grey standing-stones surrounding her – like the ones you see at Stonehenge. 'Together the three cards give you an answer to your question.'

'So what's the answer?' I asked, leaning forwards. 'What do they mean?'

'This first card, The Chariot, tells me that in the past you've had to summon a great strength from inside yourself, one that you previously did not know you had. You have been driven by fear, but have overcome that fear. And yet your fear still haunts you, it's still a driving force for you now. And where you stand now is represented by this card here.' She tapped the central card. 'The Magician is a place of great strength. You sometimes find it difficult to understand that you are in control, Suzy. You have the power to transform old situations. You must use that energy buried deep inside yourself to evolve, you must focus your will. And if you can do that, then the path ahead for you is a very interesting one. You're very special, Suzy. That much is obvious to anyone, and it's here for me now in the cards you have selected. This card here –' she pointed to the card with the girl on it, the card that represented my future – 'is The Daughter of Stones. This is what we tarot readers refer to as a Minor Arcana card. The Daughter of Stones represents great energy, sacred energy. Energy harvested through rituals and visions.' My heart gave a sudden jolt at the words she used. 'Rituals', 'visions' – it made me think of Ouija boards, seances, candles and chanting, the very things that had brought about my 'visions' at school. Visions I'm not sure I wanted to ever have again. 'You must use your strength to take responsibility for a power greater than yourself,' Nell said, her eyes burning with intensity as she looked straight at me.

'What do you mean?' I asked, hearing my voice catch in my throat. 'What power greater than myself?'

'You have great love and courage and inner beauty, Suzy. But you also have an ability to see the world in a way that others can't. This is both a great gift and a great burden. You're walking a path that is very special, but also very lonely. It's a path that most people cannot follow you down. You must learn to be very strong if you are to survive the road ahead. I'd say …' She paused and stared at me for a beat. '… I'd say that you already know what lies ahead. You know what your visions mean. Being a visionary will stand you apart from others, but that is not something that should be feared.'

'*A dreamer is one who can only find his way by moonlight, and his punishment is that he sees the dawn before the rest of the world,*' I whispered. 'Oscar Wilde said that. Maybe that's me, someone who must find their way by moonlight.' I blinked the glaze from my eyes and looked up to see Nell smiling at me fondly. 'Who owned this house before my aunt's husband?' I had no idea where the question came from – I'd never really thought about it before – but as soon as the words were out of my mouth, the answer suddenly seemed important.

Nell stared me straight in the eye and said, 'After the Dudley family fell into debt and sold off the house in the 1800s it became a school. A school for orphaned young ladies run by a charity. The school closed in the 1950s and the building stood empty for decades after that. The charitable trust that once ran the school still owned the building, and your uncle Richard bought it from them.'

'Why did the school close?'

Nell shrugged. 'I guess there weren't enough orphaned young girls in the country to keep it going.'

'Seems sad,' I said quietly, 'for a building to stand empty for so long. How do you know so much about the house?'

'My sister and I grew up in the village; in fact, our mother was one of the girls who went to Dudley Hall School. She used to hate us coming up here as children and playing in the grounds. She used to tell us that a building can hold more than just dust and furniture.'

My heart rate spiked at Nell's words. No one knew that to be true as much as me – sometimes there was so much more to buildings than what we could see. There were stories and darkness and spirits that lingered and haunted. 'What did she mean?' I asked in a whisper. 'What's here?'

'Bad memories. Mum didn't like to talk about the years she spent here. It's hard to imagine this place as a school, isn't it? Your room would have once been a dormitory with four or five girls in it.'

The reminder that the house had once been a school and that my bedroom had once been a dormitory made me feel sick. The walls of Dudley Hall had witnessed stories and lives that I could never know about. Ghosts that were somehow still trapped here.

'Nate's been asking after you,' Nell said, looking back down at the cards. I looked at her blankly, suddenly forgetting who Nate was and why he would ask about me. 'My nephew,' she reminded me.

'Of course,' I muttered, remembering exactly who Nate was and the fact that he thought I was some kind of lunatic.

Nell smiled. 'I told him you're fine, and keeping yourself busy doing lots of writing. He gets so bored during the college holidays,' she said without me asking how he was. 'His mum's got him working hard around the house to try and keep him busy. I feel sorry for him if truth be told. Dudley-on-Water is a lousy place to be a teenager, nothing to do here. Meredith did wonder if the two of you might become friends, but I guess you can lead a horse to water ...'

'I'm sure Nate can make his own friends,' I muttered. 'He doesn't need me.'

'You should come over for dinner some time,' she said.

'You live with him?' I asked, surprised.

'And my sister, his mother. They moved in with me when Nate's father left them.'

I hadn't given Nate's family much thought. I'd tried not to think about Nate at all since my run-in with him in the village over a week ago. I knew Nell was his aunt but I hadn't even wondered about his mother and father. 'Does Nate have any brothers and sisters?'

Nell shook her head. 'No, it's just him. So will you come then, to dinner?'

The thought of sitting around a dinner table with Nate, the boy who'd called me 'mental', was the last thing I wanted to do. He'd made assumptions about me and he didn't even know me. But then again, maybe I'd done the same to him. Both times I'd met him he'd seemed arrogant and rude, but I'd never really given much thought as to why he might have been like that. Maybe I should give him another chance.

'Dinner might be nice, thank you,' I smiled.

'Tomorrow night?'

'Okay.'

I watched as Nell scooped up the cards on the kitchen table and began to shuffle them again. 'Is it true what Toby said,' I asked curiously. 'That you never go upstairs?'

'I told you before,' she replied. 'Toby is many things but he's not a liar. It's Katie up there now cleaning the guest rooms. I like to stay down here.'

As I opened my mouth to ask more Aunt Meredith walked into the kitchen. 'Suzy, can I have a quick word with you?' She approached me and paused as she came close, looking at me with a mixture of anger and worry. 'You all right, Suzy? You look like you haven't slept. Have you eaten yet?'

'I didn't sleep,' I admitted. 'And no, I've not eaten yet.'

'Well, that won't fill you up.' She nodded at the hot chocolate in my hands. 'Let me fix you some food and then you can go back to bed and try to snooze for a couple of hours.'

I watched as she opened the fridge and started to pull out bacon, eggs and milk. 'What did you want to talk to me about?' I asked.

'One of the guests said a red-haired girl came charging into the library in the early hours of the morning and interrupted a private party.'

'If by "private party" you mean "scandalous liaison" between two guests, then yes I suppose I did interrupt them.'

'What were you doing stalking around the house in the small hours?'

'I just told you, I couldn't sleep last night.' I winced at the memory of barging into the library in the hope of finding an explanation for my misplaced notepad.

'Well, next time you feel like a midnight adventure please try not to involve the guests. And if you must talk to them then please make sure you do so in costume.'

I nodded and turned away from Aunt Meredith, aware of Nell's eyes on me as I shuffled my feet about on the floor awkwardly.

After a cooked breakfast I went back upstairs. I showered and crawled into bed, too tired to bother with the pretence of closing the curtains. I knew I'd only find them open when I woke up.

84

As I lay there I thought about what Nell had told me, about the house once being a school and a building holding more than just dust and furniture. I wondered if that was why she wouldn't venture upstairs. Maybe she knew something about how Dudley Hall wasn't quite right. Whatever presence I could feel in the house – the cold breath on my cheek, the crying in the attic, the ghostly girl who walked in the moonlight – maybe she felt it too. As I drifted off to sleep with the afternoon sun shining through my bedroom window, I wondered what would be worse – to be mad, or for this to be real.

8

I slept right through until the next morning – a deep and dreamless sleep. After I woke I showered and went downstairs. I liked the feel of Dudley Hall without the murder mystery guests filling the place with noise; the house had an emptiness to it which suited it. An emptiness that matched my mood.

Toby was eating cereal alone at the breakfast table. I poured myself a bowl and sat down next to him. 'Hey, Toby, what's up?'

'I'm bored,' he said.

'You should never be bored,' I smiled at him. 'There's far too much to explore in the world. Music, poetry, art – you can always find some way to entertain yourself.'

'Are you going to be writing today?' he asked.

I thought for a moment. 'No.' I didn't feel ready to go back to *The Ghost of Dudley Hall*, not yet. 'Wanna hang out?'

He looked at me cautiously. 'Okay. What do you want to do?'

'I don't know.' I lifted my eyebrows playfully. 'What do you want to do?'

'Play detective.'

An idea quickly popped into my head. 'Cool, detectives. Great idea, Toby.' I smiled. 'Let's investigate the top floor of the house.'

'It's spooky up there,' Toby said, looking slightly embarrassed.

I agreed with him, and even in the cold light of day I didn't particularly want to go up there alone, but somehow going up there with my kid cousin seemed bearable. 'But we'll be together, we'll look out for each other.'

'Okay,' he smiled back. 'I'll get my fingerprint kit after breakfast.'

So after breakfast, fingerprint kit in hand, Toby and I ascended the top flight of stairs up to the third floor. I looked along the long corridor to my right, which I'd foolishly walked down two nights before. I wasn't quite ready to go back there.

'Let's go this way first.' I walked in between the rusted hinges on the broken door frame to the left. The corridor beyond the door looked smaller than it did the other night. And lit by daylight, not flashes of lightning, it almost didn't look creepy. Almost.

'You go first.' Toby pushed me further into the corridor.

Full of bravado, I charged straight up to the first door on my left and reached for the door handle. It swung open easily. Behind it was a small empty room, nothing but dusty wooden floorboards and an old fireplace. No pictures on the walls, no old furniture, nothing. 'Let's go to the next room,' Toby announced.

The next two rooms along the corridor were exactly the same. Floorboards, fireplaces and dust, nothing more. The windows looked out into the sprawling grounds, the winding river and, from up this high, you could just about see the rickety old boathouse.

'Let's investigate the other corridor too,' Toby said, obviously enjoying himself. 'I've wanted to explore up here since we moved in, but no one would come with me.'

'You were sensible not to come up here on your own,' I said seriously. 'Exploring should always be done in teams.'

'But I'm the detective and you're my assistant,' he reminded me.

'Lead the way, Sherlock.' I gestured to the other corridor.

Toby merrily skipped past the staircase and along the other corridor, the same corridor I'd walked down the night I'd heard crying coming from the room at the very end. The corridor door was still open, pushed back against the wall. I shuddered as I walked over the corridor's threshold; it seemed colder in there than the rest of the house.

Just as we'd done with the first corridor, we investigated room by room. And just like the first corridor, the first two rooms were empty. Dusty floorboards and fireplaces, that's all we could find. I stood staring out of the window in the second room, studying the grounds, the river and the boathouse, trying to put off the moment we approached the third room – the locked door I had heard crying seeping through. My fingers moved over scratches in the wooden window frame. I looked down and noticed there were letters and words carved into the rotting wood. Girls' names, mostly: Catherine, Caroline, Beth, Mary, Lavinia. The room had once been a dormitory. I'd forgotten that for the briefest of moments. So many other lives had passed through these rooms and halls.

I heard the rattle of a door handle, pulling me from my thoughts. 'Toby, wait ...'

'This room is locked,' he announced in frustration. I walked out into the corridor to see Toby battling with the locked door at the end. 'I'll see if I can pick it.'

He pulled out a little pouch of screwdrivers and tools from

his pocket. 'Part of my detective kit,' he informed me, as he began to try to pick the lock. He fiddled with the stubborn lock for several minutes before he gave up in frustration. 'Let's dust the other rooms for fingerprints instead.'

'Okay, you do that and I'll have another go at picking this lock,' I told him. He disappeared into the room next door and began to try and lift fingerprints from the windowsill.

Alone in the corridor, I pushed one of Toby's pins further into the lock but nothing happened. Toby moved on to the next room and I stayed where I was, struggling with the door. Suddenly, the only thing in the world that was important to me was getting into that room and seeing what was inside. I stood up and pushed my weight into the door, then I kicked it, hard. It wouldn't budge.

Toby emerged from the room at the end of the corridor. 'Don't break the door down, Suzy. Richard will be mad.'

'No, he won't,' I reasoned. 'He's going to have to break it down eventually anyway to renovate the room. I may as well do it for him.'

Toby shook his head. 'You'll make him angry. Maybe there's a key downstairs.'

'Fine, I'll go and ask.'

'I'll stay here and look for more fingerprints,' he said.

I frowned. 'You sure you'll be okay on your own?'

He nodded and smiled. 'It's not scary up here. It's just rooms.'

I flashed Toby a false grin. I wanted more than anything to agree with him.

I left Toby upstairs as I went down and into the kitchen. I found Aunt Meredith hunched over a juicer, working her way

89

through a pile of fresh lemons. 'I'm making lemonade for this weekend,' she said as I came into the room. 'Here, try some.'

She passed me a glass of pale, cloudy liquid. It was sharp and sweet. 'Great, thank you. Aunt Meredith, is there a key for the attic rooms?'

'What?' She looked up from the juicer.

'I need a key for the attic rooms. Toby and I are exploring.'

'No, I shouldn't think so. Although Richard will be back later this week and we can check with him then if you really want.'

'I could just break the door down ...'

'No, you won't. I don't want broken legs and sharp wooden spikes to worry about, thank you very much. I promised your mum I'd look after you,' she said sternly. 'Like I said, Richard will be back soon, you can ask him about a key then. There are plenty of other rooms for Toby to explore in the meantime.'

I huffed loudly. 'Fine, I'll wait.'

I spent the rest of the day helping Toby dust the other attic rooms for fingerprints. The only ones we found in the thick layers of dust were his and mine. The frustration I felt at not being able to go into the room at the end of the corridor was subdued slightly by Toby's obvious enjoyment of the day. After he'd collected the prints he lovingly taped them into a scrapbook and I helped him label them all up. Before I knew it the day had passed and it was time for me to get ready for dinner at Nell's house.

'Thank you for keeping Toby entertained,' Aunt Meredith said as she caught me on the second-floor landing, just about to go into my room. 'He likes you.'

'I like him too.' I grinned.

'It's good to see you smiling, Suzy,' she said gently. 'Sometimes you remind me of your mum when she was younger. She had that same twinkle in her eye.'

What happened to her? I wanted to ask, but Aunt Meredith reached forwards and pulled me towards her. She held me tightly in her arms and squeezed me. 'I'm glad you're here, Suzy,' she whispered. 'I'm sorry Dudley Hall's not the most exciting place in the world, and I'm sorry your mum couldn't look after you, but I'm glad you're here.' I wasn't sure how to respond, so I just smiled and awkwardly wriggled out of her arms, putting space between us.

'There's more than enough excitement at Dudley Hall,' I said, trying to sound positive. Aunt Meredith had been nothing but kind to me since I arrived, even though it wasn't her job to make sure I was well – Mum should have been doing that. In that moment I couldn't bear to let her know just how much I hated the house and how difficult I found it living there, how I'd leave in the blink of an eye if I could.

'You better hurry up and change for dinner.' Aunt Meredith nodded at me. 'I know Nell's looking forward to having you over tonight.'

I walked away to my room feeling suddenly deflated at the thought of dinner with Nell and Nate. Sitting around a table making small talk with them was the last thing I wanted to do with my evening. Still, at least it would only be for a few hours. I showered quickly and picked out a short black skirt and a bright blue vest I'd stitched a peace sign onto the front of last summer. I put on my heavy DM boots and wrapped a fake ivy wreath I'd bought from Camden Market around my

91

head. I painted on my make-up, taking the time to draw small flowers at the corner of each eye.

With every minute that passed I felt myself grow less sure that leaving Dudley Hall was what I wanted. Instead of feeling relieved at leaving the house I was beginning to feel dread. Dread at having to see Nate again, dread at having to make small talk and answer questions I didn't want to answer. As the sun set in the sky and the evening grew colder, I felt my stomach tighten up in knots as if I was about to walk onto a stage in front of a room full of people.

'Suzy, Nate's downstairs.' Aunt Meredith banged on my door, making me jolt with nerves.

I felt my stomach fall through the floor, and my legs shook beneath me as I walked slowly out of my room and down the stairs.

Turning the corner of the grand staircase, I saw Nate standing just inside the front door wearing his uniform white T-shirt, leather jacket and jeans. His eyes met mine before looking me up and down. I gave him a nervous smile that wasn't returned, and a scowl quickly spread across my face as I realised Nate was obviously dreading the evening as much as I was. All of a sudden I had no idea what I was doing – why on earth was I leaving Aunt Meredith and Toby to spend the evening in the company of someone who thought so badly of me? My feet numbly moved towards him, and I noticed that he held a motorbike helmet in each hand. 'This is for you,' Nate said, pushing one of the helmets towards me. I took the helmet from him and looked down at it with a frown. I opened my mouth, desperate to tell Nate where he could stick his helmet, I was staying right where I was. But my voice froze in my throat and I looked up at him blankly. His expression had softened, and there was the faintest hint of a smile upon his lips. 'You'll need a jacket,' he said, looking me over once again. 'It's cold outside. Let's go.'

9

Nate's bike pulled up outside an old cottage next to the village church. He stopped the engine and pulled his helmet off. 'We're here.'

I hopped off the bike, my legs still shaking from the ride, and removed my helmet. I turned away from Nate as I tried to mess up my hair and give it some body before I put back the ivy wreath that I'd had to take off to wear the helmet.

'Very pretty,' Nate said, walking around me.

'Oh, ha, ha,' I joked. 'Motorbike hair is such a good look.'

Nate began to walk towards the house. He stopped abruptly and turned around. I just managed to stop myself crashing into him and looked up to meet his eye. 'Look, you should know that this wasn't my idea.'

'What?' I asked, confused.

'Dinner, here, tonight,' he said, looking me dead in the eye. 'Trust me, I can see you don't want to be here and I don't particularly want you here either.'

That stung. I could tell by his behaviour that Nate didn't want me here, but he didn't actually have to say it out loud. 'Well, I'm here now,' I said bitterly. 'So get over it.'

He shook his head and opened his mouth to speak but then quickly stopped himself. There was something in his eyes that I couldn't quite make out – an apology? An explanation? 'Look, Suzy…' he said slowly. I waited for him to finish, but his words hung in the air unspoken. The hazel flecks in his eyes glinted in the twilight, and his gaze burnt into me as if there was something I should magically understand. 'Come on,' he said eventually. 'You'll see for yourself.'

He led me down a cobbled garden path and then through a narrow arched door into a warm, softly lit hallway. He hung his leather jacket on a wall hook and put his helmet down on the hall table. I put my helmet next to his, shrugged my jacket off and hung it up. I cast him a cautious glance, still feeling hurt by what he'd said to me outside, but Nate didn't look back at me.

After spending over a week at Dudley Hall the cottage felt incredibly small. The tiny rooms and low ceilings were such a stark contrast to the cavernous and endless rooms I'd grown familiar with. Nate led me into a space that was both a sitting room and a dining room. A fire roared in the grate on one side of the room and a door leading to the kitchen sat on the other. Nell poked her head out from the kitchen. 'Hi, Suzy. Take a seat.' She gestured to the dining table that had been set for supper. 'Dinner's almost ready.'

I sat down opposite Nate and picked up my serviette, placing it over my lap. I looked up and caught him staring at me. I widened my eyes and mouthed, 'What?' at him.

'You make your own clothes?' he asked.

'Yes,' I replied proudly. 'Fashion is an important form of self-expression. What you wear says a lot about you.'

He raised his eyebrow at me mockingly. 'Really?'

Before I could knock out a witty reply a woman walked out of the kitchen with a bowl of mashed potato. She was willowy and pale, her clothes hanging off her in a way that they shouldn't have. Her tired eyes cast me a quick glance as she said, 'Hi, Suzy. I'm Fiona, Nate's mum.'

'Nice to meet you,' I replied automatically. I looked over at Nate but his head was cast down; he was picking at the table cloth, his forehead creasing in a frown.

Nell came out of the kitchen with a large plate of sausages, a bowl of baked beans and an array of condiments on a tray. 'I thought I'd keep it simple.' She grinned at me. 'Sausages and mash.'

'Perfect.' I nodded, silently thankful that I wasn't currently going through one of my vegetarian phases. Fiona and Nell dished up the food and Nate poured us all glasses of juice. I noticed that Fiona was already drinking wine. It was Nell whose voice filled the silence; she chatted on about the trials and tribulations of cooking dinner on their ancient oven. Fiona moved through the room like a ghost, never looking at anyone or speaking. She eventually sat herself down and began to pick at her food. Once or twice I tried to catch Nate's eye, but he seemed to be looking anywhere in the room but at me.

Once my plate was piled high with steaming food I began to tuck in. 'This is lovely,' I said after my first mouthful.

Nell smiled as she chewed. 'I get so bored of cooking up at Dudley Hall when it comes to dinner here it's all I can muster to mash a potato and put a few sausages under the grill.' She was wearing her trademark orange turban and dangling gold earrings. Her pink top clashed loudly with the red coral she had draped around her neck.

Nell and I exchanged small talk for a while about food and the guests that she would cook for up at Dudley Hall. 'I once had a fruitarian at one of Meredith's parties,' Nell told me. 'Ate nothing but fruit – I couldn't even cook her an apple pie because she refused to eat the pastry.' Both Fiona and Nate remained silent, Fiona pushing her food around her plate as though it were poisoned and Nate eating so quickly I doubt he even tasted it. I could only assume his haste wasn't because he was starved but because he couldn't wait to get away. As he shovelled the last forkful of mashed potato into his mouth he let his cutlery fall onto his plate and he pushed his chair back to go.

'So, Nate,' I said before I could stop myself. He looked over at me, startled. 'You're at college?'

He cast his mum a nervous glance before looking back at me and answering. 'I'm doing my AS-levels at a college in the next town.' He leant forwards in his chair, resting his arms on the table, and I felt suddenly glad that he wasn't about to leave. 'I get to drive my bike there every day,' he continued, looking straight at me. 'I used to have a moped but I graduated on to the bike this year.' Fiona tutted and shook her head in disapproval as she raised her glass to her lips. I realised that whilst she'd barely touched the food on her plate, she seemed to have poured herself another glass of wine since we'd all started eating. 'You studying for AS-levels?' Nate asked me.

'Not quite yet,' I replied, suddenly wanting to change the subject. I didn't want to have to talk about myself. I hadn't been in school for months, thanks to my breakdown. I had no idea if I'd finish my GCSEs or not, let alone ever graduate to AS-Levels.

'You like living at Dudley Hall?' Nate asked me quietly, as if we were alone in the room.

I finished the last of my food and placed my knife and fork in the centre of my plate. 'It's okay. Better than being at boarding school, which is where I was before.' I skipped out the part about the lunatic asylum in between school and Dudley Hall.

'If you knew what's good for you you'd get yourself back to school as soon as possible,' Fiona said quietly. I looked over at her, feeling slightly annoyed, expecting her to launch into some kind of lecture about the importance of education, but that wasn't what I got. 'It's not right, a young girl living in that house. It's bad enough that Nell goes there every day, but at least she knows what to expect.'

I stared at Fiona, dumbfounded, unsure what to say, as silence fell across the table. Nate stood up, reached for my plate and began to tidy up the table, a mild look of embarrassment on his face. Nell just looked down at the table, studying the food on her plate silently.

'I don't like being here in this village but we've got nowhere else to go,' Fiona added, completely unaware of how her words were making everyone else feel so awkward.

'What have you got against the village?' I asked without thinking.

'It's not the village. It's the house,' Fiona replied.

'That's enough, Fiona,' Nell said gently.

'What's wrong with the house?' I asked.

Nate walked away into the kitchen and I heard him drop

the plates down onto the kitchen counter with a loud clang. Fiona and Nell exchanged a look and I noticed Nell give her sister a warning glare.

'It's...it's nothing,' Fiona said, standing up. She drained the rest of her wine before pouring herself another full glass. 'Excuse me, I'm overtired. It's this weather – I don't know if we're having thunder or blue skies. It makes me anxious. It was lovely to meet you, Suzy, good night.' And then Fiona turned and left the room, taking her wine glass but leaving her untouched plate of food behind.

I looked at Nell for an explanation, and Nell just shrugged as if that explained everything. She hadn't warned me that her sister had obviously nothing good to say about Dudley-on-Water and especially about Dudley Hall. Nate had tried to warn me about his mum before I came into the house. And now Nell just wanted to shrug off Fiona's behaviour as though there was nothing strange about it at all.

'Is the reason Fiona doesn't like Dudley Hall the same reason you won't step foot upstairs there?' I asked Nell.

Nate came back into the room with a steaming teapot and mugs on a tray. His mouth was set in a hard line. 'They're both superstitious old biddies,' Nate said quietly, pouring the tea. 'They got it from my grandmother, she was even worse. She was a schoolgirl at Dudley Hall back in the day, and she used to say that the house was cursed.'

'Nate,' Nell warned. 'Suzy has to live there. Don't go filling her head with your grandmother's mumbo-jumbo.'

'They're just stories, Aunt Nell, you said so yourself,' Nate replied.

'What stories?' I pressed.

'Enough,' Nell warned Nate, before he could say anything else.

The three of us took our tea onto the sofas and sat around the fire sipping it. Nell worked hard to steer the conversation away from Dudley Hall. She asked me about the clothes I made and the screenplay I was writing. Nate sat there quietly, staring off into space and seeming to be lost in his own thoughts. I noticed Nell didn't ask me anything about school or about my time in Warren House. She obviously knew it was something I didn't want to talk about, and I was incredibly thankful that I didn't have to answer any awkward questions in front of Nate, even if he didn't seem interested in anything I said.

The light outside had completely faded and the fire was dying out when Nate offered to give me a lift back to Dudley Hall. I thanked Nell for dinner and made her promise to say goodnight to Fiona for me – she hadn't come back downstairs again since walking off.

I lifted my jacket from the hook in the hall, picked up Nate's spare helmet and took my ivy wreath from round my head before I put the helmet on and clambered onto the back of Nate's bike. I wrapped my arms around Nate's waist and squeezed my knees against his hips as the bike began to power down the road. I'd never been on the back of a motorbike before that night. The feeling was intoxicating. I loved the sensation of the wind rushing against my limbs and the gush of air hitting the helmet. The cobbled houses and streetlights of Dudley-on-Water moved past us in a blur as we sped through the night together. I closed my eyes and imagined I was flying.

The ride was over too quickly, and before I knew it Nate was pulling up in front of Dudley Hall and switching off the engine. I passed him back his helmet and smiled before I could stop myself. 'Thanks for the lift, Nate.'

I turned around and began to walk towards the house, stopping when Nate said, 'Suzy, wait.' I spun around. 'I'm sorry about what I said earlier, about not wanting you to come for dinner.'

I shrugged at him and looked away, staring off into the dark night. 'Your mum seems nice,' I muttered.

He let out a small laugh. 'My mum *seems* crazy.'

I looked back at him. 'Is that why you didn't want me to come over tonight?'

'Can I have your number?' he asked without warning, ignoring my question.

'I don't have a phone,' I replied quickly, feeling slightly confused. Nate hadn't seemed interested in a word I'd said all evening, he hadn't even wanted me there, and now he was asking me for my number.

'Who doesn't have a phone? Well, do you have an email address?'

'Not one that I check.' My teeth began to chatter in the cool night air.

'Well, you are a mystery, aren't you?' He smiled – a genuine smile, one that I hadn't seen on him all evening.

I smiled back. *'The true mystery of the world is the visible, not the invisible.'*

He laughed. 'Excuse me?'

'Oscar Wilde,' I explained, shivering in the moonlight.

He nodded his head, his eyes softening as he looked at me. 'Well, *I'd rather die enormous than live dormant.*' He looked at me expectantly and I shook my head in confusion. 'You can quote Oscar Wilde but I can quote Jay-Z.' He laughed and shook his head. 'I want to know what *you* think, Suzy, not some dead guy.' Nate put his helmet on and revved up his bike engine. I stood back as the bike prepared to speed away, wishing I could think of something clever to say. Maybe Nate was right, maybe I shouldn't hide behind other people's words. But in truth I had no idea what I was thinking, and no idea what to say to him. I'd only met Nate a handful of times, but I couldn't quite work him out. One minute he was cocky and full of it, the next he was quiet and lost in thought. And in one evening he'd gone from telling me he didn't want me over for dinner to asking for my phone number.

'Well, I guess I'll just see you around then, Suzy,' Nate shouted over the noise of the engine.

'I guess so, Nate,' I whispered into the wind as I watched him spin the bike around on the gravel and speed away into the night.

IO

The next day I felt ready to write again. After breakfast I took myself into the garden with my notepad and pen. I didn't fancy being alone in the boathouse, so I stayed close to the house. I ran my hands over the pentagram scar on the side of the weeping willow tree as I sat down next to the flowing brook. I leant my back against the tree and wrote away for a couple of hours.

As I dotted the end of a sentence a huge black bird swooped down and landed on the ground a few short paces away from me. A raven. I'd seen them before when I visited the Tower of London on a school trip. Legend said that if the ravens ever left the Tower then England would fall. Whatever that meant. I idly worried if the bird in front of me had flown all the way from London, and if England was due to fall because of him. I watched as he pecked at the ground and jerked his head about. He fluttered his wings and launched himself into the air. I followed his flight as he swooped up towards the house, towards an open window on the top floor of the building. The last window on the right at the very top of the house. The room that was locked. The room that I so desperately wanted to see inside.

I absently got to my feet and walked towards the house, all the time not taking my eyes from the window I'd seen the raven disappear into. I came closer to the house and shielded my eyes from the sun as I looked up. The window to the locked room was wide open. It was large enough to climb through if you could get up there.

If I wanted to get into the room then that was my way. I had to follow the path of the raven. He was showing me the way. My eyes traced a route down from the window onto the ground below. There was an old drainpipe running down the side of the house. The drainpipe looked new; it must have been put in there when they renovated the roof. It would hold my weight, I was certain of it.

Before I could convince myself it was a bad idea I threw my pen and notepad to the ground, walked over to the drainpipe and prepared to climb.

The drainpipe was as sturdy as it looked and firmly fixed to the side of the house. I placed one Converse trainer on the drainpipe's bottom support and propelled myself up. There was another support at head height, I grabbed onto that and placed my other foot onto the ground-floor window ledge. The window looked into the lounge, which I knew would be empty at that time of the week without party guests to sit in it. Anyone who caught a glimpse of a red-haired teenager shimmying up a drainpipe would have done something to stop me. But as I reached for the next support on the drainpipe and pulled myself higher, using the top of the ground-floor window as my next foothold, there was no one there to force me back down. Once I'd cleared the first storey I knew nothing would stop me from reaching the top. I was already a good two metres from the ground – there was no turning back now.

I couldn't let myself look down as I continued to scale higher up the side of the house. The drainpipe ruts and windowsills provided me with sure and steady footholds and I took my time with each move. All the tree-climbing practice I'd had as a tomboy child had put me in good stead. Like a pawn in a game of chess I moved myself up the side of the house with careful precision. Soon I was level with the first-floor windows. I was halfway to the roof and halfway to the open attic window. My arms were starting to ache with the tension of heaving up my body weight. The tips of my fingers were numb from gripping the smooth edges of the drainpipe, and the inside of my thighs were beginning to fatigue from clenching the pipe tightly between them as I climbed.

I took a moment to rest as I cleared the first floor window. Just a few more moves and I'd be over the gargoyles and onto the roof. I pressed my weight into the drainpipe, gripped the pipe between my aching thighs and relaxed my hands for the briefest of moments. My heart was pounding, and I closed my eyes and took a deep breath to try to steady my nerves. As I opened my eyes, a movement in the corner of my vision nearly swept me off the side of the house. A black raven swooped down from the roof. The motion of the bird made my stomach drop like a lurching elevator. I felt the urge to vomit and suddenly all I wanted was to feel my feet flat on the ground. I was aware that my hands were shaking, and my thighs wobbled where they gripped the pipe. I needed to keep moving or I'd fall to my death.

I looked up and saw my next handhold, a drainpipe support just a foot above my head. Shakily, I stretched out my left hand and reached for it. I looked for the next foothold – a small air vent cut into the house. Before I allowed myself to think I pushed onwards, higher. Next step was another drainpipe support. Before I knew it I was reaching for the face of a stone gargoyle and shakily heaving myself up onto the gently sloping roof. The roof tiles were new and firm, not a scrap of slippery moss in sight. The window to the attic room was now within reaching distance.

Not thinking about what I might find inside the room, I launched myself up. I scrambled over the roof tiles, running up the sloping roof like I was a child scrambling up a sandbank. Just as I felt gravity try to pull me down, I reached for the crumbling window ledge. I grasped it between my numb fingers and somehow pulled myself towards it. Next thing I knew I had both hands on the window ledge, then my right foot was pushing at the rusted edging of the window pane. I can't remember how I got myself in through the window, all I remember was lying flat on my back on the attic room floor. Panting for breath and shaking from head to toe like someone who'd just escaped the gallows. I was in, I'd done it.

I pulled myself up so I sat below the window I'd just climbed through, my back pressed against the attic room wall. My eyes scanned the room I'd spent the last few days obsessing over. I was finally inside.

It wasn't like the other rooms in the attic. This room was crammed full of things. There was a small bed pressed up against the exterior wall. There was no mattress on the bed, and the rusted springs and metal headboard looked ancient. At the foot of the bed was a rotten wooden wardrobe, the door hanging off the hinges. On the other side of the room was a large piece of furniture covered by an old dust sheet. Beside that was an old wooden trunk, the lid secured in place by a padlock. This must have been one of the schoolgirls' bedrooms. It looked as though nothing had been touched for a long, long time. Decades, maybe longer. I slowly stood up and walked towards the small table next to the bed. It was scattered with dust-covered cut-out shapes stuck on to sticks. I picked one up. It was a black figure of a woman, parts of her dress and face cut out. As I held it up to look closer I noticed the shadow it cast on the far wall – an elegant maiden. A long, medieval dress and flowing thick hair. 'A shadow puppet,' I whispered.

The sound of something rustling in the wardrobe made me jump. My fingers closed tightly around the shadow puppet's stick as I turned around to face the old wardrobe. Something was inside it, inside and moving about. Nervously, I stepped towards the wardrobe doors. The rustling sound intensified and I reached forward, ready to pull the rotten door wide open and see what was inside. At that moment a black bird burst out of the wardrobe, nearly crashing into me as it flew past and out of the window into the fading daylight.

I turned away and tried to catch my breath, feeling so stupid for letting myself be scared. I'd known the ravens were nesting in the room before I'd come up here – they'd led me here. There was nothing to be afraid of. Resolute, I walked over to whatever was covered by the dust sheet in the corner of the room. With the shadow puppet still in one hand, I reached for the edge of the dust sheet with the other. I tugged it hard and pulled the sheet clean away. Beneath was a child's dressing table and small stool. Propped up on the table top, lying against the wall was a shattered mirror. It looked as though someone had struck it in the centre – all the cracks began at a central point and bled out to the edges. The room behind me reflected in the mirror shards, and I could see a dozen red-haired girls looking gormlessly back at me.

The mirror was framed with dark wood, and there were words scratched into the bottom of the frame. I moved towards it, my reflections getting bigger as I tried to read the words someone had scratched into the wood.

I am half sick of shadows

No sooner had I finished reading the words than there was another sound behind me. This time it wasn't coming from the wardrobe. It didn't sound like the rustling of a bird. It sounded like the quiet crying of a child. Slowly, I turned away from the shattered mirror and looked around the cluttered room. There was no one there. I was all alone. The sound of crying came again, louder this time. I could hear it behind me, as if it were coming from the mirror. I spun around and froze in horror as I saw the reflection of a small grey girl in the shards of mirror. She was crouched on the floor and scratching manically at the floorboard beneath her feet as she sobbed. I could hear the sound of her nails tearing at the wood. I closed my eyes and counted to ten, just like a doctor had once told me to do if I should find myself having a delusion.

I opened my eyes, hoping the grey girl would have vanished. But she was still there, reflected in the shards of the broken mirror. Only now she wasn't crouched on the ground scratching at the floor, she was standing and staring straight at me. Her face was stained with tears, her hands outstretched towards me. Reaching for me. In the mirrors' reflections she was standing behind me, at my shoulder. I turned around again and for the briefest of moments I saw her in front of me. Her face a mask of desperate horror, her lips parted, and in between her sobs she cried, 'Help me. Help me.'

The next thing I heard was the sound of my own screams.

The girl vanished and I was alone in the room.

I bolted for the door, desperate to get out.

I rattled the handle violently. The door wouldn't open. There was no key in the lock, no bolt to pull aside. I screamed and screamed. 'HELP!' I yelled at the closed door. 'SOMEONE HELP ME!' I desperately shook the door handle as I shouted and cried. I turned towards the window, half expecting to see the girl again as I ran towards it. I screamed into the garden. 'HELP ME!' The walls felt as though they were closing in on me. Every piece of furniture in that room loomed in like some kind of nightmare. I ran at the door with all my strength, screaming, screaming. But it wouldn't budge.

I banged against the door again and again.

Soon I was blind with panic, my whole body frantically convulsing with a primal fear that consumed every part of me. I pounded and pounded against the door until it felt as though my bones were breaking. When that didn't work I began to scratch at it, as if I could somehow claw my way out.

As though the door was a coffin and I had been buried alive.

Once again I reached for the impotent handle and gripped it hard. The door handle began to shake beneath my hand and I stepped back in horror as it rattled without me touching it. Just as I thought I would pass out from fear, the door swung open.

Monday 22nd September 1952

It's the class recital coming up, and today we were put into pairs. We have to work together on a poem of our choice and perform it in front of the other girls. You'll never guess who I'm paired with – Tilly. Lavinia and Sybil are working together, and I was secretly grateful that I wasn't paired with Margot – the Goddess still hasn't cured her of her lisp and there's no way we'd stand a chance of winning with that. But Tilly? The ghost girl who never goes outside and is as pale as ash? I'd rather compete on my own!

Tonight we had our first rehearsal. 'You better not be nice to her,' Lavinia had warned me. I assured Lavinia that I had no intention of being nice to Tilly, but that I couldn't avoid speaking to her – we had to choose the poem we wanted to recite.

Tilly was waiting for me in one of the cold music rooms after school today. 'Maybe we could walk around the grounds as we talk,' I said to her. 'I find fresh air helps me think.'

'I can't go outside,' Tilly said quietly. She'd fallen right into my trap; this was exactly the admission I had wanted her to make. I didn't have to be as nasty as Lavinia, but at least I could report back to my friends the real reason why Tilly can't go outside.

'Why?' I asked her.

'I'm cursed,' she said seriously. 'I have been all my life. When I go outside in the sun my skin burns up and I come out in painful blisters. Before they died my parents would pray for me each night, but that didn't help. Now they're dead I pray for myself.

111

But God hasn't answered my prayers.'

I didn't know what to say to Tilly. I had never heard of such an affliction before. To not be able to go out in sunlight must be such a terrible curse. To never see the blue sky, or feel the wind or rain on your face. 'But you can go out at night?' I asked her without thinking. Tilly studied me closely and an unspoken understanding passed between us – she knew that I had seen her.

She nodded. 'I'm a Moonchild.'

Tilly the Moonchild.

Maybe she shouldn't be praying to God, she should be doing Rituals to the Goddess instead, maybe she'd hear Tilly's prayers. Lavinia would strangle me in my sleep if I said anything to Tilly about the Goddess or the Rituals, so I stayed quiet. But I wanted to do something that might help her, I wanted to do something kind. 'You can choose the poem,' I said. It was the only thing I could think of. 'What do you want to do?' I asked. 'What's your favourite poem?'

Tilly smiled and answered me in a clear and confident tone, 'The Lady of Shalott.'

'Excellent choice.' I smiled, and I meant it. I've always adored that poem.

Until I write again,

Annabel

I I

'Drink this.' Aunt Meredith pushed a cold glass of cloudy, fizzing water into my hand. 'It'll help with the headache.'

'I don't have a headache,' I lied. 'And I don't need to see a doctor.'

'Richard didn't manage to catch you in time,' she said with worry, perched on the end of my bed. I was sitting upright with pillows propped behind me. My head was pounding. 'He said as soon as he managed to get the door open you fainted. Smacked your head on the old dresser as you fell. The doctor will be here any minute, Suzy. Nell's going to bring him up as soon as he arrives.' I closed my eyes and rubbed at my temples. I had no memory of how I got from the attic room into my bed. 'You were screaming the house down. What happened?' my aunt asked softly.

'I don't remember.' Another lie. I remembered exactly what had happened once I was inside the room. I remembered stupidly climbing up the side of the house to get into the attic room. I remembered the raven in the wardrobe, the shadow puppet and the cracked mirror with writing etched into the frame. And I remembered her. The grey girl. Scratching the floorboards. Standing at my shoulder. Her hands outstretched towards me, reaching for me. Pleading. 'I don't remember anything. One minute Richard was knocking down the door, next minute I'm here in my bed.'

'How did you get into the room?' she asked, her face telling me she knew the answer before I gave it. 'You climbed up?'

I stayed silent and looked down at my hands. They were red, sore and grazed from where I'd tried to claw my way out of the locked room. I looked away from my hands in horror as something on my bedside table caught my eye. It was the shadow puppet from the attic room. I couldn't remember bringing it downstairs with me; maybe I'd been clutching it as they dragged me unconscious from the room. Some kind of sick reminder that I hadn't imagined the whole thing. I picked it up and began to twirl it around between my fingers nervously.

'Oh, Suzy.' Aunt Meredith leant forwards on the bed and reached for one of my bloodied hands. 'You promised you'd behave if you came here. And I promised your mum I'd look after you.'

'I'm sorry,' I said quietly, trying not to cry. 'I don't know why I did it. I just wanted to see what was inside the room. And when I saw the window open I thought I could climb up. And it was perfectly safe, I didn't ...'

'Climbing up a four-storey building is never safe, Suzy. What is wrong with you?' The last sentence stung, and hung in the air as if it echoed off the stark white walls. What was wrong with me? Had I imagined the whole horrid scene in the room?

There was the sound of footsteps coming towards my bedroom door. A short succession of knocks and then the door swung open. Nell came in, wearing a green headscarf wrapped around her grey head of hair and a long, beaded dress. Behind her was a tall, slim man in a smart suit. 'This is Dr Carter,' Nell said softly, leading the doctor into the room.

'I've just been speaking to your husband,' the doctor said to Aunt Meredith. 'He told me he found your niece in a locked attic room. She'd been screaming hysterically before collapsing.'

'You could ask me what happened,' I said, annoyed. 'I'm right here.'

'Where is he?' Aunt Meredith asked the doctor. 'My husband, is he downstairs?'

The doctor nodded as he made his way to my bedside. 'He's with your son. Toby was quite … disturbed … by the girl's screams. I believe your husband is trying to calm him down.' I hated the way he spoke about me as if I wasn't there. Suddenly it was like being back in Warren House all over again. It felt like I was some kind of animal in a cage that everyone spoke about but never to. The doctor put his box of tricks on my bedside table and clicked it open. As he rummaged around for a stethoscope Aunt Meredith mumbled something about needing to call my mother and then left the room. Nell took her place, perched at the foot of my bed.

Nell looked around my room nervously. I suddenly realised that this might have been the first time she'd ever come up the stairs. She sat on the end of my bed and watched silently as I lied to the doctor. Just as I'd told my aunt, I swore I remembered nothing from my time in the room. 'I think I was just scared I was locked in.' I tried to shrug. 'I have a history of panic attacks. I don't like confined spaces.'

115

'Well, your heart rate's normal,' he said. 'So is your blood pressure and temperature. Your uncle tells me you have a history of mental health problems.'

'He's not my uncle,' I said quickly, trying to change the subject. I felt embarrassed that Nell should have to listen to this. I wasn't sure how much she knew about my mental health history – as little as possible, I hoped. 'He's my aunt's husband.'

The doctor ignored my attempt at diversion and ploughed on with his questions. 'I understand you recently spent some weeks in a rehabilitation facility as a result of paranoid delusions.' I looked down at the bed. I couldn't bear to look him in the eye. I gave him the tiniest of nods. 'I'd like you to make an appointment to come and see me in my surgery. For the time being I'm prescribing you something for the anxiety, and something to help you sleep. I'd like you to come back to me in about a week and have a chat. Do you think you could do that?' God, I hated the way doctors spoke to me like I was stupid.

'Yes, I think that I can do that,' I said petulantly.

'I'll see myself out,' he muttered to Nell.

The doctor left the room, leaving Nell and me alone.

'Suzy, what were you thinking? Climbing up the building like that?'

'I know, I'm stupid. You don't need to remind me.'

'You're not stupid. Far from it. I can see that.'

'Then you think I'm crazy?' I looked down at the bed, dreading her answer. I felt warm ribbons trickle down my face and I hurriedly brushed away the tears that I couldn't stop from falling.

Nell shook her head and spoke in a whisper, 'No. I don't

think you're crazy, Suzy.' I looked up and saw the fear in her eyes. And at that moment I understood perfectly. I understood why Nell never went upstairs at Dudley Hall. I could tell by the look on Nell's face that she knew what I'd seen in that room. 'I don't need a deck of tarot cards and a crystal ball to see that something about this house has deeply affected you,' Nell said quietly. 'And that's what drove you to climb that drainpipe. You needed to see the inside of that room, didn't you?'

I felt my hot tears slide down my face as I nodded.

'Why, Suzy?' Her eyes filled with concern.

'You know why,' I whispered.

'Don't listen to stories and gossip, Suzy.'

My hands flew out in exasperation. 'What stories? What gossip? No one's told me anything about this house and what really goes on here. I know something's not right. Just tell me the truth, Nell, please! I know I'm not crazy, even though everyone thinks I am.'

'It doesn't matter what other people think,' she said softly. 'What do you believe?'

'I believe in ghosts.'

She stared at me thoughtfully for a long moment. 'So do I,' she said quietly. 'But I also believe that you should let the dead stay sleeping. And don't go looking for trouble. The ghosts you chase you never catch, remember that. Don't go meddling in things that you have no way to control.'

'What if I don't meddle with the dead, what if they meddle with me?' I said, trying so hard not to sob. 'Maybe I just see things that other people can't?'

Nell smiled at me – the very smile that I had found so

117

irritating when I first met her. 'I like you a lot, Suzy. I want you to think of me as a friend. You can trust me, talk to me. Okay? Look,' she said, leaning forwards. 'Richard's back for a few days. Try and pull yourself together for your aunt's sake. Once he's gone then maybe we can talk some more. But if anything else is bothering you, I want you to come to me first, do you understand? Don't go climbing up the side of a building next time. Just come to me and we'll kick the door down together, okay?'

I nodded and a small smile touched my lips before I could stop it. 'Please don't tell anyone what I told you. Don't tell them about ghosts and seeing things that aren't there. Please don't tell Nate.' I couldn't bear the thought of Nate finding out what had happened to me. I'd started to like the idea of getting to know him better.

'Try and get some rest.' Nell nodded, rising from the bed. 'We'll talk again properly soon, I promise.' She handed me the glass of sparkling water that Aunt Meredith had put by my bed, and one of the sleeping pills the doctor had given me. I quickly swallowed down the tablet, wanting nothing more than to drift off into oblivion and not remember a thing about that day. Nell got up from the bed and began to walk towards the window. 'I'll close your curtains.'

'No!' I said loudly. She turned around, alarmed by my tone. 'No,' I said again, trying to sound calmer. 'I don't want them closed.' Nell looked again at the open curtains, and then back to me and nodded. She closed the door behind her and I was alone.

I put the shadow puppet on the pillow next to me and twirled it between my fingers. The last rays of the day's sunbeams were streaming through the window. The puppet caught the fading light between its cut-out shapes and patterns, and a shadow of a beautiful maiden cast itself on my bedroom wall. I wished I could be a shadow. Untouchable. Unbreakable.

My eyelids began to flutter closed as I let the doctor's sleeping pill take hold of me.

Words echoed in my head as I drifted into sleep. Words I'd seen in the attic room.

I am half sick of shadows

I knew those words. I'd read them before – long before I'd stepped foot in Dudley Hall.

Those words weren't new to me. Their rhythm, their flow – I'd read them, spoken them before. As I drifted off to sleep those words hung in the air like beams of fading sunlight.

'I am half sick of shadows,' said
The Lady of Shalott.

Everyone was quiet at breakfast the next morning. Nell had made some excuse not to come into work at Dudley Hall that day, and I didn't blame her. I'd want to stay as far away from Dudley Hall and its ghosts as possible if I had a choice. It was just me, Toby, Aunt Meredith and Richard sitting around the breakfast table. The sound of Richard buttering his toast and then munching loudly was like a cheese grater rubbing against my fragile head. I clanked my knife against my plate and closed my eyes, trying not to get angry. I felt as though I had the shortest fuse in the world. I searched my brain for something that might calm me down and remembered one of my favourite quotes from *Othello*. '*How poor are they who have not patience,*' I said aloud.

I took a deep breath and opened my eyes, ready to force myself to eat some toast. Toby was staring right at me as though I was a total stranger. After our day exploring the attic I thought we'd made friends, but right then he was looking at me as though I was the most frightening thing in the world.

'No book on spies to read at breakfast this morning?' I asked him, trying to smile.

Toby's gaze flickered nervously to my hands. I glanced down at them. My fingertips were still red-raw from where I'd tried to claw my way out of the locked attic room. I made a mental note to put on a long-sleeved sweater after breakfast, one that I could pull down over my hands and hide my bruised and bloody fingertips from the world.

'I prefer Toby not to read at the breakfast table,' Richard said. His steely gaze bore into me like ice. 'Bad manners to read whilst eating. A dinner table should be used to hold engaging conversations around it. Toby will never learn to do that if he is forever reading.'

'More tea, sweetheart?' Aunt Meredith said briskly. She seemed different this morning – on edge. I wondered if it was because of what had happened to me yesterday or if she was always like this around Richard. There was something forced and rigid about her demeanour, and she was wearing more make-up than normal and had made more of an effort with her hair. Maybe it *was* Richard to blame for her unease, not me. The thought only made me more annoyed that he had come back to Dudley Hall.

Richard nodded sharply and Aunt Meredith leant over Toby and began to pour tea into his cup. Richard lifted the cup and took a loud slurp. I looked at him with unbridled disgust.

'So, I've been working on a new idea for a murder mystery party with a flapper theme,' Aunt Meredith said brightly. 'Prohibition America,' she continued. 'Everyone could put on American accents. I've got a wonderful Charleston dress that would look lovely on you, Suzy. Suzy's been doing a marvellous job of playing the murder victims,' she said to Richard.

Richard nodded. 'Yes, I hear you want to be an actress one day.'

'Actually, I'm going to be a writer,' I corrected him. 'Although I might act in my plays and films. A lot of people do that.'

'Do they?' He smiled patronisingly. 'Well, I think it's wonderful that you're managing to be so focused, despite all your difficulties.'

'Maybe you'd like to put that creative brain of yours to use coming up with ideas for new murder mystery parties,' Aunt Meredith said before I had a chance to react to Richard's words.

'And can I write it?' I asked quickly.

'Umm … you can certainly have a stab at it,' she replied. 'Actually, we have a different sort of party arriving this weekend.'

'Different how?' Richard asked, sounding as if he wasn't the least bit interested in the answer.

'The group is younger than we usually have,' Aunt Meredith replied. 'It's a hen party. I've told them to come dressed in school uniforms – I thought we could base the murder mystery during the time that Dudley Hall was a school.'

'I have the perfect storyline you could use for them,' I blurted out.

Richard sighed and crossed his arms over his broad chest, leaning back into his chair and smirking at me as though I was about to prattle out some kind of nonsense.

'I've been writing a story set here in the house, whilst Dudley Hall was still a school,' I said, ignoring Richard.

'Is it a murder mystery?' Aunt Meredith asked, sounding genuinely encouraging.

I shook my head. 'Not exactly. It's more of a ghost story.

But I could tweak it slightly, and maybe you could use it this weekend? It's called *The Ghost of Dudley Hall*.'

'Original,' Richard muttered to himself.

'I think it sounds wonderful.' My aunt smiled at me. 'Why don't you do some more work on it and then come and show it to me?'

'Honestly, Meredith,' Richard said, sounding bored. 'You're not helping the girl. Letting her think that some silly story is good enough to use is only going to damage her more when you don't –'

'Damage me more?' I interrupted, feeling as though a weight was suddenly crashing down upon my chest.

Richard looked at Aunt Meredith and rolled his eyes. She cast me a nervous glance and opened her mouth to speak but stopped short as the sound of the telephone rang out around us.

'Not while we're eating,' Richard said, glancing towards the ringing phone in the hallway. Toby cast his eyes down to his plate and Aunt Meredith studied the table in embarrassment. I looked at Richard incredulously. Who did he think he was? Yes, this was technically his house that he'd spent a small fortune buying and renovating. But he had no right to tell people how to live their lives. He had no right to tell me what to do. He wasn't my father. He wasn't my teacher. He wasn't even my real uncle, he was my aunt's fourth husband.

The phone continued to ring and ring. It sounded like a chainsaw in my head. Whoever was ringing was certainly persistent. My head throbbed and it rang and rang and I knew I'd throw my plate across the room in frustration if the noise didn't stop.

I pushed my chair back and got to my feet.

'Suzy ...' Aunt Meredith said in warning.

Without looking at her or Richard, I quickly made my way out into the hall towards the blaring telephone.

I violently picked up the receiver. 'Hello,' I said, relief flooding through me that I'd made the unbearable racket stop.

'Suzy!' came a voice, a male voice down the end of the phone. The way he said my name made my stomach plummet. I recognised the voice instantly; it was a voice I hadn't particularly ever wanted to hear again.

'Sebastian Cotez,' I said into the receiver. I felt eyes boring into the back of my head and turned around to see Richard standing in the hallway glaring at me furiously. I turned my back to him and walked off with the phone. I sat down on the bottom of the grand staircase next to the shining suit of armour. The satisfaction I briefly felt for annoying Richard was quickly replaced by the dread of hearing Seb's voice. Just like Frankie, Seb was someone I did not want to hear from. He was someone who reminded me of everything that had happened at school, everything I needed to forget. 'Why are you calling me?'

'I'm worried about Frankie,' Seb said slowly. It's always annoyed me that Seb takes forever just to say one single sentence. He thinks about every word before he says it. I like people who just speak their mind, to hell with the consequences. 'I don't know what to do to help her. Frankie really needs a friend right now and –'

'Yeah, and I really need to distance myself from anything that reminds me of what happened at school, Sebastian. There's a reason I'm locked away in a country house in the middle of nowhere. There's a reason I don't want to speak to Frankie, or you or … hang on, how did you even get this number?'

He sighed and spoke slowly. 'Frankie told me where you were staying. Your aunt's murder mystery business lists this number on the internet. Look, Suzy, I know what happened at school was horrible. But you weren't the only one who has to deal with it. Frankie's not coping. She's –'

'I don't care if you think I'm selfish, Sebastian. The doctors said I need to do what's right for me. And that's being away from school, and Frankie and you and anything else that reminds me of what happened. Frankie has you to talk to if she needs someone.'

'Suzy, please, if you could just call her – maybe visit her. I really think –'

'Goodbye, Sebastian. Don't call me here again.' I hung up before he could argue with me. Good job I was speaking to him on a phone and not face to face. Sebastian had always made me feel nervous. He has these deep blue eyes that stare right into you when he speaks to you. He never smiles, he's always so serious. He unnerves me. Frankie thinks he's hot, but he's way too intense for me.

'Who was that?' came Richard's voice from the corridor. My head was splitting and I needed air. If I didn't get out of the house quickly the next murder mystery party would be trying to piece together fragments of Richard's skull instead of the jigsaw pieces of a fake murder.

'I'm going for a walk into the village,' I announced, walking towards the front door. I grabbed my hoodie from a peg on the wall and slammed the heavy oak door behind me as I left.

As I marched away from Dudley Hall I pulled the hood over my head and buried my hands into the sleeves. I didn't care if I looked like a teenage extra from *Crimewatch*. Good. Maybe that would make people stay away from me. I found my iPod in my hoodie pocket and blasted loud music into my ears to drown out the sounds of the world around me. A world I no longer trusted. I marched in the middle of the road to the music's punishing beat, getting a buzz every time a passing car beeped and swerved to miss me.

In the middle of Dudley-on-Water was the ancient church. Every English village has an old church – the village my school was in had one too. And they all look the same. Crumbling stone walls, faded stained-glass windows. Crooked gravestones surrounding it. The church in Dudley-on-Water had one solitary bell tower that reached up into the grey sky. Surrounding the small church was the obligatory sprawling graveyard. At school I'd read somewhere that if you were being haunted you should go to a graveyard, collect some soil and sprinkle it in the place where you see the ghost. Apparently, the soil acts as a reminder to the spirit that their place is in the world of the dead, not the living, and it will then leave you alone. Walking into the Dudley-on-Water graveyard, I remembered the time I'd made Frankie traipse into town with me in the darkness one night. She watched me gather up soil from the local graveyard and take it back to my dormitory at school. It hadn't worked. The haunting only got worse after that. I wished banishing ghosts was as simple as scattering graveyard soil, but the reality couldn't be further from the truth.

126

I absently took my headphones from my ears as I walked through the gate of the graveyard. I strayed from the pebbled path and began to weave my way through the moss-covered graves. The crooked headstones were blackened and smooth with age. 1798, 1821, 1876 – there were some really old graves in there. I guessed that some of the graves were even older, but were unmarked, forgotten. As I walked I wondered about all the dead bodies that I might be walking over. Mothers, brothers, children, cousins. Every person had once been alive and had a story to tell. But at the end of the day we all end up the same, dead and buried. I only wished I knew why some of us came back to haunt when others were content to stay sleeping.

A figure crouched over a grave in the far corner of the graveyard and scraping away at the gathering moss caught my eye.

It was Nate.

He didn't look like he normally did – shoulders pulled back, head held high. He was on his hands and knees, carefully tending to a grave. I felt like I'd stumbled on a very private moment, as if I was seeing the real Nate for the first time – all his bravado stripped away.

I walked between the graves towards him. He must have heard me approach but he didn't look up. I came and stood beside him and looked down at the grave he was tending to.

Annabel Dixon
1945–2012
Mother, Grandmother, Friend

'Come here often, do you?' Nate said without looking at me.

'Was this your grandmother?' I asked before I could stop myself.

He nodded. 'You okay?' he asked.

'Why are you asking me that?' I knew I sounded prickly, but I hated the fact that he was asking if I were okay. He must have heard what had happened the day before. I felt a sudden stab of betrayal – I thought I could trust Nell not to tell him.

Nate looked up at me, his eyes wide. 'No reason,' he said. 'I just wondered what you were doing in a graveyard – it's not exactly a normal place to go for a walk.'

I walked over to a bench a few metres away and sat down. I chewed at my lip as I watched him rise to his feet and walk towards me. Maybe he didn't know what had happened yesterday. Nate sat down next to me and we both stared out into the graveyard in silence. 'I just needed to get out of the house, get some fresh air,' I said eventually.

'So you came to a graveyard?' he asked softly. He seemed quieter today than the other times I'd seen him.

'It's not like there's anywhere else to go,' I shrugged. 'Is this where you come too, when you need to get away?'

He shook his head and looked towards the church. 'If I need to get away then I get on the back of my bike and *really* get away. It would have been my grandmother's birthday today, that's why we came here.'

'We?'

He gestured towards the door of the church as Fiona appeared through it. She looked up and smiled at Nate and started walking towards us. 'Your mum?' I asked.

Nate nodded silently, and I noticed the pain in his eyes as he watched his mum approach. He seemed like a completely different person to the boy I'd first met at Dudley Hall. Sitting next to him on the graveyard bench there was no bravado, no cocky jokes. It was as if his mask had slipped, as if he no longer had to pretend.

Fiona walked up to us. 'Mum, you remember Suzy?'

'Hi, Suzy,' Fiona smiled. I could tell she'd been crying. Something passed across her eyes as she looked at me. 'You've seen her, haven't you?' she said quietly.

I stared at her blankly, unsure I'd heard her correctly.

Nate stood up from the bench and walked towards his mum. 'Come on, Mum, let's go home.' He tugged at her arm, trying to move her away from me but she wouldn't budge. She stood rooted to the ground, her eyes locking onto mine.

'You've seen her, haven't you?' she said to me again. There was no mistaking her words this time.

'Seen who?' I asked, getting to my feet.

'Mum, come on,' Nate said urgently, trying to steer her away.

'Who?' I repeated loudly, my heart beginning to splutter about inside me.

Fiona's eyes softened. She shook herself free of Nate's grasp and stepped towards me, whispering in my ear so only I could hear. 'I know just by looking at you that you've seen her. She's appeared to you, hasn't she? The grey girl.'

Monday 6th October 1952

You'll never guess what happened today. Something truly amazing and unbelievable! We won the class recital! Can you believe it? Tilly and I won the class recital! Mistress Johnson praised us for our 'ambition, sensitivity and dramatic flare', and told us, in front of everyone, that it was simply the best recital she had seen in years. Lavinia and Sybil (whose spots look worse than ever today) came in second with their Wordsworth recital, and Margot and Alice limped in at third place with their performance of Kipling's If.

The other girls were jealous, but I don't care. They can't take this away from me. I've never won anything before in my whole life, and Tilly and I deserved it. We've been working tirelessly, practising every moment we could find these last few weeks, and all the hard work certainly paid off.

The recital went exactly to plan. We didn't perform ours like the other girls, we didn't act out the words as though we were actresses on a stage. Oh no. Tilly had the idea of creating shadow puppets, one for the Lady of Shalott and one for Sir Lancelot. We dimmed the lights in the classroom, closed the curtains and asked for special permission to light a candle (which I told Mistress Johnson I had borrowed from the village church, but actually it's one we use for the Rituals upstairs in the dorm). Tilly and I used our shadow puppets to tell the story of the poem as we recited it. Tilly spoke the first line, 'On either side the river lie,' and I recited the second, 'Long fields of barley and of rye.' I operated the puppet of Lancelot and

Tilly's puppet played the part of the Lady of Shalott, and together we told the story of The Lady of Shalott...

Everyone in the class stayed as silent as the grave from the first line of the poem right up until the last few verses, where the lady releases the boat and floats down to Camelot, to her death.

When Mistress Johnson announced the winner Tilly and I leapt up to embrace one another in excitement. Lavinia sneered at us and looked on as though she was sucking a sour sweet. I just ignored her, though; nothing could have stopped me feeling as though I was soaring through the sky with great wings. And as I looked at Tilly I knew she felt it too.

'As you know, girls,' Mistress Johnson said after our win had been announced, 'the prize is to name the new boat that has been kindly donated to the school. The boat that shall live on the river and be available for all girls to use during the weekends.'

Tilly and I looked at each other, smiled and then said in unison, 'The Lady of Shalott.'

Tilly won't be able to go to the naming ceremony this evening, which makes me sad. It will still be light outside. But she'll watch from her window, like she always does when we're out in the grounds. I said that I would represent us both and not let anyone forget that she helped win the prize and name the boat too. Tilly smiled sadly at me when I said this. 'I'm pleased we have a school boat,' she said. 'I shall look out of my window upon it and imagine that I'm lying down in it, bathed in sunshine, the river taking me to a better place, far, far away from here.'

So I stood on the river bank after school today and thought of Tilly during the naming ceremony. I silently prayed for her as we christened the boat and I recited a few suitable lines from the poem.

Down she came and found a boat
Beneath a willow left afloat,
And round about the prow she wrote
The Lady of Shalott.

'She's not your friend, I am,' Lavinia reminded me as we were
preparing for the Rituals this evening. 'Don't let one poxy poetry
recital make you forget that, Annabel.' Then she lifted up my cloak
sleeve and pressed down on the star-shaped scar on my forearm.
'This mark means that we are bound together. We are sisters and
servants of the Goddess. Tilly isn't, don't forget that.'

How could I ever forget that? How could I ever forget the promise
I made to Lavinia and to the Goddess? How I scarred myself so
I should never forget?

But tonight, during the Rituals, as we lit candles and chanted our
prayers to the Goddess, all I could think about was Tilly. I secretly
prayed that she would one day be cured of her terrible curse, that
one day she could really lie down in The Lady of Shalott in the
sunshine and float far away. The strangest thing happened as we
were chanting to the Goddess tonight – there was a gust of strong
wind and it blew the window right open. I wonder if that means
she's finally heard me. I wonder if the Goddess will answer my
prayers. And I wonder if, soon, Tilly will finally be free …

Until I write again,

Annabel

13

The grey girl.

She was real. Not real in the sense that I could reach out and touch her. My fingers would pass through her misty form as though it were smoke. But she was real – she existed. Fiona had seen her too.

I stood shivering in the graveyard long after Nate had mumbled some excuse and taken his mother away. Part of me wanted to run after them, to shake Fiona until she told me everything she knew about the grey girl. Who was she? How did she die? And why would she not leave Dudley Hall?

Somehow the whole day passed before I found my feet scrunching down upon the gravel driveway of Dudley Hall. I must have walked for miles around the village and the surrounding countryside, going around in circles and trying to make sense of what Fiona had said. *I know just by looking at you that you've seen her. She's appeared to you, hasn't she? The grey girl.*

Whatever Fiona had seen in me, I wondered if Nate had seen it too. Did I wear my memories like a mask, is that really what people saw when they looked at me? Did I look haunted, frightened, unhinged?

As I pushed open the heavy oak door to Dudley Hall I knew I had to find a way to ask Fiona what she knew. Nate seemed so protective of his mother, I doubted he'd want me asking her about such things. But I had to, I didn't have a choice.

Aunt Meredith appeared in front of me as I was about to climb the grand staircase. 'Suzy, you've been gone all day,' she said softly. 'I've promised your mum and Richard that this is the best place for you. You can't just run away like that.'

'If I'd run away I wouldn't have come back,' I said flatly.

She frowned at me with concern. 'Go and freshen up for dinner, I'll see you in the kitchen in ten minutes.'

I moved around my room like a ghost. I felt so numb being back there, where I knew the grey girl could be watching me. How could Aunt Meredith possibly think that Dudley Hall was the best place for me? She must have really fought to bring me here. I felt so betrayed. If she had any idea what was lurking between the crumbling old walls of the house, if she cared for me at all, then she'd try to keep me as far away as possible.

We sat around the dinner table in silence. Toby nervously pushed a few pieces of penne around his plate and Aunt Meredith's gaze flittered towards Richard every few seconds as he bulldozed his way through his food without a word to anyone.

'I saw Nate in the village today,' I announced clearly.

'The cook's nephew?' Richard said gruffly.

'Nell's a bit more than just a cook,' I corrected him. Richard ignored me and carried on eating. 'Nate was in the graveyard with his mother, Fiona. Do you know her, Aunt Meredith?'

'Fiona is nothing but trouble,' Richard grumbled without giving my aunt a chance to speak. 'Whatever she may have said to you you're to ignore it. The woman is as mad as a deranged hatter.'

'Why?' I pressed. 'Because she thinks this house is haunted?'

'Suzy,' my aunt warned.

'You knew that, didn't you?' I said to Aunt Meredith, my anger beginning to rise to the surface. 'You knew that everyone thinks this house is haunted.'

'*Everyone* does not think Dudley Hall is haunted,' Richard said curtly, putting his knife and fork in the centre of his empty plate. 'No one thinks that because it's not true. Don't be so childish. That woman is insane, everyone knows that.'

I ignored Richard and directed my hurt right at Aunt Meredith. 'If you knew the rumours about this house then why did you bring me here? After everything I've been through you think I'd want to be *here*?'

'That's enough!' Richard slammed his palms down on the table. Toby winced and shrank back in his chair.

Richard looked at me coldly and said, in a measured voice, 'It would do you good to remember whose house this is, Suzanne. You're staying here because we let you, because you have nowhere else to go. I understand that you may be ill, but dredging up such nonsense will do no good for your recovery. I won't have you filling young Toby's head with superstitious mumbo-jumbo, and I won't have you speak to your aunt like that. There's no such thing as ghosts.'

I narrowed my eyes and threw my best quotation at him, '*There are more things in Heaven and Earth, Horatio, than are*

135

dreamt of in your philosophy.'

Richard grinned a slow, cat-like grin. 'You really are a few sandwiches short of a picnic, aren't you? Do you always quote Shakespeare when you have nothing else to say?'

In that moment I'd never hated anyone more in my life. I hated the way Richard treated my aunt, the way he was with Toby, and the way he spoke to me as if I was so broken I couldn't be fixed. And it was all his fault. If he hadn't bought Dudley Hall then Aunt Meredith would never have brought me there.

I got up, picked up my plate and calmly walked over to the kitchen bin. I scraped the entire contents of my food into it, then walked over to the sink and quickly washed my plate, putting it on the drying rack. 'Thank you for dinner, Aunt Meredith. It was delicious but I have an issue with the company. Next time I'll eat in my room.' I dared a glance at Richard; it looked as though his blood was about to boil, like his eyeballs would pop with the pressure of his steaming head.

Toby stared at me, mouth agape. I'm not sure if I saw admiration or fear in his eyes. I felt a momentary wave of regret that he should have to witness such an outburst. He was only a kid, after all, he should be sheltered from all of this. He didn't need to know that ghosts exist, and that Dudley Hall was haunted. But as I walked away I reminded myself that it wasn't my fault. I hadn't bought Dudley Hall, I hadn't forced Toby or anyone else to live here. If anyone was to blame, if anyone should feel sorry, it was Richard.

I marched out of the kitchen with my head held high, through the dark corridor, up the grand staircase and straight to my room on the second floor.

Less than a minute later the door swung open and Aunt Meredith stood on the threshold. 'Suzy, that was uncalled for.'

'Was it?' I glared at her.

'Richard is right – if it weren't for Dudley Hall you'd have nowhere else to go. And neither would me or Toby – we'd all be out on the streets.'

'Wouldn't be such a bad thing. I'd take a cardboard box over this ghost house.'

Aunt Meredith walked further into my room. 'Look, Suzy, I've been thinking about what you were saying earlier.' I looked at her blankly, not knowing what she was referring to. 'About that story you were writing, *The Ghost of Dudley Hall*. Maybe we could use your story this weekend. The guests are already coming in the perfect costumes – all we'll need to do is give them your characters when they arrive. And I meant it when I said I'd love to have a read of what you've –'

'I don't know if I can do it,' I cut her off. 'I don't know how much longer I can stay here.'

'Suzy,' Aunt Meredith said gently and walked towards me. She took a deep breath and looked me dead in the eye. 'I'm so sorry, but you can't go home. Your mum's not well enough to look after you.'

'Not well enough?' I shouted. 'There's nothing wrong with her! She chugs down prescription pills and spends the day in bed – she cares more about herself than she ever has about me. I swear she was glad when I was carted off to Warren House – if I'm mad then I must have got it from somewhere. Now she can hold her head high and think that I'm just like her – a crazy old bat who nobody cares about.'

I waited for Aunt Meredith to slap me, to shout back or tell me to pack my bags and leave. But she just stood there, concern etched on her face and her eyes watering up. 'Suzy, people care about you. I care about you, and I want you here. I'm sorry if you've heard upsetting stories about Dudley Hall, but they're just that – stories.'

She reached out to touch me and I flinched away. 'I want to be on my own please,' I said, trying not to cry.

'I don't want to leave you, Suzy,' she said, taking another step towards me. 'I know you must be lonely here. Why don't you call your friend Frankie – it might do you some good to –'

'I want to be on my own!' I shouted.

Aunt Meredith stared at me for a long moment before nodding and turning away. I watched, my eyes stinging with tears, as she gave me one last sorry glance before leaving the room.

I locked the door behind her as she left. Frustrated and angry, I headed towards my notepad, kicked off my shoes, sat on my bed and flicked it open at the first clean page. I put the nib of my pen to paper and began to write whatever came into my head. I wrote a hate-filled letter to Richard that I then screwed up and threw violently at the locked door. I wrote a poem about how betrayed and disappointed I felt in Aunt Meredith for allowing me to come and live at Dudley Hall. And when I'd finished that then I poured my angst and hurt into *The Ghost of Dudley Hall*. Whether I was ever going to show the story to Aunt Meredith or not, whether it would ever be anything more than words on a page, I didn't care. I just needed to write it. I wrote about the girls in the boarding school, about the ghost they'd seen – it was the ghost of a girl who'd been murdered at the school, and the girls had to discover who had killed her in order for her spirit to rest. The evening passed in a frenzied blur of writing. That evening I discovered that there's nothing like the feeling of boiling blood to really inspire my creativity.

After hours of furious writing I leant back against my bed's headboard and rubbed at my tired eyes. I was suddenly exhausted. My hand ached from gripping my pen, my arm was numb from pressing down hard on the notepad. Too wired to sleep, I decided to fire up my laptop and distract my busy brain from the angry thoughts still whirring about inside it. I spent a while looking at internet gossip sites before I went onto Facebook. I couldn't bear to scroll through the pages and pages of inane status updates from the lives of people I didn't really care about. I would have logged straight off but I saw that I had over a dozen private messages waiting to be read. They were all from Frankie. I only read the most recent one.

Suzy.

I know you don't want to hear from me. I know you think it's better to just walk away and try to pretend that nothing happened. But I can't do that.

I went back to St Mark's. I had to see the school again. I had to see if anything had changed. They wouldn't let me in. They shut me out just like they did to the Blue Lady all those years ago. I may as well have laid down and died on the school steps, just like she did.

I just don't see the point of anything any more.

I think Seb is starting to hate me. He was so angry at me for going back. If I lose him too I don't know what I'll do.

Please call me, Suzy. I really need a friend right now.

Frankie xxx

I slammed the laptop shut, wishing I hadn't read Frankie's message. How dare she contact me? How dared she think that I was the answer to her problems? I couldn't help her! I couldn't even help myself. Besides, Frankie was the strong one. It was me who fell apart after what happened at school. Me who had to go into the loony bin. I was the one who should have been asking her for help, not the other way around.

Frustrated, I walked away from my desk and paced around the room. It was dark outside, the night was warm and I hadn't yet shut the windows from having them open all day. The curtains flapped about in the night-time breeze. Yawning, I went over to the bed and sat on the edge of it. I picked up the shadow puppet from my nightstand and twiddled it between my fingers. I moved the puppet so it sat in front of my bedside light. I slowly twirled it around and watched as a silhouette of a woman appeared on my bedroom wall. She looked like a medieval maiden. I made the puppet walk and skip along the wall, twirl about and fly through the air.

A gust of cool air swept into the room and I shuddered. I placed the puppet on my bed and walked over to the window to close it.

As I got nearer to the window I could see movement outside in the garden below.

I recognised her straight away.

A small grey girl, running away from the house. She was

shrouded in a heavy winter cloak, and she ran over the grass as if she was desperately fleeing from something. She was running towards the river, running towards a boat.

I leant out of the window, my heart fluttering like an angry caged bird in my chest. I rubbed at my tired eyes and blinked furiously to try to clear them of any haziness. She was still there when I opened them. It wasn't the moonlight or my weary eyes; I was seeing her. She was real. Every beat of anger, frustration and disappointment I had felt that evening suddenly fell away from me. All I could feel was an enveloping exhilaration at what I was seeing. The grey girl – she was real. As real as the last time I'd seen her from my window, and clawing at the floorboards in the attic room. This was the same girl Fiona had spoken of, the girl she could see painted onto my face. The grey girl.

In that moment all I wanted was to know who she was and why she was there.

Without bothering to put on my shoes or a jumper, I turned and ran for my bedroom door. I unlocked it and flew down the stairs, and down the corridor to the kitchen. I rummaged around in the dark for the back door keys. I soon found them, opened the door and let myself out into the cold spring night.

I ran, barefoot, down to the stream. It was dark but there was enough moonlight to see the rippling water trickling through the grounds.

As I got down to the river bank I walked along the edge of it like a tightrope. I came to the weeping willow and ducked beneath the bowing branches, all the time my eyes searching the water for a boat, for the girl. I needed to see her, to be close to her. In that moment I could have stood face to face with her and looked her dead in the eye. I could have reached out and touched her; adrenalin was pumping through my veins like fire. My eyes wide with terror, my skin rippling with exhilaration, I followed the stream as it wound through the grounds. Sharp rocks and twigs on the ground snagged at my naked feet, but I could barely feel a thing. I was driven by a primal fear to confront whoever she was – the demon that haunted me. All I wanted was to look her in the eye and unlock her secrets.

But there was nothing. I looked around me in desperation as I walked and saw nothing but the dark night and the lonely grounds of Dudley Hall. There was no trace of the girl and no trace of the boat she had been fleeing in. I looked around desperately, wishing her to appear. I wanted to shout out for her, I wanted to summon her back from whatever dark realm she was hiding in.

My body began to shake with the cold night air and the feeling of defeat that crashed down upon my shoulders like a boulder. Suddenly all I wanted was to lie down and sob. I felt so ready to face her, I didn't think I'd ever feel that brave again. I didn't have the strength inside me. The next time she appeared I would want to run. I'd hide in shadows, withdraw from the world. I'd lose myself.

Nell was right. The ghosts you chase you never catch.

Shaken, I turned and made my way back into the house. I locked the door behind me and tried not to cry as I walked back towards the staircase on numb feet.

The first footprint was on the bottom step.

Moonlight flooding through the glass roof and bounced off the wet little puddle. The next footprint was on the step above, and then one above that.

Shaking, I followed the footprints as they led me up the stairs. They wound around the first-floor landing and up the second flight of stairs. My throat tightened painfully as I followed them along the second-floor corridor. The footprints came to a stop outside my room. Slowly, every fibre of my body shaking with fear, I raised my hands and pushed my bedroom door open.

I knew what I'd find inside my room. This was how the dead worked. How they communicated. They came for you in ways you couldn't predict or understand. I didn't know what she wanted, but I knew one thing for certain. She was coming for me.

My teeth chattered violently, and my legs vibrated beneath me as I stood in the doorway.

The small, wet footprints trailed all the way to my bed.

Quivering and cold, I followed the footprints into the bedroom and up to my bed. There was a rectangle of old brown leather propped up neatly on my pillow. It was a book.

Tuesday 14th October 1952

Lavinia caught Tilly and I laughing together outside French class today. We had been talking about our perfect knights in shining armour. Tilly says that she would prefer Sir Galahad to Sir Lancelot, and I joked that whoever her 'Loyal knight and true' might be she could borrow his suit of armour and wear it to dance around in the sunlight. 'Only if he wears my winter cloak in the moonlight!' she laughed.

'I'm glad you think it's so funny that you're such a freak,' Lavinia spat, as Margot and Sybil sniggered behind her. 'And Annabel's laughing at you, not with you.'

'That's not true!' I shouted back.

This made Lavinia really mad. That's when she grabbed Tilly's school jumper and began to drag her along the school corridor.

'What are you doing, Lavinia?' Tilly shrieked, as Lavinia pulled her towards the school entrance.

'I don't believe that you're ill,' Lavinia snarled, reaching for the door handle. 'I don't believe that you're allergic to sunlight. There's no such thing as a sunlight curse. You only skip out on Games because you're lazy. And you only sleep on your own up in the attic because you're such a freak no one else will share with you.'

I tried to pull Lavinia back as she swung open the door and dragged Tilly out into the sunlight. As soon as Tilly was outside Lavinia slipped back in and slammed the door shut, bolting it locked. I argued with her to open it, I pleaded with her as Tilly

144

banged on the door, begging to be let in. 'I thought we were friends, Annabel,' Lavinia said to me as Tilly begged desperately from outside. 'But friends don't desert one another, especially when they are bound together like we are.' She dropped her voice and whispered in my ear, which only made Tilly's cries from outside sound louder. 'Don't you remember what you let me do to you? You let me burn you. Not only that but you let me give you the Kiss of Death. Don't you remember, Annabel? It was me who did that to you, not her, not some little freak who's too lazy to play hockey.'

'Let her in, Lavinia!' I shouted, finally managing to push her aside.

I unbolted the door and Tilly fell into me as it opened. Her face was red and swollen and her eyelids fluttered as she murmured in pain. Lavinia took a step back in horror and the other two gasped in shock. 'Fetch the nurse!' I demanded. 'Now!'

The nurse came and took Tilly away. We haven't seen her since.

'It'll be your fault if she dies,' Lavinia said to me. 'If it wasn't for you I wouldn't have done it.'

I hope Tilly doesn't die.

I prayed to the Goddess tonight that she doesn't.

I would never forgive myself if she does.

Until I write again,

Annabel

14

I spent that night on my bathroom floor. I left the wet footprints – I couldn't bring myself to mop them up. And I left the book. I didn't even get close enough to touch it. I didn't want to know what was printed on its pages. I didn't want to think about what it might mean and who might have put it there and why. There may have been a fleeting moment the night before when I'd felt brave, when I felt that I could face her. But that had disappeared as soon as I realised I could never have the upper hand. She controlled this, whatever *this* was, not me. I hated myself for being so weak, for being so terrified. If Frankie had been there she would have picked up the book and read it cover to cover, she would have done anything to make this stop. And what had I done? I'd cowered away in the bathroom behind a locked door. I may as well have been a child hiding under the bed from nightmares. Except I couldn't even bring myself to go anywhere near my bed. I had edged around the room and locked myself in the bathroom like I was trying to avoid a wild animal.

I curled up in a corner of the bathroom on the cold tiles and hugged myself for comfort. I stared into space. My mind yo-yoed from being as blank as an empty page to as busy as a speeding highway. There were moments when I tried to convince myself that this wasn't happening. I was imagining the whole thing. But in my heart I knew the truth. Dudley Hall was haunted by the ghost of a small girl, 'the grey girl', as Fiona had called her.

It was only when bright daylight streamed in through the bathroom window that I realised the whole night had passed and I hadn't moved from my spot on the cold tiled floor. The only time I'd moved throughout the night was to scratch at my hands. They were red-raw from where I had picked and clawed at them anxiously as I sat catatonic on the bathroom floor. Summoning all the strength I had inside me, I pulled myself to my feet and took my aching body over to the sink. I gently scrubbed the blood from my hands and then patted them dry with a towel. I found some lotion to rub into the wounds, which only made them sting worse than they did already.

Slowly, exhaustion consuming every cell in my body, I made my way towards the bathroom door and unlocked it. For a brief moment I wished that I was mad. I wished that I'd open the bathroom door and find an empty room with no sign that someone other than me had been there the night before. I wished it was all in my head, that the book and the footprints had never been there at all.

I opened the bathroom door with a violent jolt of my hand. I stood in the open doorway and studied my bedroom. The footprints had vanished – evaporated in the morning sun. But there on my pillow, just as it had been last night, was the old book.

In a series of swift movements I crossed the room, picked up the book and threw it at the far wall. Its pages splayed wide as it fell to the floor with a gentle thud. I stared at the crumpled heap for a moment before running from the room.

I bolted along the landing, down the stairs, through the great hall and along the back corridor.

No one was sitting in the kitchen as I marched through it. From the pale, fresh light outside I knew it was early, far too early for anyone to be up and eating breakfast. I had no idea what I aimed to achieve by running through the kitchen back door, into the garden and heading for the river. I knew there was nothing to see there. There had been nothing to see the night before when I ran down to search for her. She was gone with the passing night, evaporated like the footprints on my bedroom floor.

My bare feet took me along the river bank towards the boathouse. I pushed open the rusty hinges and embraced the smell of rotting wood and stale river water that wafted up my nose as I entered.

In the old boathouse lay the remains of the ancient boat I'd sat and written beside a dozen times. The shape of the hull was exactly the same as the boat I'd seen the girl with on the river. Staring down at the rotting wood, I knew it was the same boat I'd seen the girl desperately clamber onto in the dead of night, the boat that was to be her escape. This was the relic of a story that I so desperately wanted to know.

The Lady of Shalott.

And then I remembered.

The line I'd seen scratched into the mirror in the attic: *I am half sick of shadows.* The line had been taken from the

148

poem of the same name. My eyes widened and I backed out of the boathouse and onto the muddy ground at the sickening reminder of what was haunting Dudley Hall. I turned around and started to run. I needed to get away.

My legs took me back through the garden, inside the house and up to my room again.

The book I'd thrown from my bed minutes before sat crumpled on the floor where I had left it. The golden embossed lettering on the book's cover glistened at me in the morning light.

The Complete Works of Alfred, Lord Tennyson

My heart jolted inside me. I knew what I'd find within the pages of the book before I opened it. Whoever – whatever – had put the book on my bed wanted me to look inside. There was one poem they wanted me to read.

I bent down and picked up the ancient book with quivering fingers. The book's well-worn spine fell open on the poem I knew I was meant to read: *The Lady of Shalott*.

Still shaking, I perched on the edge of my bed and began to read: '*On either side the river lie, Long fields of barley and of rye…*' I read the poem until the end, and then went back to the beginning and read again. The poem told the tale of a beautiful maiden who was cursed to live her life in a tower. The curse forbade her to look out the window, instead she could only look at reflections of the world outside in a mirror. I read and re-read the poem countless times, never moving from the bed. My fingers flicked the thin and delicate pages back and forth with care as I read the lines again and again.

As my eyes moved over the words of the poem I searched them desperately for meaning. There must be something hidden in between those lyrical lines that would provide the clue I needed. The clue that would lead me to discover why the grey girl wouldn't rest, and how I might help her to move on. When staring at the book felt fruitless, I moved over to my desk, booted up my laptop and searched the internet for answers. I typed all manner of words into the search engine: *Lady of Shalott – meaning. Who was the Lady of Shalott? Dudley Hall – Ghost. Lady of Shalott – Ghost.* I read each new page as it popped up with fascination. As the minutes slipped into hours I felt myself being dragged deeper and deeper into my new obsession. I hadn't eaten, I hadn't washed, I hadn't slept. All I could think about was the link between the poem and the house, and what it had to do with the girl who must have died there. My mind drew blanks at every new internet page that popped up. I knew that the grey girl had scratched words from the poem into the mirror upstairs, I knew an ancient boat at Dudley Hall was named after the poem, but beyond that I couldn't see a link.

Out flew the web and floated wide;
The mirror crack'd from side to side;
'The curse is come upon me,' cried
   The Lady of Shalott.

As I read through the poem I was vaguely aware of the doorbell chiming. It chimed and chimed until I heard my aunt run through the house to answer it.

The sound of muffled voices grew louder as I read the poem for the umpteenth time. The voices became even louder. My aunt was leading whoever it was up the stairs. She was taking them through the house, towards my room.

'She's just in here,' I heard my aunt say. 'Suzy!'

The door pushed open and I turned around to see Frankie standing in my doorway.

15

My best friend stood in my bedroom doorway looking like a lost orphan. Her hair had grown longer since I last saw her and it hung loose around her shoulders, framing her delicate face. She wore black trousers and a tight black vest top. Frankie always wore black, and I always liked the way it made her look like the tortured artist she was.

'What are you doing here?' I blurted out.

'Suzy!' Aunt Meredith gasped. She was standing behind Frankie in the hallway, her flannel dressing gown tied at the waist and her hair a mess. 'That's no way to speak to your friend.'

'Does your mum know you're here?' I asked Frankie. 'Does Seb know?'

She nodded her head slightly. Frankie has always been a bad liar, it's one of the reasons I always liked her. I can always rely on her to tell the truth. I lifted my eyebrow sceptically. 'Really?'

Frankie jerked her head, no.

'Sweetheart.' My aunt put her hand on Frankie's shoulder and Frankie turned around to look up at her, her large brown eyes pleading with a woman she didn't know. 'You need to tell your mum where you are. I'll get the phone, you need to call her.'

Aunt Meredith left us and hurried away to retrieve the phone.

'I tried to call you,' Frankie said timidly, coming further into my room. 'And you never replied to any of my emails or Facebook messages.'

'I…' I didn't want to apologise. I still didn't think I'd done anything wrong. 'I just needed space, Frankie.'

'And I just needed to get away from home,' she said. She walked up to my bed and paused by my bedside table. Her eyes went straight to the Victorian shadow puppet resting on the nightstand. She picked it up and twiddled it between her fingers thoughtfully. Trust Frankie to gravitate towards the one thing in the room I didn't want to speak about. She was always way too perceptive for her own good. 'Please, Suzy.' She turned to look at me, her eyes wide and afraid. I hated seeing Frankie look that way. She was meant to be the strong one. 'I really need a friend right now.'

'Frankie!' my aunt called from downstairs.

'You need to call your mum,' I said, standing up and walking towards Frankie. 'Do that and then we'll talk, I promise.' Frankie nodded in resignation.

Before I led Frankie out of my room I quickly grabbed my notebook and the pages I'd written *The Ghost of Dudley Hall* on. With my notebook in hand I led Frankie down the stairs and into the kitchen. Aunt Meredith was standing by the oven with the telephone in her hand.

'How did she know my mum's number?' Frankie whispered to me.

'You gave it to her, remember? When you wanted me to call you back.'

Aunt Meredith passed Frankie the phone and I heard Frankie's mum start to shout down the other end of the line. 'Suzy, come with me.' Aunt Meredith pulled me into the back garden. She closed the kitchen door so that Frankie could have some privacy, and I found myself standing outside for the second time that morning. 'Leave her to speak to her mum for a moment. I've told her Frankie can stay the night. She's going to pick her up tomorrow.' Aunt Meredith watched as I took a long deep breath and tried to contain my frustration. 'It'll be good for you to have a friend stay for the evening. Here.' She opened up her purse, which I hadn't realised she'd been holding, and handed me a wodge of notes. 'For you. Think of it as payment for all the brilliant murder victims you've played. Go into the village today with Frankie and have some fun.'

'I'm not sure they take twenties at the duck pond,' I said dryly. I suddenly felt ashamed for being ungrateful, so as I took the money from my aunt I tried to give her an appreciative smile and say gratefully, 'Thank you. Aunt Meredith,' I added tentatively, 'you said if I worked on *The Ghost of Dudley Hall* then you'd look at it.' She gave me a warm smile and nodded. I pressed my notebook into her hands, feeling suddenly nervous at the thought of her reading my story. 'Here it is. I've written up the story as though it was a murder mystery, and written descriptions of all the main characters. Maybe you could use it at some point?'

'I'll use it this weekend,' she said, without even glancing at the pages. 'It'll be perfect. I'll give the party your characters when they arrive and we'll use the story you've written. I'll take a look at it today and type it up so we can use it this weekend.'

'I'm going to stay here tonight,' came Frankie's voice from the kitchen door. 'Mum's picking me up tomorrow.' Aunt Meredith smiled at me and walked back into the house, *The Ghost of Dudley Hall* in her hands.

'My aunt's going to use a story I wrote for the murder mystery party this weekend,' I told Frankie. She smiled at me, and I noticed that her eyes were full of tears. I felt horrible for not noticing before – Frankie must have thought I only ever cared about myself. 'Is everything okay?' I added.

She shook her head. 'No, not really. Mum's so mad at me for running away. But I couldn't stay there a minute longer. I had to see you.'

I nodded. 'Come on, I need to get dressed then we can walk into the village. I'll buy you lunch.' I flashed the money my aunt had just given me at her and winked playfully.

'I've missed you.' She lunged at me and threw her skinny arms around my neck. Before I could stop myself I hugged her back, squeezing her bony ribs and burying my face into her hair. In that moment I never wanted to let her go. Every tiny emotion I'd bottled up inside me threatened to crash out into the world like a tidal wave, destroying everything in its path.

'I've missed you too,' I whispered back. She pulled away from me and smiled brilliantly. She gently brushed away the tears rolling down my face. 'How did you even get here?' I asked, feeling stupid that I was crying.

'Got the train from London and then walked from the nearest station. It took me nearly two hours with nothing but Google

155

maps on my iPhone to find my way. And the reception is terrible around here. But then I guess you wouldn't know that, seeing as you don't have a phone ...'

I smiled bashfully. Now that Frankie was standing in front of me, I felt stupid for not wanting to speak to her for so long. She was the best friend I'd ever had, the only person who wanted to see the world in the same way I did. And she was the one I'd shared that terrible time with at school, the only one who could possibly understand. 'Come on, let's go ...'

I quickly showered and threw on some clothes. I had an old shirt of my dad's that I'd made into a dress a couple of years ago. It still fitted me, and I teamed it with my DM boots and a quick fluff of my hair and a lick of eyeliner. Frankie smiled in approval as I pulled myself together and grabbed her hand to lead her downstairs and out of the house. We followed the gravel path away from the house and into the small village of Dudley-on-Water. We caught up as we walked. She didn't ask me any questions about Warren House, thank God. I skipped over the whole period I spent there and instead told her about the few weeks I'd spent so far at Dudley Hall. I told her about my new-found passion for writing and how I dressed up and played the murder victims at my aunt's parties. Frankie listened to every word I said as if it were the most interesting thing she'd ever heard. I secretly adored the way that Frankie always seemed so fascinated by me.

After I'd finished speaking Frankie told me about her mum's marriage breaking down after she left school. 'Now Mum's got a new boyfriend,' she explained. The new boyfriend was Scottish and her mum wanted to move Frankie to Edinburgh.

'I can't bear the thought of moving again. I've begged her to send me back to boarding school. Mum said she'd think about it,' she said hopefully.

'Sebastian rang me,' I admitted, as we walked into the village. I steered Frankie towards a small tea shop. The bell chimed as we entered. I ordered us two cream teas and found a seat in the corner where we could talk without being listened to. 'He's worried about you,' I said, as we sat down.

Frankie stared out of the window for a long moment. She smiled to herself as if remembering something. 'Do you remember that time at school when you tried to convince me to run away with you?' I nodded. 'You said we could go to London and find our fortunes. Start new lives where no one would know who we'd been before. Part of me wishes I'd just said yes. I wish we'd run away together. I'd run away now if I could. Properly, not just to your aunt's house. I asked Seb to run away with me.'

I stared at Frankie blankly. Something was definitely wrong with her. Of course I remembered asking her to run away with me. I was so desperate and unhinged at the time I would have done anything to get away from that school. But Frankie persuaded me to stay. She was always the sensible one, the one who thought about tomorrow and not just today. 'Why would you want to run away?'

She shrugged. I noticed her eyes well up with tears and she looked away, embarrassed, as the waitress came and put our tea down in front of us. 'I don't know what I want, Suzy. I just know I want to stop feeling like this.'

'Like what?'

'Like it's not over. Like any minute now I'm going to be dragged back into this dark, dark place where the ghosts of the dead swirl around me like smoke and choke me. And no one, no one believes me. Not even Seb. He doesn't believe what happened to us, that we saw … ghosts … that they led us to the truth. He thinks I'm crazy. And I don't want to lose him. But I'm worried I'm going to if I don't just accept that maybe he's right. That's why I've wanted to speak to you so badly. Because you saw it too. You know ghosts are real, that they come back and haunt you.'

'No, they're not,' I said, my voice breaking as I spoke. 'They're not real.'

'I don't believe you,' she said with conviction. 'I can see it in your eyes, you're lying to me. You know that what happened to us was real. No amount of counselling or drugs or brainwashing can take it away. You can try to forget it, Suzy, but you can't deny it ever happened.'

'It doesn't matter what happened, Frankie,' I said, almost pleadingly. 'We just need to let it fall behind into our past and try to move on.'

'You haven't moved on,' she said. 'I can see it in your eyes. You carry it around with you like a cross. Don't do that to yourself, Suzy. You're not mad. I'm not mad. Ghosts are real. They can't be ignored.'

I moved forward to the edge of my seat and looked my best friend deep in the eyes. I wanted to trust her, more than anything. She and I had lived through unimaginable pain together. We had weathered the storm once before, we were survivors. If anyone would listen to me and really understand then it was her. All this time I'd been avoiding Frankie when she was the only one I could really talk to.

Neither of us even looked at the waitress as she came and put our scones and cream on the table. We studied each other carefully, and I was sure that Frankie knew without me saying anything that I had some dark secret to tell her. I felt the words swell up inside me, ready to burst out into the world. The threat of the release felt so good. I wanted to say them. I wanted her to know. Frankie would believe me. She would believe me and I wouldn't be alone.

'Suzy,' she whispered, leaning towards me. 'Tell me what you're thinking.'

'It's happening again.'

16

Our tea turned cold as I told my best friend everything that had happened to me since I first set foot in Dudley Hall. 'I knew early on that something wasn't right.' My voice trembled as I told her about my curtains pulling themselves open each night. I told her about the strange scene I'd seen from my bedroom window. She listened, as still as stone, as I told her about the wet footprints on the stairs and the poetry book I'd found on my bed. 'The book had the poem *The Lady of Shalott* in it, you know the one –'

'Where the girl is locked up and cursed and then escapes on a boat and dies floating down the river,' Frankie finished off my sentence. 'There's a portrait of The Lady of Shalott in the Tate gallery in London. I've seen it.'

'Well, a line from the poem was scratched into the mirror in the attic room,' I said.

'What attic room?'

I told her about first hearing crying coming from the room, and about how I climbed up the side of the house to get into the room. Frankie shuddered as I told her about what had happened to me once I'd managed to get inside, how I'd seen the grey girl with my own eyes.

'You should have called me, Suzy,' she whispered. 'You could have had someone to talk to.'

I told her about Nell, Nate and his mother Fiona. 'I'm positive Nate doesn't know anything, I think he's convinced his mum's ill – he's so protective of her. But Nell and Fiona know way more than they're letting on. The last time I saw Fiona she took one look at me and knew I'd seen her. She was the one who called her the grey girl. And Nell knows something too, but she's not telling me. There's a reason she won't go upstairs in the house. Nell says I should let the dead lay sleeping.'

'But the dead don't sleep, Suzy,' Frankie warned me. 'Not if they still dream about their life. They have something unsettling them. You need to find out what happened to that girl, try to right some terrible wrong. Only then will she move on.' She sat back in her seat and her eyes softened slightly as she regarded me. 'I've missed you so much. And being here, talking about this kind of stuff in broad daylight makes it all seem manageable. It doesn't seem so terrifying if you have someone to face it with.' I smiled at her, she was right.

'Maybe when we get back to the house we can go up to the attic room?' I said. 'I haven't been able to go back up there since … but maybe together?'

Frankie nodded and smiled. 'I'll do anything I can to help you. And to prove to the rest of the world that we're not crazy. Just because other people don't see things, don't believe, doesn't mean that we don't. Someone has to lay this spirit to rest, Suzy. It needs to be us … you … you're the one she's trying to reach. Everything you've seen and heard at the house, it all

161

means something. We just need to work out what.'

'Wow, you've changed.' I raised my eyebrows. 'I remember when I met you and practically had to force you into doing a Ouija board with me. Now look at you, trying to convince me that ghosts are real.'

'I don't think you need convincing, Suzy. Look, what do you know so far?'

'Well, I know the house once belonged to the Dudley family. Rich aristocrats who lost their money and had to sell off the house. After that the house was a school, a girls' school.' Frankie gave me a shudder and a knowing nod. 'The school closed down years ago because it ran out of funding. After that the house fell into disrepair.'

'So the girl was either a member of the Dudley family or one of their servants, or a girl at the school,' Frankie said quickly.

'I'd guess she was a schoolgirl. The clothes I saw her wearing looked old-fashioned but not ancient – my guess is she died in the last century.'

'Okay, so we should find someone who went to the school and ask them if they know anything that might help. And ghost stories, legends, rumours …'

I nodded. 'Nate's grandmother, Nell and Fiona's mum, was at the school.'

'So let's go talk to her.'

'Can't.' I shook my head. 'She's dead.'

'So we ask her daughters.' Frankie shrugged. 'Which leads us back to Nell and Fiona. Or we could ask Nate – he must have heard the story, even if he doesn't believe it.'

'Actually, Nate is really cute,' I admitted, feeling the need to lighten the tone of conversation now we had a plan in place.

Frankie raised her eyebrows playfully. 'Even more reason to talk to him then.'

I shook my head firmly. 'The last thing I need at the moment is the distraction of a hot boy.' I rolled my eyes dramatically and Frankie smiled.

'Hmm,' she teased, raising a teaspoon full of cream to her mouth and licking it off. '*Love is a smoke and is made with the fume of sighs.*'

'*Romeo and Juliet,*' I smiled. 'God, it's good to see you again, Frankie. You see what I mean … love … smoke … choking … distraction! I can't have it. Nate might be cute but … oh my God, Frankie! Look over there!' I pointed to the boy in jeans and a white T-shirt walking over the village green. 'That's him.'

'He *is* cute.' She winked at me. 'And you have the perfect excuse to go over and talk to him.'

'I really don't think I'm ready, Frankie.' I watched Nate disappear down the road and out of sight. 'I'm not sure I want him to see the real me, scars and all. I'll wait and ask his mother or Nell instead – much better idea.'

Frankie got to her feet, pushing the chair away as she rose. 'So let's go and ask them.'

'Now?'

She nodded. 'Now.'

'Nell will be at Dudley Hall getting things ready for the murder mystery guests arriving tomorrow,' I said, staying sat down in the hope that Frankie would sit back down too. 'And I really don't want to ask Nell anyway – she's already warned me not to mess with this kind of stuff.'

'So we ask her sister, Fiona,' Frankie said impatiently, still waiting for me to stand up.

'Okay,' I said reluctantly, getting to my feet.

I paid for the food we hadn't touched and we left the tea shop. I filled Frankie in on what little I knew about Fiona as we walked over to their cottage. 'Fiona and Nate have been living with Nell since Fiona split from Nate's dad. Nell has a cottage by the church. The Old Rectory.'

We walked through the village towards the church. I felt brave with Frankie by my side. For a moment I let myself get lost in a daydream that we were paranormal investigators. Kick-ass girls who fought demons and ghosts and nothing ever scared us or got in our way. I saw the Old Rectory as soon as we turned the corner by the church, with its thatched roof and crooked Tudor beams appearing to hold it up. Smoke was billowing from the chimney.

'Who lights a fire this time of year? It's nearly summer,' Frankie commented. 'Shall we knock on the door?'

'Not yet,' I said. 'Let's see who's at home first.'

Staying out of sight from the windows, we snuck up to the house. We moved off the gravel garden path and onto the soft green grass that surrounded the house so our footsteps wouldn't be heard as we approached. Practically crawling on the ground, I moved towards the house and peeked into the front window. The window looked into the kitchen. No one was in there. It looked immaculate – everything neatly stacked and the surfaces sparkling clean.

Frankie made a silent gesture with her hand and I followed her around the side of the house. Rose plants crept up the trellis on the cottage walls. The garden was well kept – a large, healthy green lawn and beautiful flower beds. We approached another window, almost slithering along the ground so we could stay hidden. Once we were underneath the windowsill we slowly raised our heads so we could look into the room. It was the sitting room I'd sat in with Nell and Nate the night I'd visited for dinner. There was a woman hunched over on the floor and crying. I recognised her straight away. It was Fiona. She was crouched on the floor, her shoulders shaking from sobbing as she looked ahead into the fire blazing in the grate.

Frankie and I turned to one another and exchanged a worried look.

'What the hell do you think you're doing?' came Nate's voice from behind me.

Frankie and I both jumped and turned around to find Nate standing right behind us.

I grabbed Frankie's hand and without a word to one another we both leapt to our feet and began to bolt away from the house.

We ran and ran without once looking behind us, all the way back to Dudley Hall.

Monday 20th October 1952

No one had seen Tilly since the incident where Lavinia locked her outside. No one had heard what had happened to her or even if she was alive. Lavinia had gone very quiet this last week, and I wondered if she felt bad for what she'd done, although she would never admit to it if she did. I wondered if she was secretly praying for Tilly in the Rituals, like I did every night.

But Tilly was back in class again today. It was such a relief to see her. Her skin still looks blotchy, like a healing burn, but she's alive and that's the main thing. I would have thought that Lavinia would be relieved that Tilly was alive, but instead she just seemed angry. I think she would have been happier if she had died and she'd never had to see her again. I don't understand why she hates her so much.

'Don't even think of going up to see her,' Lavinia said with malice when I told her my intentions after lights out.

'But I promised I would,' I argued.

'Well, it was silly of you to make a promise you couldn't keep, because that just makes you a liar. You know you have to stay here with us. We need to do the Rituals. That's far more important than nursing some sick little freak.'

I didn't speak a word to Lavinia or the others as we put on our winter cloaks, drew a chalk pentagram on our dormitory floor and lit candles at the five points of the star. We held hands and began to chant, like we do every night, 'Goddess, we serve you,

166

Goddess, hear our prayers.'

It was Margot who noticed her first. The rest of us hadn't even heard the door open, hadn't heard her slip into the room and shut the door silently behind her.

'What are you doing here?' Margot lisped, pulling us all from our trance and forcing us to look towards the door.

Tilly was standing there in her white nightgown, her back pressed against the door and her eyes wide with fear and excitement. 'What are you doing?' she asked in a whisper.

'It's nothing, Tilly,' I said in panic. 'Go back upstairs, I'll come and visit you later, I promise.' Lavinia shot me an angry glare.

'Is this witchcraft?' Tilly asked, bravely taking a step further into the room. 'Is this magic?'

'It's none of your business, that's what it is,' Lavinia warned her. 'You'd leave now and forget what you saw if you knew what was good for you.'

But Tilly didn't leave. She straightened her spine and looked Lavinia right in the eye. 'If this is magic then I want to join in. No one needs a miracle more than me. And if you don't let me join in, then I'll tell Matron everything I saw this evening.'

That's when Tilly turned around and left. The four of us looked at each other in horror. Our secret is out, the Rituals are no longer just ours. No one spoke about Tilly as we blew out the candles and rubbed the chalk from the floor. We each lay in bed in silence, the moonlight pouring through the window. I took the shadow puppet that Tilly and I had made from my bedside table and silently held it up in the darkness.

It felt like the moment in the poem when everything changes. When the Lady of Shalott knows that life will never be the same *again. That Tilly discovering our secret tonight was somehow the beginning of the end. I'm not sure what will happen now. The words of the poem echoed in my head as I tried to make sense of what we should do ...*

> She left the web, she left the loom,
> She made three paces thro' the room,
> She saw the water-lily bloom,
> She saw the helmet and the plume,
>   She look'd down to Camelot.
> Out flew the web and floated wide;
> The mirror crack'd from side to side;
> 'The curse is come upon me,' cried
>   The Lady of Shalott.

Until I write again,

Annabel

17

Frankie and I spent the afternoon hidden away in my bedroom, the whole time paranoid that Nate would burst into the house at any moment and accuse us of being spies, or burglars or just downright nosy. But Nate hadn't made an appearance at Dudley Hall; in fact, Frankie and I had barely spoken to anyone else all day. We'd sat up in my room, listening to music and reading through *The Complete Works of Alfred, Lord Tennyson*.

'We should speak to Nell tonight,' Frankie said, her eyes on the poetry book.

'Nell will be busy getting everything ready for the guests arriving tomorrow,' I explained weakly to Frankie. If there was any way I could avoid talking to Nell about the grey girl then I would. Nell may have told me I could trust her, that she wanted to be my friend and that I should come to her with questions, but if there was a way to keep her out of this, to deal with everything alone, then that's what I wanted. I couldn't help but think Nell would be disappointed if she knew I was digging about in the grey girl's grave – *the ghosts you chase you never catch*. 'Besides,' I added. 'Who knows what Nate's had the chance to tell Nell by now. I'm surprised she's not called the police on us for trespassing on private property.'

Frankie rolled her eyes. 'Suzy, don't be dramatic.'

There was a knock on my bedroom door. We both stiffened and looked at one another. The knocking came again. 'Who is it?' I called out.

'Toby,' came a small voice from the other side of the door.

I walked over and opened the door. My young cousin stood there on the landing, wearing his Sherlock costume and holding on to his plastic pipe. 'Can I come in?'

I looked up and down the landing for any signs of life, and once I knew no one was watching I stood back so Toby could come into my room. He gave Frankie a small smile and she looked at him blankly. Frankie doesn't have any kid siblings or cousins so she's even more clueless about children than I am.

'Aren't you helping your mum and Nell get everything ready for the murder mystery this weekend?' I asked Toby.

He shook his head. 'He said I needed to get out of the way this evening.' I didn't need to ask who 'he' was. 'He said that everyone had too much to do and I was getting in the way. He told me to go to my room. But I don't want to go to my room yet, I'm not tired.' It was obvious that Toby hated Richard just as much as I did. Only Toby wasn't nearly as brave or stupid as I was – there was no way he'd tell Richard what he thought of him. He just suffered in silence. Poor kid. 'How long is he staying for?' Toby asked quietly. I looked down at the pained expression on my young cousin's face with pity. At least I got to walk away from Richard and slam my bedroom door – Toby was stuck playing happy families with the man.

I shrugged at Toby and smiled sympathetically. 'Not long, I hope.'

'Can I play with you this evening?' he asked timidly. 'We could play detectives again.'

'We have something important to do, Toby,' I apologised.

'What?' he asked.

I hesitated. 'We need to go back up into the attic,' I explained.

'Can't I come with you? I could help you, like I did before.'

Frankie cast me an annoyed look. 'It's not safe up there,' she said to Toby.

He furrowed his brow and looked cross. 'I won't get in your way, I promise. I want to go up there again, but I don't like it on my own.' I knew exactly how he felt.

'Sorry, Toby.' I shook my head. 'This is grown up stuff, and it's dangerous. I don't want to drag you into it. We can play detectives again tomorrow, I promise.'

Toby's eyes began to water and he blinked back his tears stoically. 'Okay, Suzy,' he whispered. I watched as he turned around, his little Sherlock Holmes cloak trailing behind him as he sulked down the corridor away from me.

'God, I'm a horrible, horrible person,' I said as I closed my bedroom door behind me.

'And you think *I've* changed,' Frankie muttered. 'Since when do you hang out with children?'

'He's not so bad,' I said. 'And I feel sorry for him. He's got no one here. He's bored out of his mind.'

'We can't have a kid get mixed up in all of this. You know that,' Frankie replied. 'You've got to be cruel to be kind, Suzy. It's best he keeps well away.'

I nodded and sighed. I knew she was right but I still felt terrible for turning Toby away. 'Ready to do this?'

'If you won't let us speak to Nell then I don't see what choice we have.' Frankie shrugged.

'I don't want to get Nell involved,' I said firmly.

'Then let's go.'

I led Frankie out of my bedroom, along the corridor and up the final flight of stairs in silence. It was beginning to get dark outside and twilight was starting to spill into the house through the large domed skylight, casting an eerie glow as we ascended the stairs.

Frankie's eyes widened as we reached the attic landing. She looked left and right, along the empty, dilapidated corridors. 'Okay, which one is the room she's in?'

I took a deep breath and walked down the corridor towards the last room on the right. The door to the haunted room hung limply on one of its hinges. It was broken and splintered from where Richard had kicked it down to rescue me when I was locked inside. I pushed the door timidly and it creaked open. My heart began to pound in my chest as I came face to face with the room once again.

I took a step further into the room, confused by what I was seeing. The room had changed – it wasn't at all as I had seen it the day I'd climbed up the side of the house. It was completely empty. There were a few twigs and bits of moss in the corner where the raven's nest must have been, but that was all there was to be seen. No wardrobe, no dressing table, no books or toys of any kind. 'It wasn't like this when I was in here before,' I said, my voice trembling. Frankie gave me an encouraging nod. 'There was an old wardrobe here where the birds were nesting. And here –' I pointed to the other corner – 'was the dressing table and shattered mirror. It had a line from *The Lady of Shalott* carved into it: *I am half sick of shadows …*'

'I love that poem,' said Frankie. 'It's so sad. *She has heard a whisper say, A curse is on her if she stay, To look down to Camelot.* I wonder if the mirror you saw is some kind of clue. I mean, it's important in the poem, isn't it? The girl was cursed to always look in a mirror. The moment she turned away from the mirror and looked out of the window she knew she had to die.'

I walked over to the window and looked down onto the grounds below. I watched the fading sunlight bounce off the river as it flowed away from the house, towards the boathouse and the world beyond. 'I swear this room was full of …' I whispered, my breath clouding up the glass on the attic window.

'There will be an explanation,' Frankie said quickly. 'Maybe Richard has already had the room cleared out.'

I nodded my head, wanting to believe her. 'There's an old boat down there, in the boathouse.' I pointed in the direction of the boathouse, beyond the weeping willow. 'It's called *The Lady of Shalott*. It hasn't been used for years, but I'm sure it's the same boat I've seen the girl climb into.'

Frankie came and stood next to me and peered out into the world. 'Probably not a coincidence that the boat is named after the poem that you saw scratched into the mirror here. The poem that's in the book you found on your bed.'

I shook my head, suddenly feeling lost. 'Unless I'm imagining the whole thing.'

Frankie grabbed my arm and pulled me around so I faced

her. 'No,' she said sternly. 'You're not imagining it. We've been through this before. We need to figure out what's happening so we can make it stop.' I nodded and drew in a deep breath as Frankie continued. 'Here, you get the Ouija board ready and I'll take pictures of the room, that way you won't have to come up here again, you can just look at the pictures if you need to.'

Frankie took out her phone and began to snap away, capturing the room from every angle. I pulled out a folded piece of paper from my pocket. We'd made the makeshift Ouija board earlier, tearing a leaf of paper from my notepad and writing the letters of the alphabet and the words 'Yes' and 'No' on it. As I spread the board flat on the ground and placed a coin in the middle of the board my hands began to shake. I hadn't done a Ouija board since the time Frankie and I unleashed the angry spirit of a dead girl at school. I'd sworn I'd never do anything so reckless ever again, and yet here I was, ready to unleash the unknown once more.

Frankie put her phone in her pocket and sat down opposite me. 'This isn't a mistake,' she said gently, as if reading my mind. 'We need to do this.'

I nodded silently and reached my hands out over the board. Frankie put her clammy hands in mine and closed her eyes. I closed my eyes too, and at the same moment we both chanted in unison, 'Spirits, come to us, Spirits, come to us, Spirits, come to us.'

I prised my eyes open and we let go of each other's hands. We each placed the tip of an index finger on the coin in the centre of the paper. 'Is there anyone there?' Frankie asked. Without so much as a beat the coin began to move towards

174

the box that said 'Yes'. My heart fluttered in my chest like a trapped bird. 'We knew this would happen,' Frankie reassured me. 'This is a good sign. It means she's ready to speak to us.'

'Are you the spirit of the girl I saw here?' I asked, my voice rattling in my throat.

The coin remained on the box that said 'Yes'.

'Why are you still here?' Frankie asked.

The coin shuffled under the weight of our fingers. I relaxed the pressure I had on the coin's surface so my finger was barely touching it. I felt Frankie's finger next to mine twitch as she did the same. The coin began to glide effortlessly over the board, towards the letters written on the edges of the paper. It paused for a moment on the letter C. Then it began to move again, this time coming to a stop at the letter U. It moved again and again until it had spelt out a word.

CURSED

I felt my blood rush to my head and my vision begin to shake as my breathing became erratic. I looked up at Frankie and her eyes were swollen with horror. She swallowed hard, staring at me as though I was about to burst into flames. 'What curse?' she asked the spirit, not losing eye contact with me.

The coin moved again. It moved so fast my eyes struggled to keep up with it. Together, Frankie and I sounded out the letters it moved to, slowly speaking the words it wanted us to hear.

THE CURSE IS COME

'What are you doing?' came a small voice in the doorway.

My heart nearly leapt out of my mouth at the sight of my small cousin standing in the doorway. Still wearing his Sherlock Holmes costume, Toby was watching us, his face a mix of confusion and fear.

I leapt to my feet, my fingers leaving the coin and the Ouija board. 'Toby, you shouldn't be here.' My voice shook as I spoke.

'I heard crying,' Toby said, sounding worried. 'It sounded like a girl crying. I came up the stairs to spy on you, to see if you were okay. Then I heard the crying coming from this room and when I looked in here you were sitting on the floor and she was standing next to you. But now she's gone. Where did she go?'

My heart raced in my chest. This couldn't be happening. My gorgeous, sweet little cousin had seen far more than he should have done.

'We were playing a game, Toby, and whatever you saw you imagined. There's no girl.'

Frankie picked the Ouija board up off the floor and began to tear it to shreds. 'We need to get out of here,' she said, her voice shaking as much as mine.

I took Toby's shoulders and steered him out of the room. We began to run down the corridor. The three of us bolted down the stairs, all the way down to my bedroom. Toby looked like someone had just told him up was down. 'You were playing a game,' he said like a dumb parrot.

I crouched down so my eyes were level with his. 'Yes, and you can't tell anyone about it. And you can't tell anyone what you saw. Not your mum, or Richard, or anyone. Promise?'

He nodded weakly.

'I'm scared,' he whispered.

I tried to smile. 'Don't be silly. There's nothing to be scared about. Look, it's nearly bedtime. Why don't you go and find your mum and ask her to read you a detective story?'

Toby nodded and ran off down the hall, calling for his mother. I felt a horrible pang of guilt that whatever was lurking in the shadows of this house had now appeared to Toby. But he was young, he wouldn't understand, and with any luck he would have forgotten every last detail of it by the morning.

'Give those to me.' I pulled the shreds of paper from Frankie's hands and took them over to the empty fireplace. I had a box of matches in my desk drawer. I rummaged around until I found them and then set the remains of the Ouija board alight.

'He saw her too, Suzy,' Frankie said, sitting down on the bed. 'Whoever she is we need to help her move on.'

'I don't want Toby involved with any of this.'

'It's too late for that. You know how this stuff works, Suzy. Once the spirit is out there we can't stop it. The more we can do to protect him and everyone else, the better. We need to find out who she is and what she wants. We need to find a way to make her disappear.'

I knew Frankie was right.

'What should I do now?' I asked, suddenly feeling exhausted.

Frankie took the phone from her pocket. 'I don't think we should go up there again. Not until we have some way of dealing with whatever's there. We don't have a choice but to ask Nell and Fiona what they know.'

I loved the way she said 'We', even though I knew that

by tomorrow Frankie would be gone and I'd be facing this alone. Frankie's face paled as she began to scroll through the pictures she'd just taken in the attic on her phone. 'What's wrong?' I asked.

Frankie didn't answer, and I walked over towards her. I stood at her shoulder and looked down at the image she was staring at on her phone. It was an image of the attic room. It was the picture she must have taken standing at the door; you could see the empty room and the window at the end of it.

And next to the window, as clear as anything, was the small figure of a grey girl, looking out on to the world outside.

Friday 24th October 1952

*We haven't performed the Rituals since Tilly caught us in the act.
And I've avoided Tilly all week. I hoped she'd forgotten about what
she saw. I thought if I ignored her and pretended that nothing had
happened then maybe she'd just forget.*

But Tilly hasn't forgotten.

*'Has Lavinia decided if I can join you?' Tilly asked me this
morning as the rest of us were putting on our cloaks and preparing
to walk down to the church for our morning service. 'If I don't
hear that she has by the end of the day then I'm telling Matron.'*

*Lavinia and I walked in silence down to the village this morning.
The air is turning colder and I can see my breath on it like clouds.
We sat in the church pews and listened to Father Molsey preach
about worshipping false idols and going to Hell for blasphemy.
I know that's where everyone will say we're all going to go, once
they know what we've been doing.*

*That's why they can't know. The teachers will expel us and
we'll all be damned to Hell.*

*I told Lavinia to follow me after school today and to my
amazement she did. Now I know she must be really worried.
As I led her down to the weeping willow by the brook I planned
what I was going to say to her in my head. I couldn't frighten
Lavinia into letting Tilly join us. I might be ready to admit that I
was afraid of expulsion, and afraid of the eternal damnation of
my soul, but Lavinia would never be.*

179

'If we let Tilly join us then we'll have five people to stand at the five points on the pentagram,' I told her as we stood underneath the old tree. 'And with all five points of the star activated then our prayers will be louder and the Goddess will finally hear them.'

Lavinia narrowed her eyes and then said, to my amazement, 'That's exactly what I've been thinking.' I blinked in confusion, wondering if I had heard correctly. Lavinia was going to let Tilly join us in the Rituals! 'But she can't join the circle unless she's initiated,' she said. I nodded in agreement. 'Tilly will need to have the pentagram burnt onto her.' Lavinia pulled her necklace out from under her cloak. 'And she'll need to be given the Kiss of Death.' My blood ran cold at the thought of small, fragile Tilly being given the Kiss of Death. 'And you, Annabel,' she said slowly, 'should be the one to give it to her.'

I stared into Lavinia's cold eyes and realised that she had me. There was no way I could reason my way out of this. And in a way there was a sort of sick poetic justice to what she was saying. If I wanted Tilly to join us then I had to be the one to kill her.

Until I write again,

Annabel

18

Frankie and I sat across from each other at the breakfast table and sipped at our coffees in silence. I tried not to wince as I drank mine, envious of how easily Frankie knocked back her sugarless black drink without so much as a frown. However bad the coffee tasted, we both needed it that morning – our eyes were framed by sunken shadows and our skin was pallid from the restless night. Neither of us had said much since the events up in the attic. The girl's spirit, summoned by the Ouija board, and the pictures Frankie took of the girl on her phone spoke for themselves. Both Frankie and I had enough experience of the paranormal to know what was happening. An unspoken understanding hovered between us as we sat at the kitchen table. Dudley Hall was being haunted by the spirit of the grey girl. A spirit that believed it had been cursed.

The kitchen door rattled and Nell came in, carrying heavy bags of food for the weekend. 'You two are too tired for words,' Nell greeted us, plonking down her bags on the kitchen floor and moving to fill up the kettle.

Frankie cast me a quick look that told me she was about to tell Nell every last detail of what had happened to us the night before. 'It's hard to get much sleep when –'

'We've got so much to catch up on,' I finished quickly, kicking Frankie hard under the table.

'*Ow*,' she mouthed, then, '*what?*'

I put my finger to my lips in warning. Now wasn't the right time to tell Nell what we'd seen.

Nell walked over to the table and stood staring down at the two of us, hands on her wide hips. Her golden dangling earrings glinted in the morning sun that streamed through the kitchen windows as she shook her head suspiciously. '*Secrets, silent, stony, sit in the dark palaces of both our hearts: secrets weary of their tyranny: tyrants willing to be dethroned,*' she said dramatically.

'Who said that?' Frankie asked.

'James Joyce,' I answered for Nell. 'And I don't know what you mean,' I continued petulantly. 'We don't have secrets.'

'Every girl has secrets.' Nell smiled, walking towards the kettle as it boiled and pulling out a mug from the cupboard.

'Have you heard crying coming from the attic before, Nell?' Frankie asked, leaning over the kitchen table and staring straight at Nell. Nell poured her tea and stared at Frankie, thoughtfully.

'Do me a favour, Suzy,' Nell asked, ignoring Frankie's question. 'Unload some of this shopping for me. I've just realised I've left my crystal ball at home.' Without another word she put down her steaming cup of tea and let herself out, her feet scrunching away from Dudley Hall on the gravel driveway.

'You need to speak to Nell,' Frankie said urgently. 'It's obvious she knows something. Talk to her today.'

I nodded my head and took another sip of my cooling coffee. Nell was going to be busy all day cooking and greeting the guests – she'd hardly have a moment spare between crystal-ball readings, tea-making and clearing up. If I was going to speak to her I wanted to do it properly, to sit down and hear the full story – I wasn't sure I'd get that from her at a weekend when the house was full of guests.

Frankie and I sank back into silence and I listened for the popping toaster, but instead the quiet was broken by the sound of a car pulling up in the vast gravel driveway of Dudley Hall.

A few moments later a petite, well-dressed woman with long chestnut hair was standing in the kitchen doorway. I studied her with a cold frown – I knew exactly who she was without being introduced. She looked just like my best friend.

'Mum, you're early,' Frankie said quietly.

'I hope you're ready to leave,' her mother replied coldly.

She looked furious, and I didn't envy Frankie her long drive home and the ear-bashing she was bound to get for running away. But in that moment all I really cared about was that Frankie was being taken away from me, and once she left I would be truly alone again. The thought was enough to make me want to cry.

I'd never actually met Frankie's mother before, but in that moment I hated her for taking Frankie away. I didn't even know her name. At boarding school our parents were nothing more than absent players in our dramas, and now Frankie's mother had strolled right onto centre stage to steal away the one ray of hope I had.

'Frankie, you look tired.' She came towards Frankie and gave her an awkward kiss on the top of her head. 'Where's your aunt?' she asked me without saying hello or bothering to ask how I was.

'I haven't seen her this morning,' I replied, looking away and gazing out of the window, trying not to cry.

'I'd like to speak to her, please,' Frankie's mother said briskly. I stood up, annoyed. 'I'll go and find her.'

'I'll come with you,' Frankie announced, also standing up. 'I need to get my stuff from upstairs anyway,' she said to her mum.

We left Frankie's mother alone in the kitchen. I didn't bother to offer her a drink; if she wanted something she could get it herself. In fact, she could blend into the wallpaper or swim down the stream to the sea for all I cared.

I ran up the stairs, Frankie following close behind. She tugged on my hand as we reached the second-floor landing. 'I wish I didn't have to go. Will you promise to keep in touch this time?'

'Yes,' I said, and I meant it. 'I wish you didn't have to go too. What about you? Will you be okay? If you need some more time away from home then you can stay here, you know that, don't you? Who cares what your mum says. Aunt Meredith won't mind if you stay.'

Frankie chewed the inside of her lip for a moment in thought. 'I wish I could stay. But from the look on my mum's face I don't think it'll be up for discussion. And don't worry about me, Suzy. I'll be fine.' She paused. 'Promise me you won't deal with this alone any more,' she said seriously. 'Call me if you need to. And talk to someone here if you can. You need to ask Nell and Fiona what they know about the girl. You may as well explain everything to Nate. Better that he knows the truth than thinks you're into breaking and entering. Next time you see him, don't run away. Promise?'

I thought about it for a moment. 'I promise.'

'Oh, and, Suzy.' Frankie smiled. 'Good luck this weekend.'

'This weekend?'

'You said your aunt was going to use a story you'd written for the murder mystery party,' Frankie reminded me. 'I'm sure they'll all love it.' I'd completely forgotten that *The Ghost of Dudley Hall* was getting its premiere this weekend. 'You get your aunt, I'll get my stuff. I'll see you downstairs in a minute.'

I couldn't find Aunt Meredith in her bedroom or bathroom. I was walking down the corridor towards the stairs when I heard her voice speaking in hushed, gentle tones from Toby's room. I walked towards Toby's door, which stood ajar, and gently pushed it open.

Toby was lying in bed asleep and my aunt was leaning over him, stroking his brow and whispering something. When she saw me she nodded in acknowledgement and gestured silently for me to walk back out into the corridor. Aunt Meredith followed me out and quietly shut Toby's door behind her.

'Poor Toby's not well,' she said. 'He's been up all night; he's hardly slept a wink. He won't tell me what's wrong. Do you know what could have upset him?'

I shook my head quickly, summoning up my best acting skills to fool Aunt Meredith into believing me. I couldn't bear the thought of Toby being so petrified by what he'd seen. But I couldn't bear the thought of telling Aunt Meredith that it was all my fault, that he'd followed me up into the attic and watched on as Frankie and I summoned the spirit of the dead girl that haunts Dudley Hall.

'Frankie's mum's here,' I said, trying to change the subject. 'She wants to thank you.'

I led Aunt Meredith back downstairs and stood there silently as Frankie's mother thanked her for looking after her wayward daughter for the evening. She opened the kitchen door and made to leave, beginning to push Frankie out onto the driveway without even letting her say goodbye to me.

I lunged forwards and pulled Frankie away from the door and wrapped my arms around her. I hugged her so tightly to me, as if I'd never let her go.

'Call me later,' Frankie whispered in my ear.

I nodded into her shoulder, not trusting myself to speak without sobbing.

'You're my best friend,' Frankie reminded me as we pulled away from each other.

I watched with a painful lump in my throat as my best friend was driven away from Dudley Hall, and away from me. I wished I could run after her, I wished my legs could carry me like a speeding bullet away from Dudley Hall, and never come back. I needed to get out of that house. I needed fresh air and daylight. I couldn't bear to be inside a moment longer, I couldn't bear the sight of Aunt Meredith's worried face as my poor cousin lay terrified in his bed.

'I'm going into the village,' I announced to my aunt, as she was making her way back up the staircase. 'Do you or Richard need anything?'

'Oh, I forgot to say, Richard left this morning.' Without saying goodbye, I thought. 'But no, thank you, Suzy, I don't need anything. And, Suzy,' she added, 'The Ghost of Dudley Hall is brilliant.' She smiled. 'You've done a wonderful job. I've typed up the character notes and we'll give them out to the guests when they arrive. You should be proud of yourself.'

I smiled weakly at her. It was difficult to feel proud of myself when all I wanted to do was run away. 'I need to go.'

As soon as my feet scrunched down on the gravel driveway I knew where I needed to go. I hadn't bothered to take a jacket with me, even though the crisp morning air was fresh and cool against my skin. I walked with blind purpose, hoping that each step would take me nearer to the truth. Frankie was right, she usually was. I needed a way to unlock the secrets of the Dudley family. And this was the only way to do it.

As I walked over the village green, towards the Old Rectory, someone in a white T-shirt and jeans caught my eye. 'Nate!' I shouted out.

He spun around and saw me running towards him; an undisguised look of annoyance quickly spread over his face. I stopped in front of him, near enough to see his hazel eyes dazzling in the sunlight and the short hairs on his arms rise as a fresh breeze blew at us. 'Nate. I was just coming to speak to you.'

'Good,' he said, although he didn't sound at all pleased. 'You going to tell me what you were doing snooping around my house yesterday? And where's your friend today?'

'Frankie's gone home.' I nodded my head towards the wooden bench on the side of the village green and he reluctantly walked towards it with me. 'I'm sorry about what you saw yesterday. I know what it must have looked like. But the truth is…' I paused as we sat down, side by side. As the breeze caught us I could smell him. He smelt like deodorant and grass. I looked over at him and was momentarily distracted from what I was about to say. He was watching me eagerly, waiting for my next words as if they were the key to some ancient riddle. 'The truth is, I wanted to speak to you. And to your mother.'

'Look,' he said awkwardly. His cheeks flushed slightly and he looked away. 'If this is about what my mum said the other day about a grey girl then I'm sorry. She's got this thing in her head about my grandmother and …'

'That's what I wanted to ask her about,' I said quickly. 'About your grandmother and Dudley Hall, and the people that lived there before us. I want to know what it was like when it was a school. I need to know who lived there, and who died there. I really need to speak to her.'

He leant forwards, resting his tanned forearms on his knees and staring out into the distance in thought. 'Look, Suzy, my mum's not well. She never really has been. I don't … I don't like people seeing that. I don't want you to see that. The things she says … you can't listen to them. That's why Dad left, he couldn't cope any more.'

Nate wasn't looking at me. He was studying his shoes as they kicked about at the ground. I reached out and put my hand on his arm. He looked down at my hand in shock and then quickly up at me, his eyes meeting mine in surprise. 'It's okay, Nate,' I said quietly. 'I'm the last person in the world who would judge anyone about something they believe in. I don't think your mum's crazy. I just really need to speak to her.'

He studied me for a long moment. I could see the conflict in his eyes as he tried to decide if he could trust me or not. The whole time I kept my hand resting on his arm. 'You can speak to her,' he said eventually. 'But I need to warn you, when she

188

talks about that kind of stuff you might not get any sense out of her. She might seem a little … strange.'

I smiled. 'Not to me she won't. Trust me, Nate,' I said, looking into his hazel eyes and making him a promise. 'I won't ever judge you or your mum.'

'I like you, Suzy,' he said quietly, holding my gaze, his eyes full of caution. 'I don't want you thinking …'

'You can trust me,' I said again, keeping a firm hold on his arm, my fingers tingling with the feel of his skin next to mine.

I felt my hope drain away. But Nate's eyes filled with warmth as he steadily reached out and took my hand in his. 'I want to,' he said, almost in a whisper. Energy pulsed through my fingertips, up my arm, rushing to my face, making it as red as a beetroot as Nate stood up before pulling me to my feet.

'Thanks,' I blushed, pulling my hand away from his and smiling.

'Come on then,' he said, beginning to walk away. 'Let's go ask my mum about the grey girl.'

19

Nate opened the Old Rectory front door by simply turning the handle. I've never understood why people who live in the countryside don't lock their doors. 'Mum!' he shouted into the house, making his way towards the lounge – the very same room that Frankie and I had peered into yesterday. The house smelt of wood smoke and cinnamon. Candles flickered on every available surface, filling the air with sweet thick smoke. 'Mum, Suzy's here to see you.'

I followed Nate into the lounge. Fiona was sitting on the sofa, her legs sprawled out in front of her on a footstool, with a book in her lap. She was still wearing her pyjamas and dressing gown, a pair of thin glasses sat on the end of her nose and her hair was pulled up into an unbrushed bun on the top of her head. Fiona closed the book she'd been reading as we came into the room, then leant forwards and eyed me with suspicion.

'Suzy. Nate's friend who lives at Dudley Hall,' she said, her voice flat and giving nothing away.

'I'm just staying there for a few weeks,' I explained, nervously moving my weight from one foot to the other.

Nate plonked himself down in a beaten-up leather chair by

the fireplace that was framed by flickering candles. He pulled a cushion into his lap and looked between me and his mum with expectation. I stood by the door feeling awkward, suddenly unsure of what to say. Now that I had what I wanted, a chance to ask Fiona everything she knew, I wasn't sure how to start.

'Mum, Suzy wanted to ask you a few questions about Dudley Hall,' Nate said. 'You can sit down,' he said to me, as if I was stupid.

'I'm not sure what you think I can help you with,' Fiona said, narrowing her eyes at me. Her voice was edging towards unfriendly. 'I don't have anything to do with that house. I don't think I'll be able to help you.'

There was a small chair in the corner of the room. I walked over and sat on it, straightened my back and looked Fiona in the eye. This was the only chance I had to discover the secrets of the house; I couldn't blow it. 'The last time I saw you was by your mother's grave,' I said. 'You told me that I'd seen the grey girl, that you could see that just by looking at me.'

Her cold eyes bore into me. 'Nate, have you offered Suzy a drink? Would you like something to drink, Suzy? Maybe some tea? Or lemonade?'

'No, I'm okay...'

'Nate, go and put the kettle on, please,' Fiona instructed him, her eyes not leaving me.

Nate lifted his eyebrows and gave his mother a nod. He flashed me a small smile as he left the room, almost as if he was wishing me good luck.

'Nate doesn't like to listen to me talk about the house,' Fiona said, leaning towards me. 'Neither does my sister. But then

191

again, she goes there every day, she doesn't need reminding of what happened there.'

'And what did happen there?' I asked, my hands suddenly cold and clammy in my lap. I brought one hand over the other and began to absently scratch the back of my hand for warmth. 'Who is she, the grey girl?'

Fiona sat back on the sofa and stared at me coldly. 'Tell me what it is that you think you've seen.'

I could have told her the truth, I could have risked it. I could have so easily told her about the times I had seen the grey girl from my window in the dead of night, running towards a boat that I knew had been un-riverworthy for decades. I could have told her about my curtains opening by themselves each day, about the poetry book I'd found sat on my pillow. About the time I'd climbed up the side of the house and scrambled into the attic room only to come face to face with the grey girl who now haunted my dreams. 'Nothing,' I lied. 'I'm just curious, I guess. I like ghost stories.'

'I think there's something you're not telling me.'

I shrugged, momentarily wondering if I should let this stranger in. If I should tell her my secrets and open myself up for her to easily pick apart. But I'd promised Nate he could trust me – I couldn't lie forever. 'The house seems to hold so much history,' I whispered, the words beginning to tumble out of me. 'The walls and floorboards seem to be imprinted with memories of a time no one is there to remember. It's like something – someone – is still there when they shouldn't be. I want to try to make sense of it all.'

Fiona studied me intently. She knew there was more I wasn't

telling her, that maybe I was holding back. Keeping my cards close to my chest until she had showed me hers. It was like some kind of unspoken game, and we were both making up the rules as we went along. 'Dudley Hall was once a school, you know that, don't you?' I nodded. 'My mother, Nate's grandmother, was a schoolgirl there after her parents were both killed in the war. The school closed soon after she left. The building stood empty for years.'

I knew all of this. I needed her to tell me something new, something I didn't already know. 'Who's the grey girl you thought I'd seen?'

'You know who she is,' Fiona said with a wicked smile. 'That's why you're here, to ask me about her.'

'I don't know who she is,' I admitted. 'I don't know what she wants, or why she died, or why she keeps –'

'Appearing to you,' Fiona finished. She paused, waiting for me to deny it, but I denied nothing. I sat still and silent and gave her the slightest of nods. 'You've seen her, haven't you, Suzy? That's why you're really here.'

'Yes,' I whispered.

'I don't know who she is,' Fiona whispered back. My heart sank. She had to be lying. She had to know. 'But I know that she's there.'

'How?'

'I've seen her too.'

'Do you take milk and sugar, Suzy?' came Nate's voice as he poked his head out from the kitchen. 'I can't remember.'

'She'll have black coffee like me, won't you, Suzy?' Fiona said.

'Yes please,' I managed to say to Nate, without my voice

shaking as much as it wanted to.

Nate disappeared back into the kitchen, leaving Fiona and I alone once again. 'When did you see her?' I asked.

'I told you my mother was a schoolgirl at Dudley Hall,' Fiona said. 'Nell and I always found it so strange that our mother never spoke about her time there. When we were younger we would ask her about her friends, her teachers, about the books she had studied and the games she had played. She told us not to ask questions. She told us not to worry about the past. The past is done, it cannot be changed. But it was obvious to us that there was something about my mother's past that had affected her deeply. I could see it, Nell could see it. You see, my mother didn't speak about her time at Dudley Hall, but she always lived in the old school's shadow. Something about that place haunted her and she couldn't let it go.'

A shiver ran through me as I remembered Frankie telling me in an email how she had gone back to our old school after we had left. She was haunted by what had happened to us there, she couldn't let it go. Maybe Fiona's mother was just like my best friend.

'Is that why your mother lived here, in Dudley-on-Water?' I asked.

Fiona nodded. 'She married a local man, my father. Even after he died she stayed here. All our lives Nell and I grew up in the shadow of that place. It was like some kind of invisible chain that bound my mother to this village. When we were younger we used to ask her about the house. How many rooms did it have? What did the bedrooms look like? Where did the schoolgirls eat their breakfast? To Nell and me, as children,

194

Dudley Hall was like some kind of forbidden castle in a fairytale. Locked up behind iron gates and closed off from the world.' Fiona's eyes glassed over as she stared ahead of her. 'We used to pretend that a twisted and tortured beast of a man lived up there – a hunchback, a cursed prince who waited for us to come and release him. We used to dare each other to climb the gates, to walk down the driveway, to peer into the windows. Before long we were setting foot inside the dark, damp old house.' A shadow seemed to fall over Fiona's face as the memories stirred up inside her. 'Old school desks, chalkboards and trunks littered the place like cobwebs. Girls' names were scratched into windowsills and the floorboards creaked beneath our feet as we grew braver with our explorations. Room by room, floor by floor, we ventured through that house as though it was some kind of theme park or film set. As though none of it was real. In our heads, in our games, Dudley Hall was a magnificent stage-set, purely there for our entertainment.'

Nate came back into the room and silently put cups of coffee in front of me and Fiona. He slumped back into the leather chair by the fireplace and looked at his mother with concern. This was a story he must have heard before, one that he hated her telling again and again.

'It was summer time when we first heard her,' Fiona continued without acknowledging Nate or the cup of coffee he'd put down in front of her. She stared ahead as she spoke, as if she was speaking to someone far away in the distance. 'Each day our parents would go out to work, leaving us alone in the house. And each day Nell and I would run through the village to Dudley Hall. We would spend hours walking through the old classrooms and dormitories, making up stories about the girls who had lived there. The, one day, we were both sitting on the stairs, our backs to the attic floor. The sound came from behind us, from the top of the house. We could hear her crying.'

A horrible shiver ran along my spine as I listened to Fiona's story. She rose from her chair and walked towards an old bureau in the corner of the room. She pulled open a drawer and took a small shoe box from it, closing the drawer again carefully. 'Nell wanted to run away,' she continued, holding the shoe box in her hands as she sat back down. 'But I wanted to investigate. I persuaded her to go with me, and together we climbed the rickety old staircase until we stood on the attic landing. We followed the corridor around to the right, and walked towards the last room. The crying got louder, it was coming from behind the door. I rattled the handle, trying to open it but it was locked. The door wouldn't budge. I remember the feeling of being very cold, of feeling every hair on my arm rise to attention. I remember feeling as though my veins were filled with ice, as though my heart would slow down and stop forever. I was so cold. Nell tugged on my arm and together we ran back towards the staircase. And on the step where we had been sitting only moments before, was this ...'

Fiona opened up the shoe box and dipped her hand inside, pulling out a shadow puppet. It was just like the one I had found in the attic room. Only this wasn't an elegant maiden, it was different. Fiona walked towards one of the flickering candles above the fireplace. She held the candle behind the shadow puppet and in the daylight it cast the faintest shadow on the wall. It was a man. A knight.

'Nell picked up the shadow puppet,' Fiona whispered. 'And I felt my heart grow even colder. As we ran back down the stairs I looked back up towards the attic floor. That's when I saw her. She was looking down at me. Right at me. It felt as though she was seeing into my soul. The grey girl.'

There was a gust of wind through an open window. The candles in the room blew out like flames on a birthday cake and Fiona dropped the candle and the shadow puppet in her hands. She sank to her knees and began to cry.

'Mum, Mum.' Nate rushed to her side and put his arms around her. She clung to him and sobbed into his shoulder.

'She looked straight at me,' Fiona whispered to Nate through her tears. 'The grey girl.'

Nate stroked his mum's head and rocked her gently back and forth. He looked up at me with a mixture of shame and sadness, and in that moment I could have sunk to my knees and embraced them both. I knew what it felt like to have your life touched by a ghost – to question your own sanity and hate the world around you for appearing one way when you knew it to be another. I could have cried with her there on the floor, rocking back and forth until my lungs gave out and I had nothing more to give.

'Suzy,' Nate said gently.

I rose to my feet and began to make my way to the door. As my feet passed the fallen candle and shadow puppet on the floor I looked back over at Nate and Fiona. He was speaking to her gently, his eyes locked on hers, whispering words I couldn't hear.

Neither of them saw as I quickly dipped down and picked

197

up the shadow puppet between my fingers. They didn't notice as I held the paper puppet close to my chest as I walked out of the living room and out of their house. And they didn't follow as I walked away from the Old Rectory with the shadow puppet in my hands – walking back to reunite the puppet with its partner, back to Dudley Hall.

Thursday 30th October 1952

Tomorrow night is All Hallow's Eve. Tomorrow night is when we initiate Tilly into our sisterhood. Tomorrow night is when I must burn her. Tomorrow night is when I must kill her.

Tilly doesn't know what the initiation involves. She's just thrilled that we've agreed to it. 'You know I would never have told, not really,' she gushed to me at dinner.

'Don't let Lavinia know that,' I said. 'She'll call the whole thing off.'

'She can't do that,' Tilly said, wide-eyed. 'I need this. This is my only hope of ever being cured. Tonight may be my last night to go out in the darkness. My last night as a Moonchild. If the Ritual goes well and the Goddess hears us, then I'll be cured. I'll be able to walk in the sunlight with you.'

I smiled at her sadly.

I remember the night that Lavinia and I initiated each other into the circle. It was the same night Margot and Sybil did it to each other too.

I remember the smell of the burning candles, and the sound of the chalk scraping over the dormitory floorboards. I can recall the sensation of my forearm sizzling with heat as Lavinia held the red-hot pentagram over it and chanted, 'Goddess of the Moon, we are your children,' until I bled. And I remember pressing my back against the cold wall and letting Lavinia place her hands over my heart. When it was my turn to do it to Lavinia my hands shook like leaves, but her hands on my chest were as steady and as sure as an executioner's. She pressed her weight into me, down onto my ribs and I felt them bow and bend within my chest. The breath was suddenly ripped from my lungs and my head clouded up. Just as my eyelids fluttered closed and I let Death take me, I remember Lavinia leaning in to me and whispering, 'The Kiss of Death.' I felt her cold lips touch mine as I sank to the floor. When I awoke Lavinia helped me up and said, 'You survived Death. Now the Goddess will listen to you.'

Once tomorrow is over then the five-pointed star will be complete. The Goddess will hear us. Margot will finally be cured of her lisp, Sybil's skin will clear up and Lavinia will one day be head girl. And me and Tilly will finally get what we want – for her curse to be lifted. One day she'll walk in the sunlight. One day she will be free.

I saw Tilly again from my window tonight. I watched as she walked down to the stream and untied The Lady of Shalott from the bank. Her last night as a Moonchild. After tonight everything will change.

Until I write again,

Annabel

20

I let myself in through the kitchen door, my heart still racing from stealing the shadow puppet. Katie was busy baking cakes for the guests' arrival later that afternoon, but I ignored her and the glorious smells coming from the oven and headed straight out of the kitchen, through the hallway and towards the stairs. I needed to get to my bedroom – I wanted to hold Fiona's shadow puppet next to the one I'd found in the attic.

I almost collided with Nell as I reached the staircase. My arm instinctively shot behind my back so the shadow puppet wouldn't be in her sightline. 'Your cousin's not well,' Nell said gravely, seeming not to notice that I was hiding something from her. 'He hasn't got a fever but he won't get out of bed. One minute he says his head hurts, the next minute it's his stomach that's upset. If I didn't know better I'd think he was faking it. I just don't know what's wrong with him. And your poor aunt…'

I felt my breath hitch in my chest. I knew exactly what was wrong with Toby. He was petrified. Too scared to get out of bed because of what was waiting for him in the shadows of Dudley Hall. 'I'll go up and see him,' I said, pushing past her and marching up the stairs, being careful to move the shadow puppet in front of me so it was still out of view.

'The guests are arriving in a couple of hours,' she called after me. 'I'll need your help.'

As I walked onto the first-floor landing I quickly glanced down at Nell. She was still standing at the foot of the stairs, watching me. I wondered if she could read me as well as Fiona could, if she could see on my face that I'd been to visit her sister that morning and she'd told me the whole story. I knew about how they'd broken into Dudley Hall as children and seen the grey girl, how they'd taken the shadow puppet from the house – the same puppet that I'd just stolen from Fiona. But I was still no closer to discovering who she was and how she died. Worried that everything was painted on my face, I quickly turned away from Nell and hurried up the second flight of stairs.

As I walked out into the second-floor landing I could hear Aunt Meredith talking on the phone. She was speaking frantically, obviously distressed. 'I just don't know what to do,' I heard her say. I walked towards the sound of her voice. It was coming from behind a closed door – her and Richard's bedroom. 'He won't even speak to me now. He's just staring off into space as if … yes, doctor. I understand. Yes … right away.'

I heard the sound of a phone click down on the receiver, and before I had a chance to move away Aunt Meredith appeared on the landing in front of me. I'd never seen her look like that before. Her eyes were red from lack of sleep and her hair was greasy from where she kept running her fingers through it with worry. It struck me how horribly she looked like my mother at that moment.

'I'm going to take Toby to hospital,' Aunt Meredith said, a

tear escaping from the corner of her eye.

'What? Why?'

'Something's very wrong with him, Suzy. He's catatonic. He won't speak to me. He's just staring into space. It's as if he's locked away inside himself and won't come out.'

I looked over towards Toby's bedroom door. Before I knew it I was walking towards it, pushing the door open and walking in. The light was dim, and my small cousin lay on his side in bed, facing the door. Aunt Meredith was right. He was catatonic. His eyes were wide open, staring into space. The whole of his little body was rigid, frozen still in terror. His two small hands were clasped in front of him, holding something tight against his chest, which rose and fell with each rapid breath. I moved towards the bed to get a better look at what he was holding, and my heart lurched with sickness within me as I realised what it was.

It was the shadow puppet of the beautiful maiden I'd found in the attic. The other half of the pair.

'Why has he got that?' I said, sounding alarmed. 'Where did he get it from?'

'I don't know, Suzy. What are you talking about?' Aunt Meredith said, following me into the room.

The earth stopped turning as I realised what had happened to put Toby into a catatonic trance. She'd been here. She'd visited him and put that thing in his hand. Seeing her again had tipped my poor, tiny cousin over the edge. He'd disappeared so far into himself to get away from her my aunt was worried she'd never get him back. I bent forwards and quickly ripped the old puppet from Toby's hands.

'I need to get him to the hospital,' Aunt Meredith said, not noticing what I'd done. She walked towards him, and started to nervously brush the hair from his vacant eyes. 'I'm going to drive him there now.' I watched in horror, the two puppets behind my back, as she darted around the room with frenzied movement, packing up a bag of Toby's things to take in to the hospital. 'Will you be okay on your own tonight, Suzy? I'm not sure when I'll be back. Nell and Katie have everything they need for the party. I've typed up your story and characters – Nell will give them to the guests when they arrive. All you'll need to do is play the murder victim and …'

'I'll be fine,' I lied. The thought of dressing up as a schoolgirl who died in Dudley Hall made me feel nothing but sick to my stomach.

After quickly putting the two shadow puppets in my bedroom, I helped Aunt Meredith load a small overnight bag into her car as she carried Toby into the back seat. She promised to call me with any news as soon as possible and then drove off with a screech of tyres upon gravel. I went back inside the house and closed the door behind me. The walls seemed to creak and the air crackled as my heart beat furiously inside me. I closed my eyes and sank my head back against the heavy wooden door. This had gone too far. This had to stop – *she* had to be stopped. For her to appear before me was horrible, but for her to taunt my little cousin until he sank into some kind of trance was unforgivable. I knew one way or another that this had to end – soon. I had to find a way to rid her from the house forever.

'Suzy,' came Nell's voice from the corner of the hallway. I opened my eyes and caught her staring at me. I briefly wondered how long she'd been standing there for. 'The guests will be here in an hour. Go and get into costume and get ready to greet them.'

My costume was simple – a school uniform comprised of a blue skirt and cardigan, a white blouse and knee-high socks. I wore my simple black ballet pumps, scraped my hair back into a neat ponytail and kept my make-up to a minimum. I stared at myself in my bedroom mirror. I hadn't worn a school uniform for months, and I'd been dreading putting one on. But staring at my reflection didn't horrify me as much as I had thought it might. It was someone else staring back at me in the mirror – I was playing a part. I looked myself in the eye and took a deep breath; I could do this, I could pretend.

As the guests began to arrive I lined up with Nell and Katie by the front door. Nell was dressed in an old-fashioned matron's uniform and Katie was in the same costume as me, only she wore a 'Prefect' badge pinned to her cardigan.

'Please each pick up an envelope from the hallway table.' Nell smiled at the guests as they streamed in to Dudley Hall with a clatter of suitcase wheels and excited giggles. They were much younger than normal murder mystery party guests – girls in their twenties. There must have been fifteen of them in total. 'Each envelope will contain your characters for the weekend, along with smaller envelopes containing the clues to be revealed throughout the weekend. Don't open these smaller envelopes until you're instructed to.'

'Which way are our bedrooms?' one of the girls asked.

Katie dutifully led them up to their rooms for the weekend. An hour later the hen party were dressed in their blue school uniforms and standing in the library, awaiting further instructions. 'Welcome to Dudley Hall,' Nell boomed loudly. 'The year is 1952. King George VI has just died and his daughter, the Princess Elizabeth, has come to the throne. Winston Churchill is Prime Minister, 1.4 million people in Great Britain own a television set and Team GB has won a gold medal at the Winter Olympics. You are all schoolgirls at the Dudley Hall boarding school, having been orphaned during the Second World War. And amongst your lessons and games of hockey this weekend you may want to keep your eyes peeled for something far more sinister … because we have a murderer in our midst.' The obligatory 'ooh' and 'aah' sounds echoed throughout the library. 'Now, please help yourselves to tea and cake and be ready to be seated for dinner at seven o'clock sharp.'

The flurry of activity over the next few hours was exactly what I needed. I helped Nell and Katie prepare the guests' dinner and ply them with endless cups of tea and pieces of cake. It was a fantastic distraction, but every now and then my mind would wander back to the two shadow puppets sitting upstairs in my bedroom, and I worried about how this would all end. I couldn't bear the thought of Toby lying in a hospital bed, Aunt Meredith holding his hand and praying he'd be okay.

Nell and Katie served the guests their dinner, and once they had finished their dessert course I opened the front door and quietly stepped out into the night. I hadn't noticed it grow dark, but the evening was pitch black, with only the faintest glow from the moon. Just as I had written in *The Ghost of Dudley Hall*, I stood outside the dining room window and gave the guests my best blood-curdling scream. I then lay on the cold

206

gravel ground, bending my arms and legs into as uncomfortable a position as I could manage so I looked more authentic.

'She must have jumped from a top-floor window!' one of the guests cried as they ran out to find my lifeless body on the driveway.

'Someone pushed her from her dormitory window!' another person added.

'This is so exciting!' gushed the voice of another girl. 'Murder at Dudley Hall!'

The party soon complained of the chill in the air and quickly disappeared back inside the house to get warm, happy that the body had been discovered and the murder mystery was under way. Once the front door had been shut behind them I opened my eyes and stared up into the starless sky, watching as my breath made small puffs of white cloud above me. Lying on the ground, looking up at the Dudley Hall gargoyles looming over me, I felt strangely peaceful. But my peace was quickly ended by the sound of motorbike wheels scrunching down on gravel. As the bike pulled to a halt I got to my feet and began to shake off the stray stones that had clung to my school uniform.

'You promised me I could trust you,' Nate growled at me as he jumped from his bike and pulled his helmet off. I watched, speechless, as he stormed past me into the house. 'You stole that stupid puppet from my mum, Suzy, didn't you? It's not yours to take – it belongs to my family.'

'You shouldn't be in here.' I ran after him. I pulled at his white T-shirt so he spun around to face me. We stood opposite one another in the grand hallway as the sound of the party guests seeped underneath the closed dining-room door. 'The house is full of murder mystery guests – they can't see you.'

'I'll be gone as soon as you give me the puppet back.' He glared at me.

I nervously glanced towards the back corridor, praying that Nell wouldn't hear us and come out to see why Nate had driven up here to confront me. 'I need it,' I admitted to him quietly.

'What could you possibly need an old piece of junk like that for?' Nate asked me, his voice still hard and his eyes unforgiving.

'You wouldn't believe me if I told you.'

'Try me.'

I stood silently for a moment, weighing up whether to tell him the truth or not. 'I need to show you something,' I said eventually.

Silently, I led him up the grand staircase, onto the second-floor landing and into my room. Nate's eyebrows raised as I reached to close my bedroom door behind him. 'You wanted to show me the inside of your bedroom? Suzy, don't think you can distract me with …'

'Oh, shut up, Nate.' I rolled my eyes and made my way over to the computer. 'The house is crawling with murder mystery guests and Nell's just downstairs. I don't want them to see you. Besides, it's time I told you something.'

Nate shook his head at me and exhaled loudly. 'Fine. Nice room by the way,' he said, glancing about. He opened the door to the bathroom and looked in there, then peered out of the window onto the grounds below. 'Very posh.'

'Here, look at this.' I pulled up one of the pictures from Frankie's phone onto my computer screen. The one with the girl standing by the window.

Nate looked at the computer screen for a second, and then looked back at me. 'What exactly am I meant to be looking at here?' he asked.

'Er, the ghostly girl by the window.'

'It's an empty room,' he said with a raised eyebrow. 'There's no one there.'

I looked down at the computer screen again. I was not imagining it. Frankie had not been imagining it. There, in the centre of the picture, as clear as the window she stood next to, was the little grey girl. I pointed to the screen in frustration. 'She's right there.'

'You're pointing at a wall.'

'No, I'm not,' I said, feeling irritated. 'Can't you see her?'

'Er, there's nothing there to see.' He laughed nervously.

'There!' I shouted at him, thrusting my finger towards the grainy image of the grey girl in the picture.

'It's a trick of the light,' he shrugged. 'Okay, it looks a bit like the shape of a girl, but it's probably just a shadow or ...' He stopped and studied me. A slow smile spread over his face and something passed over his eyes, as if he was suddenly shutting down. 'You're letting my mum's stories get to you, Suzy. Don't listen to her.'

'Your mum's not crazy. The grey girl really exists – she's here in this house. This photo is ...' I stopped talking as something out of the window caught my eye.

It was her.

The grey girl, running away from the house. Her cloak billowed behind her as she ran as fast as her legs could carry her. Running towards the river, towards *The Lady of Shalott*.

'What are you looking at?' Nate moved beside me. His voice had dropped its cocky arrogance and he suddenly sounded concerned.

'You can't see that, can you?' I whispered.

'See what?'

I looked across at Nate. His eyes searched mine for answers.

'I can see a girl, running from the house towards the river. She's running for her life. She's untying the boat…' I said, as I watched her untie *The Lady of Shalott*. 'I just wish I knew what it all meant.' A single tear began to trickle down my face.

'Suzy, you're kind of freaking me out…'

'She's trying to get into it, can't you see?' I began to cry. I couldn't stop the tears. This was it. I was seeing something that he couldn't. She was appearing to me and not to him. I didn't know why. I didn't want this. I wanted the darkness of the spirit world to be invisible to me too. 'Can't you see her?' I sobbed.

'Suzy!' Nate took my arm and tried to pull me away from the window.

'No!' I fought with him as he tried to lead me away. I struggled to see more. I hung on to the window frame and watched, my eyes wide with horror at what I saw.

I'd seen it all before. The girl waded into the water, her cloak spreading out behind her. She pushed the boat further out into the stream and began to climb in. 'What's she running away from?' I cried, feeling Nate's hands come around my waist as he tried to pull me back from the window. I fought against him. 'She's running away. Look at her!'

Nate's arms suddenly went limp around me. Then I felt his

chest rise quickly as he took a sharp intake of breath. He had seen her. I spun around and looked up at his face. His eyes followed her as she began to row herself downstream.

'You can see her?' I whispered up at him, tears streaming down my face.

He nodded silently. His eyes met mine and he nodded again. 'I see her.'

I turned back around towards the window, but she had gone. Vanished into the night.

My whole body shook and my hands gripped the windowsill for support. I'd seen her again. And Nate had seen her too. Now he knew as well as I did, as well as Fiona did, that the grey girl was real.

Nate began to mutter and whisper something in my ear but I couldn't hear him. I wasn't listening. All I could hear was the howl of the wind outside. I felt Nate's arms close around my waist once again, and I let myself sink back into him, my body pressing against his.

The next thing I knew my legs gave way beneath me and I collapsed into his arms.

21

I woke up still dressed in my school uniform costume, the sunlight streaming violently through my bedroom window. My eyes were swollen and sore, and as I lifted my hand to rub at them I felt something resisting me. There was a pair of strong, warm arms wrapped around my waist, pinning my arms to my side. The arms were pulling me close to a warm, hard body. I could feel breath rising and falling; I became aware of soft exhales tickling the back of my neck.

'Nate?' I whispered.

He gave no answer.

Mortified, I tried to wriggle out of his vice-like hold. Memories of last night came flooding back to me. I'd sobbed my heart out to him. Tears and snot had streamed down my face as he'd tried to console me. He hadn't asked me any questions about what we'd seen. He didn't ask me if I'd seen her before or if I knew who she was, if it was the same girl his mother had always spoken of. I wouldn't have been able to answer him if he had asked. All I could do was cry. I cried myself to sleep and Nate rocked me back and forth in his arms as I drifted off. It was the first time I'd ever spent the night with a boy by my side and I'd fallen asleep with snot encrusted on my face. Brilliant.

As the harsh morning sunlight invaded the bedroom I just wanted to slip out of the room and never see Nate again.

Slowly, I managed to prise one of Nate's arms from around my waist. He stirred slightly as I lifted it up and gently crawled out of his grasp. I swung my legs off the bed and sat up, careful not to make any sharp or sudden movements that might wake him.

Nate murmured something in his sleep, and as I stood up I turned around and looked at him. He was fully clothed and sleeping on top of the duvet, lying on his side facing where I had been. I took a moment to study his relaxed features. His hair had grown slightly since I'd first met him – I could tell that it might grow into thick blond curls if he were to let it grow out any more. His skin was perfect, his lips puckered, kiss-like, in his sleep. His eyelids twitched as if he was dreaming. It was the first moment I truly appreciated just how handsome Nate was. And that realisation only made me more feel more mortified about the fact that I'd practically fainted on him the night before and then cried on his shoulder for hours.

I silently pulled out fresh clothes from my drawers, crept to the bathroom, and locked the door behind me. I jumped in the shower and let scolding hot water pour over me until I was numb. When the water started to run cold I got out, dried myself and put on the clean clothes. I stared at myself in the mirror as I brushed out my wet and faded red hair. My eyes were slightly less swollen, but I still looked like something that had crawled out of a nightmare.

With a deep breath, I opened the bathroom door, feeling slightly more human and better prepared to face Nate. The bed was empty. For a moment I thought I'd dreamt the whole thing. Wishful thinking perhaps. As I walked up to my bed, I noticed a page of my notepad had been torn out and written on, the note sitting on top of my pillows.

See you downstairs. I make a mean bacon sandwich.

I smiled to myself as I carefully put the note back down where I'd found it. There was something I knew I had to do before I went downstairs to face Nate. I quickly fired up my computer and logged into my Facebook account. I typed out a private message to Frankie and quickly read it through before pressing 'send'.

Dear Frankie,

It meant so much to have you here the other day. I'm sorry I was such a bitch to you for so long before. You're the best friend I've ever had, and I'm sorry if I don't tell you that enough.

Things here are coming to a close. I can feel it. Everything has changed. And soon everything will be over. I spoke to Fiona – she'd seen the grey girl too. I'm still not sure who she was, and why she's still here – but I'm going to find out if it kills me.

If I never see you again I want you to know how important you are. You're important to me and to the universe, Frankie, never forget that.

Suzy xxx

It was late and the guests had already eaten their breakfast and were busy reading clues and occupying most parts of the house, rendering them out of bounds. Katie and Nell were nowhere to be seen as I came into the kitchen to find Nate pottering around. With any luck no one had seen him come downstairs this morning – who knew what kind of conclusion people would come to if they knew he'd spent the night in my room.

Nate busied himself around the kitchen with his back to me. With one hand he flipped over charred bread under the grill, and with the other he turned the heat down on the stove. I stood in the doorway, silently watching him. 'Grab some plates, will you,' he said without turning around. 'And some ketchup – breakfast is ready.'

I hesitated for a moment, slightly bewildered by the sight of Nate so at home in Aunt Meredith's kitchen, and slightly confused by the fact that he was acting so normally towards me. After what he'd seen last night I couldn't believe he'd still want to step inside Dudley Hall, and still want to be anywhere near me. He turned around and stared at me; I stared back. He raised his eyebrows and lifted the sizzling frying pan towards me. 'Plates.'

Swiftly laying the table, I sat down and waited for Nate to join me. He landed a very crisp-looking bacon sandwich in front of me, and then poured a steaming pot of thick, strong coffee into a couple of mugs. It was the first time coffee had ever smelt so appealing to me, and I greedily picked up my mug and blew on it to cool it down.

Nate sat down opposite me and hungrily lifted the sandwich

to his mouth and began to devour it. 'Eat up,' he said with his mouth full. 'That'll get cold.'

'Did you, um, sleep okay?' I asked, not looking at him.

'Eventually. You took a while to go to sleep. And you seemed to be having nightmares.'

I closed my eyes, just wanting the kitchen floor to open up and swallow me whole.

I could feel Nate staring at me, as though he was waiting for me to speak. *'I could be bounded in a nutshell, and count myself a king of infinite space, were it not that I have bad dreams.'*

'It's a bit early for *Hamlet*, isn't it?' He was smiling at me when I looked up at him.

'You know *Hamlet*?' I asked, briefly forgetting how humiliated I felt.

'We studied it in college, it's pretty cool.' He smiled.

'It's my favourite play. I love Shakespeare.'

'Suzy, can I ask you something?' I lowered my coffee cup and braced myself. 'When you don't want people to know how you feel you start reeling off lines from plays and poems – am I right?'

I took a swig of my coffee and lowered the cup to my lips, letting it hover there for a moment before I thought of the best thing to say. 'Maybe I say those things when I want people to know how I feel but don't know how to put my feelings into words,' I said slowly, choosing my words carefully. I'd never wanted to explain myself before, not really. But for some reason I found myself wanting to be completely honest with Nate. 'I have so many thoughts rattling around inside my head, sometimes it's hard to give them shape. Sometimes other people's words are easier to use. And I find them … comforting. It's good to know that other people have seen the world in the same way that I do. It makes me feel as though I'm not alone.'

'You're not alone,' he said gently, reaching across the table towards me. He took my hand in his and gently stroked the backs of my knuckles. 'You know you can talk to me, don't you?'

I nodded and took my hand away, clasping my coffee cup and bringing it to my lips once again.

'I think I'll go and visit Toby today,' I said quietly.

'Do you want a lift?' he asked, his hand still reached out on the table where I'd left it.

'Yes please,' I replied, looking down at his outstretched hand. He suddenly seemed to realise that his hand was still there, and quickly moved it back to his coffee cup. 'Won't your mum wonder where you were last night?'

He shook his head. 'I told her I was coming here to visit you last night. She knows where I am.' My cheeks blushed at the thought of Fiona knowing that Nate and I had spent the night together in Dudley Hall. I felt a momentary jab of annoyance that Nate might let them believe that he and I were more than just friends.

'I hope you're going to tell them nothing happened,' I said sharply.

'Don't worry,' he smirked, biting into his sandwich. 'Your honour will remain intact,' he said through a mouthful of bacon.

'Is your mum really mad with me then?' I asked awkwardly, taking another swig of my coffee. With each sip I was gradually feeling more human.

'Why would she be mad at you?' he asked, confused.

'Because I stole her shadow puppet.'

Nate shook his head. 'She doesn't know it's gone.'

'But you told me...'

'I told you what you needed to hear so you'd give it back to me, which you still haven't done. It's not yours to take, Suzy.'

'Did you know that the puppet your mother has is one of a pair?' I said quickly, trying to sidetrack him. 'There's another one. I found it here, in one of the attic rooms. In the room that I saw her in one time. It's a puppet of a woman.'

Nate looked at me and shrugged. 'Mum has a box of old things like that. Most of them belonged to my grandmother.' I thought of the shoe box that Fiona had pulled the shadow puppet from. 'I don't know what that thing you took – the shadow puppet – is for or why she has it. And if you've found another one here at Dudley Hall then I have no idea what that means. It's just junk, Suzy, it probably doesn't mean anything. But for some reason that puppet, and everything else my mum keeps in that stupid box, is important to her. I need to take it back. You can't have it.'

'Okay,' I said quietly. The mention of his mum and the shadow puppet had quickly turned Nate from kind and sympathetic to prickly and cold.

'Now eat your breakfast,' Nate said, looking down at the bacon sandwich sitting untouched on my plate. 'Before it gets cold and before I eat it for you.'

I began to eat my bacon sandwich, soon realising how famished I felt and devouring the thing in a few monster-sized bites. 'That was delicious, thank you.'

Nate sat back in his chair and took a loud slurp of his coffee.

'I thought you could do with a descent breakfast … after, you know … last night.'

I looked down at my empty coffee mug, wishing I had more to drink. I placed it down on the kitchen table and rubbed my tired temples with my fingers. 'Nate, I'm so sorry about last night. I didn't want you to see any of that. I hardly know you – the last thing I wanted to do was cry in front of you like that. And I'm grateful, really grateful that you stayed with me. Thank you. Although, honestly, right now I'm kind of mortified by the whole thing and I kind of wish you weren't here.'

'Mortified?'

'Yeah, now you know how crazy I am.'

'Crazy?' he echoed. 'I don't know about crazy, Suzy. I saw her too, remember? My mum used to tell me about a grey girl who haunts this house. I never believed her. But that was her, wasn't it?' I nodded. 'I've never believed in ghosts before.'

'I have,' I said, looking up at him.

'Has this happened to you before?' he asked, leaning forwards and staring right into my eyes.

I nodded, hesitating for a brief moment before I told Nate my story. 'I used to go to an all-girls' boarding school,' I said. 'My best friend, Frankie – the girl you saw me with the other day – she and I thought it would be fun to do a Ouija board. We wanted to summon up the spirit of a girl who'd supposedly died at the school hundreds of years before. A girl who everyone said haunted the school. The Ouija board worked, but it wasn't her we contacted. It was another girl. A girl who'd been murdered at the school – buried alive. Once we'd awoken her spirit she wouldn't leave us alone. It was horrible. I thought I was going crazy, no one believed me. It nearly killed me. Frankie was the strong one – she managed to uncover the truth about who had killed the girl. I just fell apart. The doctors all thought I'd gone mad. That's why I was in hospital before I came here. They locked me up for "delusions".'

'But they weren't delusions, were they?' Nate said, his voice soft and worried. 'What you saw was real. This girl, the ghost at your school, she was as real as the grey girl at Dudley Hall.'

'As real as a ghost can be,' I shrugged. 'Whoever she is – the grey girl – she's dead, she doesn't belong here. But where is she when she's not in front of me? Is she watching, invisible in the shadows? Is she sleeping? Is she waiting? Is she nowhere at all, like before you're born? Nate …' I said slowly. He nodded, wanting me to go on. 'Do you ever wonder if there's any truth to what your aunt does?'

'Fortune telling?'

'No, not that. I mean, do you ever wonder if there's really a way that we can contact spirits of the dead? A dimension beyond our own that some people can access – by tarot cards or Ouija board, or crystal balls – and others can't see?'

'Honestly, Suzy, I'm pretty much a man of science. I believe in what I can see. I believe that when you die, that's the end. No Heaven, no Hell, no coming back and haunting. But then, I guess I've always thought of myself as having an open mind. I'd never judge someone like my mum because of what she believes. I'd never judge you, Suzy, no matter what you told me. And after what I saw last night, I honestly don't know what I believe.'

'It's all true, Nate. All of it,' I said quickly, not wanting to hold back. 'Ouija boards and ghosts, tarot cards and seances. It's all real. It's all true. And something terrible once happened here at Dudley Hall, something that no one wants to talk about or try to look into. But whatever it was was so bad that the memory just won't go away. It's haunting this house. *She's* haunting this house. I don't know how to get rid of her, but something has to be done.'

We were interrupted by Nell walking into the kitchen. 'Is there any coffee left in that pot?' she said. 'I've been hunched over my crystal ball all morning and I'd kill for some caffeine right now.'

'Sorry, it's empty.' Nate shrugged.

I couldn't bring myself to look up at Nell. She knew that Nate had stayed over last night; God only knew what she thought of me. I waited for her to pass comment but she simply picked up the empty coffee pot and tutted. 'I'll make some more. You both want some?'

'Actually, we were just about to go.' I pushed my chair back and stood up abruptly. 'Nate's giving me a lift to the hospital so I can visit Toby.'

Nell nodded and gave me a sad smile. 'Send him my love.'

I smiled briefly before rushing out of the kitchen and making my way towards the front door to grab my coat. I swung open the heavy door and walked towards Nate's motorbike without looking back. It felt good to get out of the house. Inside I felt so lost – I had no idea what to do or how all this was going to end. But as soon as my feet stepped onto the gravel all I cared about was getting to Toby, and as far away from Dudley Hall as I could. At least outside the house I had some kind of focus.

As Nate clambered onto the bike in front of me and pulled on his helmet, passing me the spare one, I wrapped my arms around his waist and pressed myself into his back. I closed my eyes and let my arms squeeze around Nate's waist gently. He lifted his helmet visor up and turned back around towards me. 'I meant what I said, Suzy,' he whispered. 'You're not alone.'

22

I saw Aunt Meredith as soon as I stepped onto the ward. She was deep in conversation with one of the doctors. She clutched a styrofoam cup to her chest and hung on every word the doctor was saying to her. I walked up slowly, waving at her first so she could see me coming.

'Suzy.' She said my name with surprise, clearly startled to see me there, as if she almost didn't recognise me out of context.

'Nate dropped me off,' I said. 'How's Toby doing?'

'I'll come and check on him again within the hour,' the doctor said to Aunt Meredith, walking away.

'The doctors still aren't completely sure what's wrong with him.' She looked exhausted; she clearly hadn't slept since Toby had been brought in. 'They've ruled out meningitis, or flu. But they think it's shock. He's gone into shock, Suzy. Why? I just don't understand. It's almost as if his body is just shutting down for no reason. And I'm afraid that if they don't figure out what's wrong...'

I awkwardly put my hand on her arm to calm her. Aunt Meredith caught herself and stopped herself from saying whatever was coming next. Instead she took a deep breath and said, 'It's good to see you, Suzy, thank you for coming. Knowing you're here would make Toby so happy.'

I bit down on my lip, hoping to suppress the tears that were threatening to spill. How was I ever going to make up for what had happened to my small cousin? 'The murder mystery's going well,' I said, hoping to distract her. We walked over to two plastic chairs propped next to the corridor wall and sat down on them.

'Of course it is,' Aunt Meredith smiled. 'Your story is brilliant, Suzy. You'll be a fabulous writer one day.'

'I promise I won't forget you when I'm rich and famous,' I joked.

'Oh, Suzy.' Tears began to trickle down her pale cheeks. 'You've always wanted to be famous, ever since you were a little girl.'

'I guess I just don't want to be forgotten,' I said before I could stop myself.

Her eyes softened and she reached forwards and brushed a rogue strand of fading red hair behind my ear. 'How could anyone forget you? You're so special, Suzy, everyone can see that.'

'Can they?' I asked, my voice wobbling. I'd come to the hospital to see Toby, not hold a mirror up to my self-esteem. 'I'm easy to forget,' I added sadly. 'It was so easy for my parents to ship me off to boarding school and forget about me there. And they didn't want me to come home after I left Warren House, even after everything I've been through. You were right when you told me before that if it wasn't for you and Richard I'd have nowhere else to go.'

A storm cloud seemed to pass through Aunt Meredith's eyes. 'Look, Suzy, we need to talk.'

'Talk?' I echoed, startled. 'About what?'

'About you living at Dudley Hall.'

'I have nowhere else to go,' I reminded her. 'I know I've been difficult, and I'm sorry. And I know Toby's ill, but I promise to help out however I can. I'll help with the parties and –'

'I spoke to your mum last night,' she said, cutting me off. 'We both wondered if the time is right for you to go back to school. You can't stay at Dudley Hall for ever, and –'

'You can't send me back to school,' I said loudly. A nurse looked up from the clipboard in her hands and gave me a stern frown. 'Please don't send me back to that school. Please let me stay with you, just for a while longer.'

'Suzy.' Aunt Meredith closed her eyes and tears streamed down her face. 'Something terrible happened to Toby in that house. I don't know what. But I've heard the stories, I'm not stupid. Village gossip about the ghost of a girl who haunts the house.' I stared at her in disbelief. She knew about the grey girl – all this time, she knew. 'I wouldn't have let you come to stay if I had thought for one moment that the stories were true,' she said pleadingly. 'All I wanted was to care for you when your mum couldn't. I just wanted to help you. I didn't believe in ghosts. But after everything that's happened – to you, to Toby – I can't ignore it any more. I can't let you stay there any more.'

'I'm going to find a way to make her leave,' I said urgently. 'I promise you, Aunt Meredith.'

Aunt Meredith closed her eyes again, a sigh of pure

exhaustion escaping her. 'We'll talk about it again when Toby's better.' She sniffed. She pointed to a single room off to the right of where we were sitting. 'Toby's in there. I'm going to get another coffee. Do you want one?'

'Yes please,' I nodded.

Slowly, I made my way towards the room that Toby was being kept in. The lights were dim and as I opened the door I could hear the beep, beep, beeping of the monitor he was strapped up to. He looked so tiny. I walked over to his bed with a sick feeling in my throat. Just like the day before, he was staring off into space. His eyes were wide open in shock and his little chest rose and fell in rapid movements. My feet wanted to turn around and run as far away as I could from him; he just looked too sick and I wasn't sure how to deal with that. But I owed it to my little cousin, the boy who had followed me around and made me play spy games with him. Who had shown me his books and talked to me with trust and affection. Seeing him lying in a hospital bed, looking so tiny and helpless, I felt the hatred for the grey girl well up inside me and threaten to spill out and flood the room in angry waves. She had done this to him. This was her fault. In that moment, if I could have found some way to send her restless spirit to eternal Hell then I would have done it.

'Hey, mate,' I said meekly as I came near to Toby's bed.

All I had in response was the beeping of the machines.

'I'm so, so sorry, Toby,' I whispered. 'I should have warned you about her. Maybe then you wouldn't have come up into the attic after us. This should never have happened. You should never have been dragged into this.'

Something on Toby's bedside table caught my eye. My stomach lurched as I recognised the book – it was the book of Tennyson's poetry, the book that I'd found on my pillow back at Dudley Hall. The book that she had put there. I'd last seen the book back in my bedroom. I had no idea how or why it had come to be at the hospital. Toby was too young to read or understand poetry like that, and if Aunt Meredith was going to sit by his bed and read, surely she'd be reading spy stories to him.

Feeling like the ground was shaking beneath me, I slowly reached for the book. As if in slow motion, I held the book in front of me and let it fall open. I knew what I'd see before I looked down.

She left the web, she left the loom,
She made three paces thro' the room,
She saw the water-lily bloom,
She saw the helmet and the plume,
    She look'd down to Camelot.
Out flew the web and floated wide;
The mirror crack'd from side to side;
'The curse is come upon me,' cried
    The Lady of Shalott.

I snapped the book shut and nearly knocked into Aunt Meredith as I turned around quickly. 'What's this doing here?' I asked, holding the book up in front of me.

'It was in Toby's room,' she replied, alarmed at my tone. 'I thought I would read –'

'What do you mean? Where did he get it from?'

'I don't know where he got it from. I would have thought he was too young for Tennyson, but I found it by his bed so he must have been interested in it. I thought he might want to read it when he woke up so I brought it here.'

I stepped backwards, away from her.

'Suzy, what's wrong?'

'This shouldn't be here. Toby shouldn't touch it,' I said, edging for the door.

Aunt Meredith looked at me with wide-eyed shock as I ran from the room, the book still in my hand.

I pushed my way past nurses, doctors and porters as I ran through the hospital and out into the warm afternoon air. I still had money in my purse left over from when Aunt Meredith had given me a wodge of notes to go out for lunch with Frankie. I'd have enough for a taxi to take me away from the hospital and back to Dudley-on-Water.

I climbed into a waiting cab at the taxi rank, my eyes wild with fear.

'Where to, love?'

'Dudley-on-Water,' I said quickly. 'The Old Rectory.'

The car sped off and my blood rushed through my veins with exhilaration. I knew what I had to do. This was it. I was turning the pages of the last chapter of this story; my drama was moving into the final act.

One way or another, it would all soon be over.

23

I walked up the garden path to the Old Rectory as the taxi pulled away. I knocked hard on the door and waited for someone to answer. Nobody came.

I turned the front door handle and it opened beneath my fingertips. Gently, I pushed the creaking door open and walked into the house. 'Hello?' I called out, shutting the front door behind me.

There was no answer. The house, as always, smelt of wood smoke and candles. But as I walked through the small hallway and into the lounge I noticed that there were no candles burning, and no fire blazing away in the grate. 'Hello?' I called out again.

Once again there was no reply. The house was empty. I hadn't planned on coming to an empty house, and couldn't believe my luck that I'd managed to turn up at a time when Fiona, Nell and Nate were all out. I walked through the lounge towards the old bureau I'd seen Fiona open the day before. With the house empty I wouldn't have to lie to anyone about why I was there; I wouldn't have to distract someone whilst I stole what I needed from Fiona's secret shoe box hidden away in the bureau drawer.

'Suzy?' came Fiona's voice behind me, just as my hand touched the bureau drawer handle. 'What are you doing here?'

My heart leapt into my throat. The house wasn't empty at all. I spun around to see her standing in the doorway, watching me like a hawk. Her hair was dripping wet and she had an old, worn dressing gown wrapped around her skinny body.

'I'm looking for Nate,' I said quickly.

'He's gone out for a ride on his bike,' Fiona said, moving towards me. Her eyes flittered towards the bureau drawer that I stood in front of. 'He said he needed to get away for a few hours. I don't suppose he'll be back any time soon. Do you want me to tell him that you dropped by?'

'No, don't worry,' I said, my voice catching in my throat. 'I'll catch up with him later.'

'Well, if there was nothing else...' Fiona stood back and opened her arm, gesturing towards the front door, implying I should leave.

'Right,' I mumbled, silently cursing to myself as I moved away from the bureau, away from the drawer and away from the box that I so desperately needed to see inside.

I walked past Fiona, trying to ignore the suspicion in her eyes, and headed for the front door. I turned around as I opened it, finding her watching me from the lounge door. I gave her a weak smile before slipping outside. I closed the door behind me and sank my back against it, shutting my eyes to the waning afternoon sun. My mind raced, trying to figure out what I should do next. There was a window next to the front door which looked into the hallway. Ivy crept over the glass and practically obscured the view into the house. Very carefully,

I pulled back a strand of ivy and peered through the window and into the hallway. I watched as Fiona walked away from the lounge and back up the stairs.

With Fiona back upstairs this was the only chance I would have to sneak inside and take what I needed.

I didn't dare go back through the creaking front door, it made far too much noise. Instead, I crept around the side of the house, almost crawling along the ground like I'd done with Frankie the time we'd spied on Fiona. When I came to the lounge window I slowly rose up and peeped in, careful that no one from the village was watching me through the hedgerows. The lounge was empty, as I knew it would be.

Very gently, I pushed at the top of the slat window, silently praying that it wasn't locked. My prayers were answered. The window slid smoothly upwards. I managed to raise it just enough to climb through into the house.

One leg at a time, I climbed into the lounge, careful not to rattle the window or make any noise. My heart leaping about inside me, I crept over to the old bureau, my eyes never straying from the lounge door, expecting Fiona to burst in on me at any moment.

With great care I delicately pulled on the bureau drawer handle, and the drawer slid open, as silently as the grave.

I pulled the drawer fully open.

It was empty.

Nothing but a few blank greeting cards and a metre or two of yellow ribbon. I frantically lifted up the greeting cards, half expecting to see the box hidden beneath them in the shallow drawer. The box wasn't there. It was the only drawer to the bureau, and definitely the same drawer that I'd seen Fiona take the box from the other day. I opened the bureau's desk, hoping to see the box in there, but there was nothing.

Panicked, I slid the drawer shut and looked around the room in desperation.

The box had to be in there somewhere. From where I stood in the corner of the room my eyes scanned over every surface, every pile of magazines and every scrunched-up jumper in the corner of a chair.

I heard the creaking of Fiona's footsteps on the stairs as I saw the box. It was sat on a side table beneath a lamp.

I only had moments before Fiona came back into the lounge and discovered me in there once again. Without a second thought I dived towards the box, grasped it in both hands and then lunged for the window. I jumped through it like some kind of acrobat, landing on the grass below with an awkward thud. There wasn't time to close the window behind me, I couldn't risk the sound of the slat scraping down the woodwork, or the look on Fiona's face as she caught me shutting it when she walked into the lounge.

Instead, I sprang to my feet and ran as fast as I could.

I ran up the garden path, out of the garden and into the village. The church loomed down at me, its sprawling graveyard an inviting place to hide away and take refuge. I sprinted for the cast-iron gate and it swung open as I hurled my full weight at it. I ran between the graves, not stopping to catch my breath or look behind me to see if I was being chased. I ran towards the bench I'd sat on with Nate that one time, the bench by his grandmother's grave.

I sat down on the bench and caught my breath, my eyes glued to the graveyard entrance, just waiting for Fiona to follow me in there.

The box felt hot and heavy between my hands. I looked down at it eagerly.

I pulled off the cardboard lid and peered in.

It was full of black and white photographs.

The photograph on the top of the pile was of four girls smiling and holding hockey sticks. They were standing in front of a building I recognised straight away – Dudley Hall. One of the girls must have been Nate's grandmother, and the photograph must have been taken when she was a schoolgirl at Dudley Hall. I turned the photo over in my hands. Four names were handwritten in faded ink on the back of the photograph: *Annabel, Lavinia, Margot and Sybil.*

I lifted up the photo and looked underneath. The next picture was of just two of the girls who'd appeared in the first photograph. A girl with dark hair and a girl with blonde hair. The blonde-haired girl had her arm wrapped possessively around the other girl's neck. They both smiled at the camera. Something around the blonde's neck caught my eye. It was a necklace shaped like a pentagram. I knew what a pentagram represented – witchcraft. It was the same symbol I'd seen carved into the weeping willow by the stream in the Dudley Hall grounds. The carving that had letters etched besides each of the pentagram's five points.

I lifted the photo of the two girls up and looked beneath. There were more of the two of them. They were wearing thick, heavy cloaks, and my heart beat faster as I recognised the cloaks as the same kind that I saw the grey girl wearing every time I watched her try to run away from my bedroom window.

The photograph below was of the four girls again – this time they were sitting around a bed in what must have once been their old dormitory. A room that looked unbearably like the bedroom I now slept in. I continued to rifle through the pictures, only finding more of the same girls.

As my fingers reached the picture at the bottom of the shoe box I felt a painful jolt of adrenalin beat through my body. With shaking hands I picked up the picture and held it to the light.

It was of two girls. They were each holding shadow puppets, one the woman, the other the man. One girl had dark hair – the girl who had been in the picture with the blonde wearing the pentagram. The other girl hadn't been in the other pictures, but I recognised her straight away.

The grey girl.

Friday 31st October 1952

Tilly is dead. I killed her.

24

There was a light in the far corridor dimly aglow as I pushed open the heavy front door of Dudley Hall. I could hear soft whispers coming from the dining room and drawing room as I walked past them. I'd almost forgotten that the house was full of murder mystery guests – young adults dressed up in school uniforms thinking it was brilliantly exciting that a schoolgirl had been murdered.

Walking towards the kitchen, I paused next to the telephone in the hallway. Something made me reach into my back pocket and pull out the scrap of paper with Nate's number on it. I picked up the telephone and began to dial. With every ring that passed I held my breath, waiting for him to answer. Eventually the phone beeped onto voicemail.

'Nate,' I said quietly into the receiver. 'I'm so sorry about everything. When you get this… I just want you to know that I'm sorry.' I put down the phone and stared at it for a long moment, wondering when he'd ever listen to the message and whether he'd believe me – I really was so sorry.

The shoe box still in my hands, I walked towards the faint light coming from the kitchen at the end of the dark corridor.

Nell was sitting alone at the kitchen table, her tarot cards fanned out in front of her. The kitchen blinds were closed, barricading the daylight out, and the room was filled with candles, flickering away in the darkness. In one hand Nell twirled the shadow puppet that I'd taken from her house a few days before.

'Did you find what you were looking for?' she asked, without looking up at me. I looked down guiltily at the shoe box in my hands, the box that contained only more riddles about who the grey girl was and why she died. Nell didn't sound angry, only tired. Maybe she felt like me, maybe she just wanted it to all be over.

'Your mother knew her, didn't she?' I asked, coming towards the kitchen table.

Nell continued to study the cards laid out in front of her, the shadow puppet whirling around between her fingers and casting blurred shadows onto the kitchen walls.

'I have no idea who my mother knew, or what she knew,' Nell said softly. 'Sit down,' she told me. I pulled back one of the kitchen chairs and placed the shoe box on the table as I sat down. Nell's eyes briefly flicked up to look at the shoe box before settling back down to the cards on the table once again. 'My mother refused to speak about her time as a schoolgirl here.'

'I know,' I admitted, one hand resting on the shoe box, as if it gave me some kind of comfort. 'Fiona told me.'

'And did my sister tell you how we used to come here as children?' Nell asked, finally looking up at me. The soft candlelight sparkled in her eyes. 'How we used to explore

237

the house when it was nothing but a ruin. It looked nothing like it does now.'

'She told me that you heard the grey girl crying up in the attic. When you went to see if you could find her you ran away. You found that on the stairs,' I said, pointing to the shadow puppet in her hands.

Nell nodded. 'Fiona swears she saw her that day. Says she stood on the landing looking down on us as clear as any living girl might do. But I've never seen her. I come here every day and she's never once appeared to me. Me with all my crystal balls and tarot cards, you'd think I'd be an easy target for a restless spirit.'

'Why did you come back to Dudley Hall to work if you knew it was haunted?'

Nell gave me an exaggerated shrug and looked down at her cards. 'The cards told me that this was where I needed to be. The cards never lie. I came here thinking that I would be the one to help her move on, but she's never appeared to me.'

'If you want to see her then why do you never go upstairs?' I asked.

'I don't want to see her. I've seen what happened to my mother and sister – they were both driven mad by her in some way. I don't want to see her, but I know that somehow I have a part to play. I don't need to seek her out to know that. I've told you before, Suzy, the ghosts you chase you never catch.'

'Did you ever tell your mother what happened that day?' I asked. 'When Fiona saw the grey girl, when she gave you the shadow puppet?'

Nell shook her head solemnly. 'My mother would have

238

skinned us alive if she knew we were coming here. This place haunted her – she carried the weight of Dudley Hall around with her all her life. Living in the house's shadow ate away at my mother like a cancer, it killed her, but she couldn't bring herself to move away or confront whatever it was that troubled her.'

'Your mother knew her,' I said, lifting the lid from the shoe box. 'She knew the grey girl when she was alive.' I pulled out the picture of the grey girl, the one where she stood with another girl, both holding shadow puppets.

'That was my mother as a girl,' Nell said, taking the picture from me. 'But I don't know who this other girl is and why her spirit would haunt Dudley Hall.'

'We need to find out,' I said, my voice as soft as a whisper. 'We need to find a way to make her go.'

'And how do you suppose we do that?' Nell lifted her eyebrow.

Holding her gaze, I reached towards the cards spread on the table and swept them into a pile. I picked up the pile from the table and shuffled it in my hands. I spread the cards out in front of me, face down, as I'd watched Nell do before. Looking down at the cards, I waited for the ones I needed to leap out at me. I repeated my question to the cards in my head: *Will she ever move on?* Slowly, my fingers moved towards one in the centre of the deck. I pulled it out and turned it over.

'Death,' I whispered, looking down on the card. 'Can't be good.'

'Death is as much a part of life as living is,' Nell said gently. '*All that lives must die, passing through nature to eternity.*'

'But some things don't pass to eternity. Some things are

trapped here.'

Nell nodded steadily. 'Pull out another card.'

I pulled out a second card, a card that seemed to glow brighter than the others in the flickering candlelight.

The five of wands.

Finally, I pulled out a third card and turned it over in front of me.

The four of swords.

'I want you to read the cards,' I told her. 'I need to know.'

Nell nodded her head in understanding. 'This card here,' she pointed to Death, 'this represents the past.'

'Her past,' I said quietly.

'The Death card represents the end of something. The end of life, the end of friendship, the end of sorrow or of happiness. And this card, the Five of Wands, the card that represents her present, is the card in the deck that means Conflict. She suffers great conflict now. Torn between one world and the next, between her desire for revenge and her need for peace. And this last card, the Four of Swords, the card for her future, represents Truce. She is ready to let go, Suzy. She is ready to leave.'

'What do I need to do?'

'You need to summon her again. She's so close to giving up her secrets. She wants to rest, Suzy. She's tired. She's been angry with this world for too long. She's ready to let go.'

'Suzy,' came a familiar voice from behind me.

I turned around to see Frankie standing in the doorway. My best friend was back in Dudley Hall. I blinked at her, feeling too confused to say or do anything.

Frankie ran towards me, worry etched on her face as she

pulled me out of my chair and flung her arms around me. 'You're okay?' she asked breathily in my ear. 'I thought… when I saw that email from you … I thought you were going to do something stupid. I came straight here.'

Frankie pulled away and I smiled at her. She really was amazing, the best friend I could have ever asked for. Someone who would drop everything and travel any distance just to see that I was okay.

'What are you doing?' she asked, looking down at the tarot cards spread out on the table.

'We need to banish the grey girl,' I said. 'And we need to do it tonight.'

Frankie nodded in understanding. 'I'll help in any way I can.'

'Let's do this now,' Nell said slowly. 'The sooner it's all over the sooner we can all move on.'

'What do we need to do?' Frankie asked, her eyes resolute. I've always loved that about Frankie, the way her eyes land on something so steadily, the way she's so dependable.

'We need to carry all these candles upstairs and put them around the attic room. That's where her presence seems to be strongest, so that's where this needs to be done. And we'll need chalk. Suzy,' Nell looked at me, 'there's some in the library, in a small box by the window. The guests sometimes use it to draw around the dead bodies.'

At that moment Katie walked into the kitchen, a tray of empty wine bottles in her hands. She smiled nervously at Nell, whose face was a mask of dread and worry. Katie's gaze moved around the candle-lit room. 'Candles and tarot cards are for the guests,' she muttered, walking over to the counter and putting the tray of empty bottles down. 'What's going on in here?'

'We're going up into the attic,' Nell replied slowly.

Katie's shoulders tensed. 'Why? You know we're not meant to…'

'There's something up there,' I said quickly. 'I know you've heard it, Katie. It's not just the wind.'

Katie nodded her head slowly, her fair hair shimmering in the candlelight. 'I've heard the stories about what's up there. I don't believe them.'

'Then you won't mind helping us,' Nell said briskly, walking towards the nearest candle and blowing it out.

Katie hesitated. 'The guests…'

'Can look after themselves for a while,' Nell finished. 'We need your help up there.'

'Very well,' Katie said unconvincingly. 'What do you need me to do?'

'Help me take the candles upstairs,' Nell said to Katie, walking towards the next candle and snuffing it out. Frankie and I watched as Nell and Katie worked to gather up all the candles scattered around the kitchen.

'I'll come with you to find the chalk,' Frankie said to me, slipping her hand into mine and squeezing my fingers.

Frankie and I walked towards the library, still hand in hand. There were no guests in there – but we could hear their voices ringing out from the other rooms in the house. It was dark when we walked into the library. I flipped the switch on the wall and bright light flooded the room. 'Wow,' Frankie gasped, looking around. 'This place is amazing. If I were you I'd never want to leave.' She looked over at me and gave me a small smile. 'Once the house is free of ghosts, of course.'

'Is anywhere ever free of ghosts?' I asked, letting go of her hand and walking towards the window.

'Maybe it's not places that are haunted,' Frankie said thoughtfully, following after me. 'Maybe it's people.'

'Who would the grey girl be haunting?' I asked. Answers to my own question buzzed around my head. The grey girl could have been haunting Nate's grandmother, she could have been haunting her daughters – Nell and Fiona. She could have been haunting anyone who stepped foot in the house that she died in. She could have been haunting me. 'We need to put her to rest,' I said.

'Tonight,' Frankie nodded. 'We put her to rest tonight.'

Suddenly the sound of Nate's motorbike tyres on the gravel driveway outside tore my attention from my best friend. I looked out of the window to see him pulling off his helmet in a rush and taking long strides towards the house. I ran through the library, into the grand hallway and watched as the front door to Dudley Hall swung open.

'You know who she is, don't you?' Nate said, walking straight up to me. 'If this is all about to end, then I'm going to help you.'

25

I stood with Nate at the bottom of the grand staircase, next to the suit of armour. His motorbike helmet rested under one arm, and he ran his free hand through his short blonde hair. I'd never seen the expression on his face before – he seemed somehow lost. 'Suzy, that message you left me ...'

'I'll meet you upstairs,' Frankie said quickly, walking up ahead of us.

'You don't have anything to be sorry for,' Nate finished.

'I stole your grandmother's shoe box of pictures,' I admitted. 'The box that your mum kept the shadow puppet in.'

He frowned at me. 'Why?'

'She was a schoolgirl here,' I told him. 'The grey girl. Your grandmother knew her – they were friends.'

'Do you ...' He put his helmet down on the bottom step and leant against the banister as he spoke. 'Do you think my grandmother had something to do with her death?'

'Maybe,' I nodded. 'We'll find out tonight. We're going to summon the grey girl's spirit. One way or another, this ends tonight.'

'Good,' he said seriously, staring me deep in the eyes. He

reached out to take my hands in his. 'All these years I thought my mum was insane for believing what she does. But after last night, after what we saw … I've been thinking about it all day. I can't think about anything else.' Nate looked down at my hands in his. 'All my life, all I've wanted is to find a way to lift the weight that's hanging around my mother's neck. The same weight my grandmother carried. It's this house and what's in it – it does something terrible to people that they can't come back from. Maybe it's too late for my mother, but it's not too late for you, Suzy. I don't want anything to happen to you. I'll do anything. What do you need me to do?'

Before I could answer I heard footsteps coming towards us from the kitchen. I looked up to see Nell walking towards us. 'It's time,' she said.

Nell stepped past us onto the stairs and began to walk up. Nate and I followed her wordlessly up the staircase, leaving his motorbike helmet behind on the bottom step. The sound of the murder mystery guests' laughter gradually fell away as we climbed higher. Every step I took felt like a mountain, as if my ankles were weighed down by an invisible force. I had no idea what to expect once we reached the attic room, and no idea what the outcome would be. But I knew that no matter what, we'd see the girl again that night. I could feel her all around me. I could almost feel her cold breath on my cheek, her cold tiny hands squeezing at my heart. My trembling hand traced the carvings on the banister as we climbed onto the first-floor landing, and then on to the next set of stairs. Not one of us spoke as we passed the second floor and continued to walk upwards, towards the attic. With each step my sense of dread grew, and the heaviness weighing me down felt more unbearable.

Nell stalled at the top of the stairs on the attic landing.

'Are you okay?' I asked, gently resting my hand on her arm.

'I haven't been up here since that day so long ago,' she whispered. 'I've revisited it so many times in my head. These steps, the landing, the long corridor. It's just as I remember it.'

'Come on.' I brushed past her, trying to stay calm, and turned right, walking down the corridor that led to the grey girl's room. I could hear Nate and Nell's footsteps as they followed me. The light outside had faded almost entirely now, and the only light in the corridor was coming from a dull glow in the grey girl's attic room.

Frankie and Katie were standing in the room as I entered. They had positioned candles all about the place. On the floor, on the old mantelpiece and on the windowsill. Candlelight flickered and glowed softly, illuminating them as they stood in the centre of the room, unsure of what to expect next.

Nate and Nell came in behind me and I turned around, waiting for Nell to tell us what to do next. Nate stood in the corner of the room, his eyes nervously casting about the place and taking in every detail. He nodded a hello to Frankie and Katie and they nodded back in acknowledgement.

'Suzy, you have the chalk?' Nell asked.

I knew what to do without being told. I took the white chalk out of my pocket and crouched down towards the floor. Slowly, I drew a large five-starred pentagram on the attic floorboards. I swept the chalk across the wooden boards, then down, then up again, drawing the pattern that I'd seen carved into the weeping willow by the brook. The shape that the blonde girl in the picture had worn around her neck. The chalk scratched at the floor and left a white trail of dust in its wake. As I brought the chalk to a stop, joining up the two last lines and completing the shape, there was a sudden gust of wind that crashed into the attic room window.

Frankie flinched forwards and then froze, her eyes wide with fear. We exchanged a panicked look – both knowing that what we were about to do, what we were about to unleash could go so horribly wrong.

'The candles,' whispered Katie, her voice trembling. I lifted my eyes from the floor and looked around the room. Every candle seemed to be burning brighter. The flames had risen into the air as though someone had poured oxygen onto them.

'The pentagram is a very powerful symbol,' Nell said, walking towards one of the five points of the star. 'It is a very ancient symbol. It is said to harness the power of the natural world. It is used to evoke the Goddess of nature, and it is used in many magical and satanic rituals. We use it here tonight to harness the power of the spirit world, so that we may contact the restless spirit that haunts this house.'

Once again another heavy gust of wind crashed into the window. Once again the five of us jumped at the sound and force of it.

'What do you need us to do?' Nate asked, looking over at Nell in the candlelight.

Nell looked around at us. 'Everyone is to stand at a corner of the pentagram. Everyone is to hold a candle.'

The four of us quickly moved to the nearest flickering candles and each picked one up between our shaking hands. I stood at the point at the top of the star, the point that sat nearest to the window. Nell and Nate stood at the points either side of me, the arms of the pentagram, and Frankie and Katie stood at the two points at the bottom.

The five of us stood there silently, candles in our hands, and looked around at each other. I could feel the crackle of anticipation in the air. Not one of us questioned what we were doing, or whether it would work or if it was stupid. Every single one of us had been touched by a ghost at some point of our lives. Every single one of us knew that this moment was important, and that we were on the verge of something both brilliant and terrible.

'To all above.' Nell lifted her candle above her head and looked up at the ceiling. 'And all below.' She lowered the candle towards the floor and looked down at the chalk markings. 'To the spirits of the afterlife, and to the Goddess of the earth. We come here to speak to you, and to seek your help. Spirits, come to us.'

'Spirits, come to us,' I echoed. As I said it again Frankie joined in. 'Spirits, come to us.' Next all five of us spoke in perfect unison, repeating the phrase I had promised myself I would never utter again. 'Spirits, come to us, Spirits, come to us, Spirits, come to us.'

A pounding silence fell across the room. No one dared speak or even breathe.

Then every candle in the room was snuffed out in a single heartbeat. In the next beat they all lit up again, burning brighter and more powerfully than before. My candle became too hot to hold and I nearly let it fall to the floor. I heard Katie curse at the heat in her hands, and Nate quickly passed his from hand to hand to avoid being burnt.

The sound of breaking glass and distant screaming filled the air. The screaming sounded as though it was coming from downstairs – the guests. 'The light bulb,' Frankie pointed above her. 'It exploded.'

'The guests are screaming downstairs,' Katie said, her face pale and clammy. 'All the bulbs in the house must have blown.'

'She can hear us,' I whispered.

Nell lowered her candle to the floor and put it down by her feet and the four of us did the same.

'She's near,' Nell said. 'Join hands.'

The five of us held hands on Nell's command, forming a circle around the pentagram. 'Keep chanting,' she instructed.

'Spirits, come to us, Spirits, come to us,' we said in unison, again and again. I felt my eyes closing as we continued to chant. The distant sound of the guests' shouts downstairs began to fade away, and all I could hear were the words of the chant. In my head I saw dancing flames lick and the room begin to spin around me. We chanted and chanted and I began to feel sick from the sound and the feeling that the room was spinning uncontrollably.

I heard the sound of someone gasping – Frankie.

I opened my eyes and looked at her. Her eyes were wide open and locked on the centre of the circle, the centre of the pentagram. There, between us all, stood the grey girl.

The air was sucked out of my lungs and I felt a horrible crushing sensation in my chest. My instinct was to pull my arms away from Nell and Nate – to break the circle, break the spell and send her back from whatever hellish dimension we had summoned her from. But I forced myself to watch her, and I forced myself to keep the circle unbroken.

Katie, Nate and Nell continued to chant with their eyes closed as Frankie and I watched the grey girl in the centre of our circle with horror. The girl turned, very slowly, until she was staring straight at me. Her hollow grey gaze burnt into me and filled my veins with ice. One by one, the other three stopped chanting and opened their eyes.

Everyone saw her.

Still looking at me, the grey girl sank to her knees and began to claw at the floor beneath her. The flickering candles snuffed out and re-lit themselves again and again, like strobe lighting in the small attic room. The air in the room grew colder and soon I could see the warm puffs of breath hover in front of my face as I laboured for air.

The image of the grey girl clawing at the floor continued to waver in and out of existence as the candlelight flickered from light to dark.

I felt Nate's hand begin to pull away from me. 'Don't let go,' I shouted at him. 'Don't break the circle.'

'What does she want?' Katie shouted into the room. Her face was wide with terror, her blue eyes alight with the flickering flames that engulfed the room.

'What do you want?' Nell shouted at the grey girl, who continued to claw at the floor.

The girl looked up at Nell and for a moment her hands were still. She opened her mouth and the sound that came out was more like the croak of death than a small girl speaking. 'I want peace.'

'We want you to have peace,' I said, my voice wobbling as much as the light in the room.

'Who are you?' Nell shouted at the girl.

'Tilly,' the girl croaked back.

'How did you die?' Frankie shouted.

The grey girl didn't answer, she looked back down at the floor and began to claw at it again. Soon her fingers began to tear and blood started to pour from open wounds.

Once again I felt Nate pull at my hand. 'Don't break the circle,' I shouted at him. 'We need to keep her there.'

'Suzy, let go!' he screamed at me, his hand pulling and pulling to be released from mine.

I tried in vain to hold onto his hand. I knew that once the circle had broken then she would disappear. This was our chance to speak to her, our chance to find out how we could finally put her spirit to rest. If we broke the circle and she vanished, we might never have that chance again.

'This is it, Nate,' I shouted at him. 'This is our chance to finally put an end to it all. For your mother, your grandmother, for Toby, for Tilly. For me. Please, Nate, keep the circle for me.' He tugged at my hand again, desperate to be released from my grasp. 'Nate, please!' I begged.

'Let go, Suzy,' he shouted at me, his hazel eyes aflame with determination.

My palm was sweaty and slippery, and Nate was so much stronger. As if in slow motion I felt his hand slide from my grasp. His fingers slipped through mine and the circle was broken.

Every candle in the room went out and we were suddenly plunged into darkness.

'You broke the circle,' Frankie screamed at Nate. 'She's gone.'

Nate sank to his knees in the darkness.

'Quick, re-light the candles,' Nell instructed.

Katie pulled a box of matches from her pocket and re-lit the candle by her feet, then she lit the candle by Frankie's and then Nell's feet. Soon the five candles at the five points of the pentagram were re-lit. Nell, Katie, Frankie and I stood at our points of the star, but Nate was crouched down in the middle of the pentagram. His fingers were moving frantically over the floorboards. He traced the edge of a board with his fingertips and then began to pick at the rusted nails that bound the floorboard to the floor.

'What are you doing?' I shouted, afraid that the vision of the grey girl had sent Nate mad. Seeing him paw at the floor in that way reminded me of the grey girl – Tilly – and how she had repeatedly scratched at it until her fingers bled.

'She was trying to show us something,' Nate muttered, his fingers running over the board obsessively. 'I need a knife, anything … we need to lift this floorboard up.'

Suddenly understanding what he wanted, I sank to my knees and joined Nate on the floor. I began to pick at the rusty nails in the floorboards, desperately trying to lift them out.

The tips of my fingers began to bleed as I picked and picked at the nearest nail. Nate's hands were bleeding too, but he was managing to lift the nail out of its small hole. Soon I'd lifted the nail nearest me out. Nate and I ran our fingers over the edge of the floorboard, trying to find a point to lift it. The other three crouched down and did the same, and with some kind of miraculous strength, the five of us managed to lift the old floorboard out of the floor and throw it to the other side of the room.

There was something beneath it. A square of leather, bound by string.

With shaking hands, I reached into the floor and picked it up. It was a book of some kind.

My bloody hands picked at the string until it fell away from the book.

The first page fell open.

It was a diary.

Friday 7th November 1952

It's been a whole week since Tilly died. I haven't been able to write in my diary these last seven days. I'm haunted by what we did. But now I feel as though the time has come for me to document our evil, evil deeds.

Last Friday night we waited until the school had fallen silent and the moon was high in the night sky. Lavinia, Margot, Sybil and I put on our heavy winter cloaks and carried the candles, matches and chalk up the stairs to the attic floor. Moonlight flooded in through the skylight and we tried our best to hide in the shadows as we climbed the stairs. We tiptoed along the narrow attic corridor like mice, afraid that we would wake one of the prefects and find ourselves expelled. We made it to Tilly's room – the room at the end of the hall – without being caught. Looking back on it now, I wish we had been caught. I'd rather be expelled a hundred times over than have to live with what I did next.

Tilly let us into her room. Her face was etched with excitement and she was wearing her winter cloak, as we'd told her to do. She had pushed her bed and chest of drawers to the side of the room so there was enough space on the floor to draw the pentagram.

Margot was the one to draw it. She dragged the chalk along the floorboards, marking out the five-pointed star. Sybil lit the candles and placed them on the five points.

The five of us held hands, the pentagram and the candles in the centre of us. Tilly joined in as we chanted in unison, 'Goddess, we serve you, Goddess, hear our prayers.'

We released each other's hands.

'Is that it?' Tilly asked. 'Am I initiated?'

'No,' I said to her. 'Come here.'

Tilly walked towards me, still unafraid and excited for what was to come. Lavinia passed me her pentagram necklace and I took it with shaking fingers. I knelt down and held it over the flickering flame of the candle. 'Pull up your right sleeve,' I instructed, staring into the flame. I couldn't bring myself to look at Tilly. I couldn't bear to see the excitement in her face. Tilly paused for a moment before doing as I said.

I rose to my feet and pressed down the scalding hot necklace into her flesh. 'Goddess of the moon, we are your children.' Tilly whimpered and tried to pull away but Lavinia moved in and held her still.

'We all have one,' she whispered in Tilly's ear.

As Tilly stepped back and fought back the tears, the four of us rolled up our sleeves to prove that we did all have the mark upon us. Binding us to one another, to the Goddess, to the Rituals.

'Is that it?' Tilly sobbed.

I shook my head. 'Now I need to give you the Kiss of Death.'

That was the moment that Tilly's eyes widened and she realised that this was more than just a game. 'We stop your heart and then bring you back,' Lavinia said wickedly.

'But I have a weak heart,' Tilly protested. 'If you stop it, it won't start again.'

I wish we had listened to her.

'Hold her down,' Lavinia whispered.

Margot took one arm and Sybil took the other, Lavinia chanted to the Goddess as I put one hand over Tilly's heart and my other hand over that. Tilly tried to scream but Lavinia quickly dived forwards and put her hand over Tilly's mouth. 'Do it!' Lavinia hissed at me. So I pressed against Tilly's heart, my arms straightened and my weight bearing down into her. I felt the air wheeze out of her chest and watched as her eyes bulged wide. Tilly tried in vain to struggle. 'Hold her down!' commanded Lavinia. The others held her down as I continued to press, press, press down upon her small, weakened heart. Soon Tilly stopped struggling and fell limp. I moved my lips towards hers. 'The Kiss of Death,' I whispered.

I've seen the Kiss of Death done three times before. I did it to Lavinia, and Margot and Sybil did it to one another. Before, the effect was always the same – after the briefest of blackouts you gasp back to life. But Tilly didn't gasp, she didn't come back to life. She lay on the ground, wheezing her last breaths. We panicked. 'Blow out the candles, scrub the chalk off the floor.'

We tried to revive her but it wouldn't work. It was me who had the idea of carrying her downstairs and outside. She was light and weighed next to nothing. No one stirred as we took her frail little body out into the moonlight, towards the river. The Lady of Shalott was tied up at the bank, like always. We arranged her body in the boat and untied it from the bank, and pushed the boat out onto the river. As the boat floated away we ran back into the house. I lay in bed that night imagining a different scene. I imagined Tilly escaping, running away from us in the night. Escaping on the boat and floating away down the river.

They found her body the next morning. The doctor said that Tilly died in the boat. She was still alive when we carried her *down there and watched her float away. We could have saved her, maybe. When she was found her lips were blue, her blood frozen, just like the poem. 'Till her blood was frozen slowly, And her eyes were darken'd wholly.'*

They assumed she had put herself in the boat and simply lay down and died. Everyone knew she was obsessed with the poem and had no hope of ever living a normal life.

This is the last diary entry I shall ever write. It is my confession. I shall never do the Rituals again. I don't deserve the blessings of the Goddess, none of us do. I'm going to hide this diary somewhere no one will ever find it, and if they do find it I hope that it is after I am gone. I hope to take this secret to the grave.

I'm sorry I wasn't a friend to you, Tilly. I'm sorry I didn't save you. And I'm sorry that I will never be brave enough to tell the truth about how you died. I hope your soul finds a peace in death that you never had in life. The grey girl, a beautiful Moonchild who was always cursed to live a half life.

'God in his mercy lend her grace, The Lady of Shalott.'
I will never write again,

Annabel

Epilogue

A ghost isn't just a spirit that haunts a building. It's an idea, or a memory, that haunts people too. A ghost is something that follows you through your life and won't let you rest, won't allow you to let go. These sorts of ghosts you wear like shadows, and some people take them to the grave.

Annabel took a ghost to her grave. She took a terrible secret too. She had known the truth about why Tilly had died; she could have saved her if she had wanted to. But that wasn't what happened. Tilly had died at her hands and Annabel had let that secret haunt her to the grave. That secret bound Tilly to Dudley Hall, and it bound Annabel to Dudley-on-Water until she died. A secret so terrible it seeped down through the generations, binding her daughters Fiona and Nell to the awful story too.

The Dudley Hall attic has now been gutted. The floorboards ripped up, the walls steamed and painted new shades of white. The windows have been replaced and the fireplaces swept. New beds, wardrobes and tables have been ordered, and a new bathroom is being put in at the beginning of each corridor. People have been up in the attic, coming and going, for weeks now. No one has ever seen the grey girl again. Some of the workmen reported a coldness in the last room on the right, but that's the only trace of her left.

Aunt Meredith hopes to move up into the attic soon, and she'll use the bedrooms on the second floor for more guests. Richard's coming back less and less, and I don't think that's a bad thing. I don't think Aunt Meredith sees it as a bad thing either. He doesn't seem interested in her or the house. I secretly hope that one day he'll never come back, and he'll leave Aunt Meredith and Toby to live their lives at Dudley Hall in peace.

Toby came out of hospital a few days after we held the seance in the attic. The first few days he was very quiet, but he was soon back to his old self. The school term started and Toby goes to the local school during the day and reads detective novels whenever he gets the chance.

The day after we had found the diary in the attic, Frankie went home and Nell and Katie cleaned the house when the murder mystery guests left. Every light bulb in the house had blown whilst we were holding the seance. Apparently the bulbs downstairs blew at the exact moment the murderer was revealed at the party, and the guests thought it was all part of the show. Aunt Meredith said the feedback she'd had from some of the guests that weekend was brilliant – and it was one of the best murder mysteries Dudley Hall has ever held. I hope she means that. I enjoyed writing *The Ghost of Dudley Hall*. I'd like to write another story like that one day. Although this time maybe I'll write about something else I know well – I'll write about hope and courage and facing up to your greatest fears.

The day after the guests had gone Nate and I went to Annabel's grave.

We lay flowers by her headstone and set fire to the diary right there in the graveyard. We watched as the wind swept away the ashes, whisking them aloft on the breeze. 'Now you can both be at peace,' I whispered into the wind. 'And everyone bound to this story can be free.'

'I'm so pleased you came here, Suzy,' Nate said to me, as we watched the last of the ashes float away on the wind. 'Not just because of all this. Not just because maybe now, after all these years, my mum and Nell will finally be free. I'm glad I met you,' he said. It was the first time I'd ever seen Nate seem shy.

I turned towards him and flashed him my best grin. 'I'm glad I met you too.'

'I love the way you see the world,' he said, his hazel eyes gazing down on me. '*A dreamer who sees the dawn before the rest of the world.*'

'Now who's been reading Oscar Wilde?' I smiled.

He leant forward and pressed his lips against mine. It felt like fireworks had erupted inside me, and I tried not to smile with happiness as Nate deepened his kiss. I kissed him back and moved closer, putting my hands against his T-shirt and feeling the beat of his heart beneath my fingertips. He lifted his lips from mine and looked down at me. 'Promise me something, whatever happens...'

'Anything,' I said quickly.

'Get a phone and keep in touch.' He smiled.

My face split into a huge grin. 'I promise. No matter what happens, I'll keep in touch.'

I bought a phone the next day. I've been using it to text Frankie and I call Nate every night, even though I see him during the day. He takes me out on his bike and we soar through the countryside like free birds in flight.

I'm leaving Dudley Hall. I knew I couldn't stay here forever. I have to go back to school. I know it's where I need to be. Not because of what's waiting for me there. I don't have scores to settle or ghosts to put to rest. But I need some kind of education if I'm going to be a writer. Aunt Meredith says I can still visit Dudley Hall in my school holidays. I can come back and visit Nate and Toby and have my own room up in the attic when I stay. Not long ago the idea of sleeping up there would have horrified me, but not any more. I can't feel her up there now. She's moved on.

I was packing up my room at Dudley Hall when a soft breeze blew through the window. I found myself walking towards the open curtains and gazed down on to the grounds below.

She was standing there, underneath the weeping willow, basking in the sunlight. The grey girl was no longer grey; she seemed to glimmer like diamonds as she tilted her head back to the sky.

I smiled to myself as I watched her fade away into the hazy sunshine. She is finally free.

Tilly just had to find a way to take centre stage, to tell her story. Fiona, Nell, Toby and I were all bit players really. '*All the world's a stage, And all the men and women merely players,*' I whispered through the open window.

I wonder what other parts I'll play during my lifetime. I wonder what's waiting for me on the road ahead. And when

I die I wonder if there will be something that binds me to the earth, preventing me from moving on. I hope not. I hope for peace. I wonder if the memory of me will haunt others, I wonder if there will be anyone who will miss me so much they won't be able to let me go.

I wish I could say that I wasn't afraid of ghosts. I wish I was immune to the coldness they cast on a room, or the way they can destroy your life and make you question your own sanity. Whether you can see them or not, ghosts are real, as real as the earth and sky and everything in between.

I'm always sad when a story ends. But another one is just beginning. Each day is like turning over the Death card in a tarot pack – the end of one tale but the beginning of the next. That's all life really is, a series of stories woven together by the people we meet and the lives that we touch. I'm the protagonist in every one of my stories, and my life is mine to live as I choose. And as Nate's bike pulls away from Dudley Hall, taking me to the train station, my bag strapped to my back, I look at the road ahead and feel a rush of happiness. I don't know what the future holds, but I know who I am. I know what I believe. I believe in ghosts and I believe in love. I believe in magic and I believe in forever. I believe in forgiveness and new beginnings, I believe in truth and friendship. And I believe in myself, no matter what.